Working It

Working It

A Love by Design Novel

Kendall Ryan

ATRIA PAPERBACK

New York   London   Toronto   Sydney   New Delhi

ATRIA PAPERBACK
A Division of Simon & Schuster, Inc.
1230 Avenue of the Americas
New York, NY 10020

First Atria Paperback edition February 2014

ATRIA PAPERBACK and colophon are trademarks of Simon & Schuster, Inc.

For information about special discounts for bulk purchases, please contact Simon & Schuster Special Sales at 1-866-506-1949 or business@simonandschuster.com.

The Simon & Schuster Speakers Bureau can bring authors to your live event. For more information or to book an event contact the Simon & Schuster Speakers Bureau at 1-866-248-3049 or visit our website at www.simonspeakers.com.

Designed by Nancy Singer

Manufactured in the United States of America

10 9 8 7 6 5 4 3 2 1

Library of Congress Cataloging-in-Publication Data

Ryan, Kendall.
    Working It : a Love by Design novel / Kendall Ryan.—First Atria Paperback edition.
    pages cm.—(Love by Design ; 1)

Summary: "A sexy contemporary romance novel set in the world of the New York City fashion industry. The novel takes place in New York City, Paris, and Milan"—Provided by publisher.
    ISBN 978-1-4767-6460-3 (pbk.)—ISBN 978-1-4767-6461-0 1. Fashion—Fiction. 2. Love stories. I. Title.
PS3618.Y3354W67 2014
    813'.6—dc23
    2013047508

ISBN 978-1-4767-6460-3
ISBN 978-1-4767-6461-0 (ebook)

For my biggest fans, my grandpa and grandma, Roy and Isie. Your love story began in Scotland in 1951 and stood the test of time. I love you always. Miss you, Grandpa.

Sometimes we know we shouldn't

and that's exactly why we do.

—*Unknown*

Author's Note

I didn't intend for this book to be dual point of view. I first wrote it solely from Emmy's perspective. But Ben wouldn't shut up. I kept hearing his voice in my head, so eventually I relented, giving him the spotlight and adding his perspective at several points within the story. It wasn't what I had initially planned, and might be a bit unconventional, but when Ben tells me to do something, I try to be a good girl and listen. He can be very persuasive. You'll see.

Working It

Prologue

Present Day

It had been a month since I'd seen him, but my body still knew when he was near. The skin on the back of my neck tingled and my hands curled around my middle, like my body was preparing itself to fall apart.

I glanced over my shoulder to see Ben Shaw striding through the glass doors with a compact carry-on bag in hand, looking devastatingly handsome. My heart pinched painfully in my chest.

Long-forgotten memories infiltrated my brain. His large hands splayed across my hips, his full mouth nipping at my throat . . . the filthy things he murmured in my ear. The way his gorgeous mouth would turn up in a lopsided smile when I tried to refuse him. My heart, though utterly destroyed, beat just for him. My hands ached to hold him; my body longed to be nestled against his. And there wasn't a damn thing I could do about it.

Last month I'd left my job and fled New York City to go back to the safety and comforts of my home in Tennessee. Now I was standing on the curb at LaGuardia, one of the busiest airports in the world, running smack into the reason I'd left. But Ben, purposeful in his stride, had yet to notice me.

Pulling my eyes away from him, I focused on getting the hell out of there. I turned away, hoping Ben wouldn't see me, snapping my fingers to get the attention of a cabdriver. He sped past as if I didn't exist. *Figures. Damn New York cabbies.* As I turned from the curb, Ben's eyes scanned the lines of waiting cars. I was only a few feet away, and he still hadn't noticed me. This both relieved and offended me. I tightened the grip around myself, though I was barely holding on.

"Emmy . . ." The deep timbre of his voice washed over me in a familiar way, knotting my stomach and making my knees weak. My eyes slipped closed.

How dare he have the audacity to speak my name? He'd lost that right awhile ago. There should be a special place in hell reserved for boyfriends who got another woman pregnant. Raising my hand in the air, I waved at a passing cab. Ugh. No luck.

"Emmy, wait." He crossed the distance between us, reaching for me.

Don't touch me. I jerked out of his reach. I couldn't handle the feel of his warm fingers grazing my skin. It'd evoke too many memories I'd been fighting to keep at bay. I watched the cars pass, unable to face him.

"How's the baby?" I couldn't resist asking; nor could I prevent the bitter tone lacing my voice.

From the corner of my vision, I saw him swallow roughly as he stuffed his hands into his pockets. "We should talk, Emmy."

"I have nothing to say to you."

"Well, I do. There are a few things you should know."

What could possibly be so important?

I spun around to confront him, my ponytail lashing him in the face. Dark circles lined his eyes. He looked terrible. His insomnia was obviously back in full swing. He'd once told me that sleeping by my side was the only thing that kept it at bay. I closed my eyes briefly, but the memories refused to stay locked away. Thoughts of his warm body curled around mine, the way he mumbled in his sleep, and the sensation of his lips rubbing against that sensitive spot at the back of my neck drifted into my consciousness.

My stomach lurched. *Hold it together, Emmy.* Guarding myself against the hot tears that threatened to escape, I drew a shaky breath.

This tall, beautiful man overwhelmed my senses. He stood with such an air of authority that I had to physically fight the gravitational pull urging me to throw myself into his arms. Even after all this time, my body had not forgotten a thing.

I couldn't believe I'd once thought he could be mine. Looking into that brilliant, hazel gaze framed by long, dark lashes, I was hit with a thousand different emotions I'd convinced myself I'd only imagined—the way he looked straight into the very center of me, the clean masculine scent of his skin that I was powerless against, the way his fingers twitched to reach out for me. Suddenly, I was delirious, overcome with emotion, and consumed by a longing so deep it owned me. And it always would. I loved him. Loved him with every fiber of my being. There was no getting over this man. It was too much to look directly at him; it was like staring into the sun. I blinked, looking down at the dirty sidewalk, needing a moment to pull myself together.

"Please. My driver's here." He motioned to the waiting black sedan parked at the curb. "Let me take you home and explain." Ben lifted my bag from beside my feet, and then those brilliant eyes locked firmly onto mine.

I felt my resolve weaken and slip away. This was why I'd left, why I hadn't answered his calls. He was going to say he didn't love her, and it had all been a terrible mistake. God help my wounded heart, I'd lap it up. I knew myself, though, knew I couldn't handle living in her shadow with the knowledge of their shared past. But being a polite southern girl, or just a complete glutton for pain, I followed Ben to the car and slid inside.

1

Four Months Earlier

Cursing my wardrobe, I grabbed a navy pencil skirt and a cream silk blouse out of my closet. Although I'd already worn them earlier this week, my options were limited. As soon as I got paid, I was going to blow my first check on clothes. If I stayed at this job, that is. I didn't know which outcome was more likely—getting fired or quitting. For the past two weeks, I'd been working at Status Model Management in New York City. Being a country girl at heart, the experience was proving to be a spectacular disaster, but at least the pay was going to be good. If I could just stick it out.

I tucked the blouse into the skirt and checked my profile in the mirror. Ugh. Bloated. I rummaged through my top drawer and dug out my Spanx. I quickly tugged them up under my skirt, cursing loudly all the while. *God, these things are awful.* I'd left my rich brown hair loose, and it fluffed out around my shoulders nicely. I could thank my mother for

having good hair. I quickly dabbed concealer on the dark circles beneath my eyes and applied lip gloss. There. Much better. Standing back, I gave myself one last look. Not bad. I was
far from a supermodel, but I looked decent. I glanced at the
clock. *Shit! I'm so late.*

I shoved my feet into my only pair of heels—nude pumps
that I pretended went with everything—and stumbled toward the door. Between the fitted skirt, tight down to my
knees, and this damn girdle cutting off my circulation, walking was going to be a challenge today. Quickly grabbing the
tray of muffins I'd baked last night as a gesture of goodwill
for my new boss and coworkers, I launched myself out the
apartment door.

A warm July breeze danced around my ankles as I walked
outside onto the bustling street. A swarm of yellow cabs
roared past me. The scents of car exhaust, warm bread, and
stale urine crammed the air, fighting for attention. A hot dog
vendor on my right smiled as I walked past. A bike messen-
ger zipped down the road, nearly hitting me as I crossed the
street, and the MetLife building loomed in the distance. I was
overpowered with an enormous sense of homesickness. This
place was nothing like Tennessee.

Even after living here a few weeks, I didn't see how the
roar of New York traffic was something I'd ever get used to.
Some days I wondered if I'd bitten off more than I could chew,
yet I kept moving forward, kept putting one foot in front of
the other.

When I arrived at work with my tray of muffins I was already late, so I shuffled as quickly as my heels in plush carpeting would allow and made a mad dash toward the executive assistant's suite outside the boss's office. A few heads looked up as I hurried past, and I wondered if my heart could give out at the ripe old age of twenty-two.

Deep, exotic perfumes mingling with the aroma of leather filled my nose and I stifled a sneeze. The agency itself was all modern, with thick opaque glass and steel beams, looking very chic and high-end. The twentieth floor provided gorgeous views of Central Park in the distance. I loved looking at those leafy green treetops. I never knew you could miss seeing trees, but New York made that possible.

The top of my desk was littered with at least a dozen Post-it notes, each one containing some nearly illegible message written in Fiona's messy handwriting. *Crap.* She'd clearly been at work for a while. Why she preferred to communicate solely on yellow scraps of sticky paper was beyond me. She never emailed me—she'd either yell something from her office or scrawl it on a Post-it when I wasn't around. It was my job to decipher the meanings. I peeled up the first one from my desk, which was fairly clear. It said, *Call Ben in.*

I dropped into my seat to start organizing her notes in case I needed to refer back to one later. I shoved one note that was presumably written in hieroglyphics into my plastic-sleeved binder and then set about dealing with the rest of them. First things first, I tried to figure out which Ben she meant. Checking the database, I saw our office had three Bens. Two of them hadn't booked a job in several months, so by process of elimination I assumed she was referring to Ben Shaw, one of our most popular models. I took a deep breath and dialed his number.

"Yeah," a deep voice answered.

"Um, yes, hi. This is Emmy Clarke from Status. Fiona would like to see you today."

"Okay." He sounded mildly annoyed. "What time?"

I opened her calendar, silently cursing myself for not having that information ready. Thankfully my computer cooperated and quickly loaded the information. She was free all morning. "You can come in any time before noon."

"Sure," he replied. "I'll be in later this morning." He hung up without saying good-bye.

I sighed and returned the phone to its receiver. Okay then. Task one complete. That wasn't so bad.

Now to take care of the few emails I had. I liked being privy to the inner workings of a modeling agency, and Status Model Management was one of the more powerful New York agencies, often winning seven-figure contracts with major advertisers. It had a fleet of fresh new faces to feed any executive's desire. The unique thing, though, was that my boss, Fiona, who ran the agency, represented only male models. Fiona made it widely known she didn't work well with females. She'd once said it was too much estrogen, or something like that.

As Fiona's assistant, my job description included maintaining the agency database of models and passing their info on to her for specific jobs. Requests would come in for certain looks, hair color, eye color, height, and weight, and I would comb through the files to find the right beautiful men for the job before sending their headshots and files over to Fiona for approval. The position certainly had its perks. Ogling delicious man candy daily was the main one. Did that make me shallow? No. I didn't think so. I'd had a bunch of crappy jobs and crappier relationships before all of this. If I wanted to be surrounded by completely delicious and highly unattainable men all day, I felt that was a God-given right. And getting paid to boot—yes, please. Sign me up.

It was my job to know the nitty-gritty details of each model, to help determine which one was right for each type of job—editorial, high fashion, fitness, lifestyle—before giving their comp cards to Fiona. This entitled me to intimate information on the couple hundred or so young men we worked with. Their shoe sizes, personality quirks, and even little-known facts, like that Nico couldn't work with Sebastian because they'd once dated and it had ended badly. Or that Leo had a phobia about anything fluffy and couldn't be around tulle or feathers.

I made sure things ran smoothly on set, and many times the photographers were worse than the models—demanding and pissy, with a tendency to degrade the models when they couldn't get the shots they wanted. I'd already learned part of my job would be to act as a mediator, helping to smooth things over and finding out about the expectations of the photographer and explaining them to the model.

Of course, my biggest challenge was dealing with Fiona

Stone, the ultra-British, ultra-bitchy head of Status Models. She was truly a rare breed. Somewhere between thirty and forty, she was stunningly beautiful. She definitely fit in among the pretty people working at the agency. Smart as a whip at business, but with the social skills and politeness of a mosquito. She was cunning, conniving, and most of all, ruthless. She negotiated hard for her models, often earning them higher rates and better contracts. But she ruled with an iron, though well-manicured, fist. And I had the distinct pleasure of dealing with her day in and day out. Lucky me.

My little desk sat right outside her office. From her immaculate red leather perch, she could glance up whenever she wanted and see my computer screen and whatever I might be looking at. So online shopping, catching up on Facebook, and personal emails were all a big no-no.

I'd applauded myself that I wasn't the receptionist out front or one of the production assistants. They seemed even more miserable than I was. Nope, I'd landed the executive assistant position—yay me! Rolling my eyes, I remembered how extremely self-conscious I had been my first day among all the toned and stylish women already working here. Little did I know that working for Fiona would prove to be a special kind of torture. She criticized everything, from my brown hair to my nonexistent sense of style to my southern accent.

My first Friday night, I'd gone out to happy hour with Gunnar and a few of the other assistants. He'd informed me that Fiona didn't hate me, that the sharp tongue was just part of her way. Apparently I'd already lasted longer than her previous three assistants combined. Gunnar was a production assistant and occasionally worked with Fiona, too, so he knew what I was talking about. After that pep talk, I'd convinced myself I could endure anything. I would win her over. I would succeed where others had failed. No way was I going to hang it up and crawl away with my tail between my legs. No ma'am. This was my first real job, and in New York City no less. I would make this work. And with the promise of the travel schedule taking us to Paris and Milan soon, I wanted to make this work. Back home, no one got opportunities like this. I would be stupid to quit just because I didn't like my boss.

Fiona's British accent cut through my thoughts like a siren. "Stop drooling over that boy, and get your arse in here."

Crap! My screen had been sitting idle on the seminude photo of a male model. Oops. I shuffled my tight-skirt–wearing self into Fiona's office. She was dressed immaculately, as always, in a Versace linen dress with a bright royal-purple scarf and a pair of the highest Prada heels I'd ever seen. Those suckers put the Empire State Building to shame. Her hair was pinned back in a loose chignon, shiny dark tendrils framing her elegant face.

"Yes, Miss Stone?" I asked.

"Do you know what time it is?" Her expensively clad foot tapped the floor and she didn't bother looking up from her computer screen. *Tap, tap, tap.*

Oh, shit. Was this a trick question? "Uh, it's ten o'clock—"

She leaned back in her chair, peering at me intently. "And?"

And? And what? She gave me an icy glare, making my heart pound and a cold sweat break out under my arms.

After ten seconds of stony silence, during which she looked me over from head to toe in disgust, making me want to hide behind the big potted plant in her office, she finally spoke.

"It is *time* for my tea." She grunted and waved a dismissive hand in my direction.

Oh. Right. Her midmorning tea. How very British of her. I dashed for the kitchenette as quickly as my restrictive skirt–Spanx-heels combo would allow to heat some purified water for her tea. I added the package of English Breakfast to the cup and scuttled back, just in time to see a man entering her office. *Great. Another blunder.* I was sure I'd catch hell later for letting a guest inside unannounced.

I stepped into her office behind him, still carrying the tea.

"Ben, love, come in," Fiona drawled and gestured to the leather seat facing her desk.

Oh. So this was Ben Shaw. Seeing his photos on the computer was one thing. Seeing this delicious piece of man meat in person was quite another. My damn mouth was watering. He was tall and poised, with dark hair, broad shoulders, an angular jaw, and a pouty mouth built for kissing.

I briefly wondered if I'd be scolded for letting someone into her office unannounced, but Fiona was all smiles where Ben was concerned.

Benjamin Riley Shaw, the agency golden boy. Our most in-demand model and top earner by a wide margin. Seeing him in person for the first time, it was obvious why. He had a certain aura about him, a glow. My eyes were unconsciously drawn to him. He was by far the most captivating thing in the room. Having just reviewed his file, I felt slightly pervy knowing so many personal details about him, but it also made me feel just a little bit smug. *Height: 6 feet 3 three inches; Eyes: Hazel; Hair: Brown; Shoe Size: 12; Suit: 42L; Inseam: 34 inches.*

I watched in stunned silence as Fiona rose and went around the desk to lean in and brush her boobs against his chest. She air-kissed both of his cheeks. He remained still, politely allowing it but not returning her affections. Something inside me liked that about him. Fiona was a grade-A bitch, and to see a fine specimen like Ben pretend to fawn all over her would have twisted the knife in my heart.

"Of course it's lovely to see you, but did you need something, darling?" she asked him, pulling back only slightly. *Ugh. Personal space much?*

Ben shifted his tall, statuesque form moving away from her in the most elegant way. "I was asked to come in today," he said flatly.

Fiona's eyes landed on mine. Panic coursed through my system and I felt the teacup rattle in my hands. Her icy glare pinned me in place, imploring me to explain.

"But your, um, note . . . said to call Ben in," I stammered.

Ben's gaze traveled to mine and my stomach did a little flip. *Whoa.* His eyes were a brilliant hazel color with flecks of deep mossy green, and they held such sadness, such mystery that I was stopped cold. As he continued to stare at me, my ovaries did a little happy dance, totally defying the strictures of my Spanx. This guy was wreaking havoc on my libido.

With difficulty, I turned my gaze and attention back to Fiona, who was sighing dramatically.

She scoffed. "I meant for you to call Ben's sizes into the designer for his shoot next week." She shook her head like I was a complete moron to mix up the message. *Crap.*

My eyes flicked to Ben's again and the cup and saucer shook in my hand. I attempted to cross the room to deliver the tea to her desk, but Ben's heavy gaze following my movements proved to be too much and the teacup and saucer went tumbling to the floor.

The teacup shattered and scalding hot water sprayed my exposed skin. *Mother, that was hot.* I winced and took a step back, assessing the damage. *Shit.* The dark stain was spreading over the beige carpet in front of me, and I looked like an overexcited puppy that had pissed itself in front of one of the world's top models. *Pull it together, Emmy!*

Ben's eyebrows drew together and Fiona let out an exasperated huff.

"It's a wonder she can even walk and talk at the same time. She's from Tennessee," Fiona said by way of explanation. Ben's attention slowly pulled back to Fiona.

My face heated with embarrassment. I liked my quaint country upbringing, and I wouldn't change it for all the glamour and designer labels in the world. So I wasn't from London, big whoop. I wouldn't let her make me feel like I was two inches tall.

"I'm sorry. I'll handle this." I picked up my chin and scurried to my desk.

Ben

Tennessee huh? That explained the sweet little lilt to her voice. She wasn't Fiona's usual assistant. First, she was female. Secondly, she was *still* female, and Fiona didn't play well with those of her own kind.

The assistant, with her tight little, knee-length navy skirt and proper tucked-in blouse, would have looked like an innocent schoolgirl if it weren't for those curves. Holy hell, those curves. A luscious ass and the swell of a generous chest. *Eyes up, buddy. No getting wood over the new girl.*

Her innocence was cute, different. A hint of pink blossomed across her cheeks and her teeth were buried deep in her bottom lip. She had dark hair tucked efficiently behind her ears, and her hands shook, unable to stop the teacup from rattling. She stared up into my eyes, looking lost before the teacup went tumbling to the floor. For a split second I worried that the city of Manhattan—or Fiona—would chew her up and spit her out. A surge of protectiveness flared up inside me, the feeling strange and foreign. Also, not entirely welcome. I didn't know this girl. Shouldn't care. Yet I did. I couldn't deny the instant chemistry and intrigue that buzzed between us, the suppressed shudder when I met her gaze, the soft inhalation of breath. I'd be lying if I said I didn't feel something when watching her fidget in front of me.

Fiona turned to face me, curling her hand around my bicep, bringing me back to the situation at hand. "Well, since you're here, love, you might as well take me to lunch."

"Sure," I responded automatically. I could see through Fiona's ploy. She wanted to see me today—but didn't want to admit it. I knew her games. This pretty young thing didn't. And she was left to feel like the village idiot.

If she understood Fiona's true motivation for calling me in, she wouldn't be staring up at me with those innocent gray-blue eyes. If she knew the depravity lurking inside me, she'd flee for Tennessee without a backward glance. I'd devour a girl like her. Own her. The thought was intoxicating. I watched her with interest, considering my next move.

"I'm sorry. I'll handle this." Tennessee picked up her chin and scurried to her desk, her confidence broken.

Watching her retreat while Fiona touched up her lipstick, I decided her assistant would be fun to play with. She'd be all soft feminine innocence, and those perfectly proportioned curves were begging for my hands. Fiona's claws would come out though, so it might not be worth it. Fiona had done too much for me. Shit, she was my manager. I wasn't about to do something stupid, like sleep with her assistant to piss her off. Bad career move. My dick would have to stay in my pants.

Emmy

The low murmur of voices coming from Fiona's office kept me from reentering. I searched my bottom desk drawer for the emergency roll of paper towels I kept there. I was waiting for them to leave before I scampered in on hands and knees to clean up the mess. But they seemed to be taking their sweet time. I couldn't hear the discussion but their postures were tense and they spoke in hushed voices.

Every time I thought about the way he'd gazed into my eyes, my heart did a funny leap. There was a certain depth to this man, one that his beauty kept hidden. I doubted most people dug below the surface. Yet strangely, I wanted to know him. It was a stupid thought and I had no idea where it came from. Perhaps it was my upbringing, southern hospitality, or something like it. But I wanted to take care of this man, ease that little worry line creasing his forehead. The depth and complexity in his eyes had held me captive a moment too long.

As if my thoughts had lured him away from Fiona's clutches, Ben came striding out of the office and hesitated at my desk. "Did you get burned?"

His question took a moment to resonate. Oh yeah, my legs. The humiliation had blocked out the pain. But now that he mentioned it, I realized they were tingling where they'd been splattered with the searing water. With his gaze so intent on mine, it took me a moment to remind my mouth how to work properly.

"Just on my legs," I stammered. *Brilliant.* Put a gorgeous man in front of me and I became a bumbling idiot. This job did not bode well for my self-esteem.

His eyes fell to my naked shins and I forgot all about the burn.

Fiona appeared, dropping a tube of lipstick into her Fendi handbag. That thing cost more than I made in a month. She lifted her chin, sniffing the air. "What is that smell?" Her face twisted in repulsion. She looked from Ben to me. All I could smell was the mouthwatering goodness of baked treats emanating from the container on my desk. "It smells like processed sugar." Frown lines deepened around Fiona's mouth.

"I baked blueberry muffins for the office." I opened the lid and the most delicious scent wafted out, reminding my stomach that I'd skipped breakfast in lieu of taking the time to dress in something presentable and straighten my hair. "Would you like one before I put them in the kitchenette?"

Ben's gaze flicked down to the floor as he tried to hide a smile. Fiona looked at me like I was mentally unstable, like I was trying to serve her a pile of manure rather than a home-made blueberry muffin.

What was her problem? Guess my gesture of goodwill was a dumb idea. I sniffled and raised my chin. I was damn proud of my muffins. But the look of disdain dripping from Fiona's pouty red mouth instantly told me bringing baked goods into a modeling agency was akin to killing a puppy. Slowly, Fiona groaned and strode away. I looked down at my burned, tea-splattered legs and my self-confidence fell to an all-time low.

"Hey, Blueberry Muffin Girl . . ." Ben's voice was low and authoritative, drawing my eyes back up to his. He fixed me with that sexy stare. "Make sure you put some ice on your burn." His expression was flirty and kind, even if his concern felt out of place.

Forming words wasn't possible at the moment, but I managed a nod. Ben followed after Fiona, chuckling to himself. I heard snickers around me. *They're probably taking bets on how long I'll stick around.*

2

Emmy

I thanked the gods it was Friday as I dragged my sorry carcass into the apartment I shared with Ellie. I wanted to do nothing more than slip into a pair of sweats, eat take-out Chinese food, and drink mass quantities of cheap wine. And after the day I'd had, I might need my own bottle.

Ellie was already in the kitchen when I arrived with apparently the same thought. She was opening a bottle of wine, or rather, wrestling the cork out of it. Our corkscrew really was a piece of crap.

"Emmy!" she called when she saw me. "Survive another week?"

"Yup." I pulled off my jacket and tossed it on the cluttered dining room table. "Thank God."

"Good, because I was a bit worried you weren't going to make it and, I mean, the chance to go live in Paris for three months? I'd work for Satan himself. I'd even have his babies."

I laughed and accepted the filled-to-the-brim glass from her. "Well, before you go spawn with Satan, I'm not cleared yet. I know for a fact she hasn't bought my ticket."

Ellie pushed her sexy-nerd glasses up higher on her nose and took a sip of her wine. "Please, if you've made it through her temper tantrums and snotty insults this far without going postal, you're golden. I would've cracked that first day. What was her comment again . . . *Kmart chic*?"

I shuddered at the memory. It was my first day. We had sat in Fiona's opulent office covering the basic roles and responsibilities of my new job. She'd brought up the dress code and said she had an image to maintain and my Kmart-chic wardrobe wouldn't be tolerated. I had been dressed according to the dress code—or so I'd thought—in black pants and a button-down top. No matter. What Fiona didn't understand was that a few nasty comments weren't going to drive me away.

I'd always wanted more out of life, and with my parents' encouragement I'd set my standards fairly high, attending a state university on a scholarship and getting my degree in communications and fashion design. I didn't need an Ivy League education and a six-figure job offer. I just wanted to break free from the financial stress of living paycheck to paycheck like my parents.

I had lived the quintessential simple upbringing while constantly striving for that ever-out-of-reach American dream. Underpaid, hardworking parents. Double-wide trailer in a one-stoplight town in western Tennessee with a jock younger brother who delivered idle threats to any guy who showed even the slightest interest in me. Climbing trees in my younger years, cheerleading and sleepovers in high school.

So after graduating from college and landing a job as an assistant at a prestigious modeling agency in NYC, I was well on my way. I would make this work.

My roommate pulled out cheese and crackers then set them on the counter, jarring me from my thoughts. She munched on a cracker and sipped her wine. I watched her and smiled.

She was spunky and fun and I was glad to be subletting a room from her, but we were from totally different walks of life. Ellie was a sassy New Yorker who didn't let anyone blink at her the wrong way without making some sassy comment in retaliation. Being the opposite, I'd been known to stop on the side of the road to help ducks cross the street and couldn't walk by a homeless person without giving him my last few bucks.

"Okay, we need to prep you for your Euro-adventure! You'll need a makeover; we'll get you smokin' for all that hot-male-model action. New clothes. Haircut. No more carbs. Wine doesn't count," she added, urging me to take another sip.

I laughed at her enthusiasm. "Whoa there! There will be *no* model action in my future," I assured her. I didn't need a one-way ticket to heartbreak city. No thanks.

Still, I couldn't help thinking about Ben Shaw again. Those intense, sexy eyes, his full lips . . .

I'd thought of him constantly since our awkward tea-spill-ing, blueberry muffin–peddling run-in earlier. Ben was the reason Fiona and I were even going to Paris and Milan. As the agency "It-boy," he'd been booked for several campaigns in some of the hottest fashion markets in the world. And Fiona, superbad at disguising her crush on the poor man, told me that she always traveled with Ben when he went on extended assignments. I couldn't blame her, though. I was pretty damn close to crush territory myself.

Ellie thoughtfully swirled the wine in her glass. "We should also make sure you get some nookie before you go; otherwise you'll be a horny mess."

"What?" I laughed again. "No, I won't. I'm a professional, unlike you."

Ellie shook her head and snorted. I didn't want to be the one to burst her bubble that many of the male models were gay anyway.

She grabbed the menu for the deli across the street, picked up her phone, and dialed. "Yes, two spinach salads with grilled chicken."

I raised my eyebrows at her.

"No carbs," she mouthed to me. It was a little disheartening to be informed by your roommate that you needed to slim down. Sure, I could probably stand to lose a few pounds, but spinach, seriously? That was ridiculous.

"You're going to be in the company of male models for the next few months," she explained after ending the call.

I didn't think Ellie understood that I'd be working, not competing on a game show to find my future husband.

But then I made the mistake of thinking of Ben.

Honest to God, I would never eat another carb again.

While he and Fiona had been out to lunch, I'd opened his file. That way I could snoop in peace without her watching over my shoulder. He was perfection. Textbook perfect. If I had to draw up the specs for my perfect man, Ben Shaw is what God, or Cupid, or whoever would've delivered to me wrapped in a bow. Tall, broad shouldered, and blessed with chiseled dark features. The pictures of him shirtless, or better yet, in a pair of briefs, really sent my pulse racing. Smooth, rounded pecs, golden skin, a well-defined six-pack, full pouting mouth, and the most intense eyes ever completed the look.

I had been ready to remove my panties discreetly under my desk when Fiona came back and my sexy reverie was over in a damn hurry. As fast as my mouse would allow, I closed the pictures of him, silently cursing myself that I hadn't thought ahead to email any to my personal account for private viewing later.

I had shaken my head clear of those horny thoughts and leaned back in my chair. The last thing I needed was a desperate crush on a male model I worked with. I would need to keep my wits about me if I expected to survive the next few months living in close proximity to him. Not to mention pack a big supply of batteries. Yes, an extra suitcase full of batteries oughtta do the trick.

3

Emmy

After a relaxing weekend watching Netflix and lounging with Ellie, it was back to the grind Monday morning. Oddly, Fiona seemed like she was in a great mood for once; her smile was sincere as she greeted me.

"Good morning, Emerson."

"Morning?" I wasn't sure what to make of her sudden shift in attitude. The number of Post-its on my desk reflected her good mood. There was just one. *Book your ticket to CDG.*

It took me a second to realize that CDG was the Charles de Gaulle International Airport in Paris. I didn't wait to be told twice. Using the credit card Fiona had given me for business purposes, I booked an overnight flight out that Friday night. Same as Fiona's. I wouldn't have a clue how to navigate Paris if I landed there on my own.

I wasn't sure when Ben was flying out but I'd overheard

that he would be there a few days before us to visit a friend.

That week leading up to our trip was crazy busy. During the day, I organized the many details that were Fiona's life: coordinating her weekly massage appointments to take place in Paris, ensuring I had a whole caseload of her favorite brand of English Breakfast tea, and arranging the Post-it note bible in alphabetical order, with subsections according to things I thought might pertain to our trip.

My evenings were spent shopping with Ellie and packing everything I owned into two rolling suitcases. It was weird to think I'd be gone for three whole months. Ellie even had someone lined up to sublet my room while I was away. My life was about to be totally turned upside down, and I couldn't have been more excited.

Pushing the strap of my duffel bag higher on my shoulder, I squeezed through the narrow aisle as I boarded the flight. I spotted Fiona sitting in the third row of first class, glass of champagne in hand, flirting with the businessman beside her. The stewardess leaned over to pass her a warm towel. Of course, I was sitting much farther back in coach, but on the bright side, I was going to Paris! Nothing could've dampened my mood right now. Fiona's mouth pursed when she saw me gawking, but she continued her conversation with Mr. Business Executive in seat 3B.

Ellie's advice to take Tylenol PM at boarding was sound. I was asleep before takeoff and only woke when we were an hour from landing. Leaving my seat, I freshened up in the tiny airplane lavatory, attempting to fluff my flat, greasy hair and dotting concealer under my tired eyes. But there was no helping the lack of color in my cheeks or the rumpled clothing. I knew I'd have a busy day ahead of me once we landed. Fiona was long gone when I finally made it off the plane. After passing easily through customs, I powered on my phone and waited at the baggage claim. Although I'd arranged for an upgrade to an international plan, I was still surprised when my cell showed a text from Fiona.

Get my bags and meet me at the hotel.

She'd left.

Well wasn't that just craptastic? I had no idea what her bags looked like, so I was forced to wait until everyone from our flight had taken theirs and then read the little tags on the dozen or so bags left unclaimed.

She had a whole fleet of luggage. Louis Vuitton, of course. It was a wonder she trusted me with it. After wrestling her bags and mine out to the curb and tracking down a shuttle, nearly two hours had passed before I made it to the hotel: an upscale, boutique affair in Saint Germain in the lovely 6th arrondissement.

Stepping from the cab, the mouthwatering smell of coffee and croissants hit my nose. People sat clustered in outdoor cafés under umbrella tables, sipping espresso and eating pastries. Water flowed down the gutters as the streets were flushed clean, and elderly people fed the pigeons. The golden glow of the sun hitting the old, stone buildings and the brilliant bright blue sky seemed to transform the city streets into something magical. Romantic, cultured, and pretty.

A place where anything could happen.

The hotel lobby was quaint and simply appointed with a large oak desk, buffed marble floors, and colorful tapestries hanging on the walls. After a quick check-in, I stepped into the antique elevator, praying it would support the weight of all the luggage.

My room was as tiny as I had expected. Though the hotel was quite upscale, my room held little more than a bed dressed in fluffy white linens. There was a wardrobe pushed into the corner and a TV mounted on the wall. Gauzy cream curtains framed the tall, narrow windows, lending the efficient room a pretty and enchanting vibe. It would be my home away from home.

Anticipating Fiona's many demands, I planned to meet with the front-desk staff to understand the Paris subway map. Best to be preemptive, since I knew I'd likely be running around the city fetching whatever Fiona needed at a moment's notice, and my learning curve was likely to be steep, having never set foot outside the United States. Plus, my French was limited to *bonjour* and *merci*. But first, I needed to get Fiona's bags to her room. They quite literally didn't fit in my own.

After wrestling them in and out of the tiny elevator, I was sweaty and more than a little grumpy as I stood at the door to Fiona's top-floor suite. The door was left cracked open, and I gave a quick but firm knock before pushing it open.

No one answered, but I could hear muted voices in the adjoining room.

Entering the living room with plush sofas and a TV, I dragged the suitcases in after me. Voices leaked from the bedroom. Fiona was with a man. And apparently they were in a heated discussion. *Awkward* . . .

I could leave the bags and sneak away unnoticed. I wasn't in the mood to face a grumpy Fiona. My agenda included a hot shower and a nap.

After stacking her bags in the corner, I froze. I recognized the man's voice. Deep and rich with a confident tone.

Ben.

My body responded instantly, my nipples hardening against my bra and my pulse jumping erratically. My body's responses to him were anything but normal.

Unable to resist getting a look at him, I tiptoed closer to the doorway, and peeked inside the room.

"What's this about, Fiona? You're mad that I saw Madeline last night? Is that what this tantrum is?"

"I'm not going to pretend I like it. But, love, you know I can never stay mad at you."

"I haven't seen Maddie in years, you know that, and we're shooting together tomorrow. I wanted to say hi. We hit one club, got a drink, and reminisced. It was no big deal," Ben said, his voice indifferent.

"Those gossip rags follow her around and I just don't want your image linked to hers." Fiona's voice was a soft whine, vaguely reminiscent of a lap dog in heat.

"Chill. It was low key, Fiona. I was back here, in bed alone, by eleven. I couldn't sleep worth shit, but I was here."

"Okay." Fiona sighed. "If you say it wasn't a big deal, it wasn't. End of story."

It sounded like Fiona was jealous that he'd hung out with a woman, and I knew she had issues with estrogen, but that couldn't be it, could it? Surely Ben was allowed to hang out with whomever he wanted. I couldn't resist peeking farther around the corner.

They stood in the center of her bedroom in front of the bed. Fiona had changed and was smartly dressed in a fitted black lace top and cream skirt. In contrast, I was frazzled, greasy, and still dressed in yesterday's wrinkled clothes. Ben, of course, looked like a walking orgasm, wearing dark fitted jeans and a black tee that showed off his muscular physique. His jaw was unshaven and his deep-set gaze was locked on Fiona's, exuding his dark boyish charm. Good Lord, did that man know how to work it.

Fiona's back was to me, and I watched as she placed her open palm on his chest and gave it a gentle pat. "I'm over it, love. I'm here now and this season is going to be terrific."

Ben's features visibly relaxed, his shoulders dropping as if her words held the power to soothe him. Just then, his eyes flicked to mine and he took a step back from Fiona, his expression weary.

"Excuse me, Miss Stone?" I found my voice, knowing I'd been discovered eavesdropping.

Fiona whirled around on her four-inch Prada stilettos. "Oh, Emerson. There you are." Her voice was laced with sour frustration and held none of the sugary sweetness reserved just for Ben. "Took you long enough. Good thing I had my carry-on."

She started toward me, seemingly annoyed by my interruption but acting as though being reunited with her precious luggage was the best thing that'd ever happened to her. Ben followed and they both joined me in the living room.

"Ben, this is my new assistant, Emerson Clarke," she introduced me, waving an absent hand in my direction.

Ben's large hand reached out for mine.

"Emmy," I added, placing my palm against his. A jolt of heat at the contact of his skin made me shudder.

Ben stared at me with an unreadable expression. Maybe he'd forgotten me.

"Blueberry Muffin Girl." He smiled. "Burn all healed up?"

"Oh, it was nothing. I'm fine." Why couldn't he have forgotten that disastrous first time we met?

"Where's my garment bag?" Fiona asked, pulling my attention away from Ben's deep hazel gaze.

"Your what?"

Hands anchored on her hips, she stood surveying the four large brown monogrammed suitcases with a frown. "I had a hanging bag of gowns. It's not here."

"I'm sorry, I didn't know about the garment bag, but I can call the airport and arrange for it to be delivered."

Fiona grabbed the smallest suitcase, heaving it past me so I had to jump out of her path to avoid being knocked over. Ben steadied me as I shuffled closer to him. His warm hand closed around my elbow, sending heat zipping up my arm at the contact. *Whoa.*

Realizing my conversation with Fiona was over, and still standing open-mouthed staring at Ben, I mumbled an apology and fled through the door.

Ben

Fiona had only just arrived and she was already exhausting me. It was going to be a long damn season if she pulled that jealous pouty act every time I talked to a female. Christ. And speaking of females, I hadn't been expecting to see her sweet little assistant. That was an interesting turn of events. Honestly, I was kind of amazed.

Fiona changed assistants more often than most people changed their underwear. And after the debacle at her office the other day—mistakenly calling me in and then shattering that teacup—it was a shocker she was still employed. Not to mention she was cute. Another strike against her. Fiona liked to be the best-looking woman in the room and certainly wouldn't have hired an attractive assistant, but then again, maybe she just didn't see it. Fiona was buffed, waxed, manicured, and Botoxed, and Emmy was au naturel—make-up-free skin that let the pink of her cheeks show, and long, straight hair that looked touchably soft.

I chuckled softly to myself. No, I definitely hadn't expected to see her again. But it was a nice surprise. Maybe this season would be interesting after all.

I dutifully kissed Fiona's cheek good-bye and strolled out of the room. I found Emmy still standing in the hall. The back of her head rested against the wall. Her eyes were closed and she drew deep breaths, her breasts rising and falling with each inhale. There was nothing merely cute about this girl. She was beautiful. I had an insane urge to hold her, to comfort her. Instantly, I changed my mind.

I wondered how much she'd heard of the conversation between me and Fiona and what she'd made of it. I certainly wasn't going to offer up any explanation. My relationship with Fiona was complicated, to say the least.

"Are you okay?" My voice startled her, and her eyes flew open and darted up to mine. She didn't answer right away; she just continued watching me. I leaned against the wall beside her and crossed my feet at the ankles.

"I'm sorry." She shook her head, looking down at the plush gold and burgundy carpeting lining the hallway. "I'm fine. I'm just overtired, hungry. . . ."

She didn't elaborate, but she was also most likely confused about what she'd just heard transpire between me and Fiona, and embarrassed for being chastised in front of me. The last thing I wanted was her thinking that it was some lovers' quarrel between me and her boss.

She remained rooted in place, pulling deep breaths into her lungs, like she was fighting for control. I wanted to reach a hand out and soothe her, brush the loose hair back from her pretty face. I wondered if her hair felt as silky as it looked. Instead, I shoved my hands in my pockets.

She looked up, pushed her shoulders back, and struggled to appear put together. She fixed me with a determined gray stare. "I'm fine. I've got to go track down that missing bag of Fiona's."

She turned to leave when I reached out and caught her elbow. A flash of heat zipped up my arm at the contact. *That was interesting.*

Emmy

His penetrating gaze held me immobile. "Don't let her get to you."

Her? Oh, Fiona.

"She's only cranky because she just turned thirty-eight," Ben said, still looking at me expectantly.

"I didn't know it was Fiona's birthday."

"Yeah, last week. But she doesn't like people to know." His hand dropped from my elbow. It was probably clear I wasn't going anywhere while this beautiful man was talking to me. "Plus, I think she's pissed at me right now, so seriously, don't worry. You'll get the bag delivered, right?"

Oh yeah, the bag. God, Ben talking to me and looking like he was actually concerned was enough to send my brain straight to la-la land. I needed to remember I had a job to do. "Thanks. And yeah, I guess I better go track down that bag."

He nodded and stepped back. I darted for the elevators

on shaky legs. It was just jet lag. It had nothing to do with him. *Yeah, right.*

Once the precious bag had been located and delivered, I spent the afternoon coordinating details for the next day's photo shoot. It would take place at a historic Paris hotel, and after confirming that the photographer, makeup artist, lighting techs, and catering would all be there, I then double-checked Fiona's notes in the Post-it bible for anything I might have missed. I still needed to email the models to give them their call times. But first, I ordered room service. I was starved and I doubted there'd be an invite from Fiona for a nice dinner out, even though it was my first night in Paris. I'd considered trying to navigate the city and treating myself to a classy meal, but dismissed the idea. A hot shower, pajamas, and dinner in bed sounded like a much better way to end the long day I'd had.

After showering, I fell into the fluffy comforter covering the bed and situated my laptop on a pillow on my lap. I double-checked their call times and sent notes to the models for tomorrow. I wasn't sure why, but the thought of emailing Ben was nerve-racking. My fingers trembled. I considered writing something funny and cute, maybe signing the note Blueberry Muffin Girl . . . but at the last second I chickened out and typed a brief, professionally worded email. No sense flirting with a model; I'd probably just end up looking like an idiot. Surely, hordes of girls threw themselves at him on a daily basis. Though a smiley face couldn't hurt, could it?

From: Emerson Clarke

Subject: Photo Shoot Tomorrow

To: Ben Shaw

> Ben,
>
> Please arrive at 58 rue de Fleurus at 9 a.m. tomorrow. See you then.
>
> ☺
>
> Emmy Clarke
>
> Assistant to Fiona Stone, Status Model Management

Someone knocked on the door. Room service! My stomach grumbled loudly. After tipping the bellhop, I settled back into the pillows with my food and typed Ben's name into my browser. Dinner and a show. What could be more perfect? Google Images was my entertainment for the night. Yes, I was developing a serious fetish for him. Sue me.

My email indicator flashed with a new message, and I silently cursed whoever was interrupting my sick little addiction. I opened my inbox.

> Ben Shaw Re: Tomorrow
>
> Tongue!

I laughed silently to myself, finding it cute that he both noticed my smiley face had its tongue sticking out and took the time to respond. I typed out a response.

> Me: Always. :)

Oh. My. Gosh. This had to be sleep deprivation talking. Who did I think I was, flirting with a supermodel? But I didn't have to wait long before my inbox informed me there was a new message.

Ben: Naughty little thing, aren't you, Miss Clarke? I approve.

I read his reply twice, savoring the fact that he seemed to be flirting back. I didn't care that I was probably living in an alternate universe. I didn't want to come back down to earth. Chewing my lip, I hesitated with my fingers over the keyboard.

Did I ignore this message, or respond? That was the million-dollar question. Obviously, ignoring him was out of the question. Hello, nerves.

Me: Glad you approve.

I wished my mind was working properly so I could've written something witty and sexy. I hit send and took a bite. Before I could even swallow, he'd replied.

Ben: What are you doing?

I was currently stuffing my face with a delicious sandwich of French bread, butter, and ham, and was pretty sure I had butter smeared on my chin, but I wasn't about to tell him that I was in bed with a sandwich, wearing my ratty sweatpants with my hair piled up in the world's messiest bun. Wiping my mouth on a napkin, I swallowed the bite.

Me: In bed. Alone. What about you?

Ben: Alone? That's no fun.

I giggled to myself. As I pondered what to write back, another message popped up.

Ben: I'm in bed, too. Just got back from dinner with Fiona.

Ugh. Her name was like a bucket of ice water on my rising temperature. Suddenly, my sandwich tasted like cardboard. Finding myself no longer quite so famished, I stood and moved the tray of food across the room, setting it on a table beside the door.

Me: Sounds like fun. Hopefully she's not still mad about earlier.

A few seconds later, his message flashed in my inbox.

Ben: No, she was fine. That was my fault earlier. She was worried I was going to get sucked into a relationship and have no time for working 24/7 like I usually do.

I couldn't resist what I typed next. I was like a giddy highschooler having an out-of-body experience. Yes, I was baiting him to get some much-needed intel. Evil. Little. Genius, right there. Ellie would be so proud.

Me: No offense, but I thought a lot of male models were gay.

I couldn't help but grin.

Ben: Don't worry. I like pussy.

Sweet baby Jesus, did he just use that word? He did. He really went there. My jaw dropped open. Suddenly the room felt much too hot and the sheets rubbed against my bare skin annoyingly. I clamped a pillow between my knees and whimpered. Ben had actually just used the p-word.

Me: Good to hear. ;)

He didn't need to know I was a hot, whimpering mess.

Ben: Is that so?
Me: Umm . . . yes?

I squealed and hid my face in my hands for a minute. This couldn't be happening.

Ben: It's fucking delicious.

Oh. My. God. This information was not helping my growing crush on him. Not one bit.

Me: I feel the insane need to admit that I'm looking up pics of you online now.

I didn't know why I told him that, but I liked this brutal honesty thing that was happening between us.

Ben: I need more shirtless pics.

Wait. Were we flirting? I didn't know how to flirt. Did I? I heard Ellie's voice inside my head. Step one: Remove his pants. I giggled and quickly typed out a response. I didn't want him to think I was a total creeper; although, to be fair, he did seem to be encouraging it.

> Me: No, actually that's not what I'm looking at. I like your lips and jaw.
>
> Ben: You like them for what?
>
> Me: Good for nibbling.
>
> Ben: Mmm. I like sucking on lips.

My heartbeat drummed in my chest. Ben Shaw could suck on my lips anytime.

> Me: :)

My only response was a smiley face, but damn. What did one say to that? There was no textbook, no manual for flirting with a highly unattainable model.

> Ben: You like that, Miss Clarke?
>
> Me: Very much, Mr. Shaw.

This wasn't me. I didn't engage in dirty talk or flirty banter with models. While they worked out and watched their diets, I ate ice cream in my sweats and slept till noon on Sundays. I pretended to go to the gym, but I really just circled the parking lot looking for a spot. But I liked this new me he was bringing out. I felt confident. Though probably just because I was hidden behind a screen where I could blush and giggle all I wanted.

> Ben: Good girl. I'll see you in the morning.

Me: Yes. You'd better get your beauty sleep for tomorrow. ;)

Ben: Done. ;)

I shut my laptop and rolled over in bed, the ridiculous-ass grin on my face refusing to fade.

4

Emmy

I was up early and had already made three trips between the hotel and the shoot location before 7 a.m. Thank goodness for the easy-to-navigate Metro. And the strong European coffee I'd downed at breakfast. Emailing back and forth with Ben the night before still seemed like a dream. My body was hyperaware that he'd be arriving soon, and though I was trying to focus, I was incredibly distracted, watching the door every few seconds.

Thankfully, everything was running smoothly. Fiona had arrived fifteen minutes ago, the photographer and creative designer were discussing the set, and the makeup and hair people were setting up their stations. Our first model, Madeline, the girl Ben had gone out with the other night, was set to arrive soon. The shoot was for a magazine layout of a luxury brand of European clothing.

We were in the courtyard of a beautiful hotel. Big green hedges surrounded a lovely fountain and lush green grass had been spray-painted to ensure it looked perfect. The morning was brisk but the sun was already shining. It was going to be a perfect day, and the elegant grounds were well suited for the sophisticated fall wardrobe look Ben and Madeline would be wearing.

We also had reserved a meeting room inside the hotel, adjacent to the outdoor space. The doors had been propped open and people filtered in and out, arranging things and preparing for the shoot.

Ben's headshot was posted next to a cluster of hangers holding dark gray trousers, a silk button-down shirt in charcoal, a woven black tie, and a deep burgundy blazer. Really, he could be wearing a burlap sack and look stunning, but these clothes were gorgeous. The shoes were classic and dressy, too—intricate brown leather lace-ups with burgundy soles. I had a feeling shoes like this would be in all the department stores next year.

Madeline's digital photo was pinned next to a plaid wool skirt and navy blouse. In her photo, she was a plain-looking blonde with high cheekbones and a heart-shaped face. But when she arrived, I dropped the croissant I'd been nibbling into the wastebasket. Madeline was stunning. Statuesque and thin, she commanded the attention of everyone in the room. She had a handler with her, and I approached the girl to point them in the direction of hair and makeup.

Fiona found me beside the catering table and shoved a

Post-it into my hands like we were passing a secret note. It said, *Always bring me a spare pair of flats!*

I looked down at her higher-than-high heels. Flats. Got it. I shoved the note in my pocket and nodded. "Madeline has arrived," I said.

"Brilliant." She smiled, though it didn't quite reach her eyes. "Slutty cow," Fiona muttered under her breath.

Fiona's attention turned from me to the spread of snacks laid out in front of her. I was proud of the array: fresh seasonal fruit, a selection of French cheeses, and the flakiest croissants I'd ever tasted. Plus, glass bottles of Perrier and various sodas.

Fiona plucked a bottle of Perrier from the stash. I sensed she was about to criticize something when our attention was captured by Ben and Gunnar entering the room. Gunnar headed to the makeup area, while Ben paused just inside the door, glancing around the courtyard. He spotted us and his eyes lingered on mine. He sized me up as he sauntered toward us. A little chill skittered down my spine. I felt hot under his gaze and the memories of his sexy words from last night. My face was flushed and my underarms felt damp. Maybe I had a fever.

I like pussy.

Okay . . . so maybe it was a Ben Shaw–induced fever.

I suppressed a shudder as Ben's eyes drifted over me. His gaze flicked to Fiona, and he stopped in front of her to allow her to press a kiss to both cheeks. "You look dreadful, love." Her hand captured his jaw to tilt his chin up. He had dark circles beneath his eyes.

"Couldn't sleep," he murmured, then his gaze danced over to mine.

Shit. No way. I couldn't be responsible for ruining his first shoot in Paris because I kept him up last night. They had concealer for that, right?

His gaze roamed my jeans-clad hips unapologetically, but he still hadn't greeted me. His gaze lifted, sliding over my chest and making my breasts ache before landing on my eyes. "Tennessee. Sleep okay?"

So we'd moved on from Blueberry Muffin Girl to Tennessee? At least it wasn't hurled like an insult the way it was when Fiona said it. I suddenly found myself wondering where he was from originally.

"I slept well. You?"

"It was an interesting night." He laughed softly, the sound rumbling against my skin, causing it to prickle with goose bumps. "Very interesting."

"Well, I've got your cure. Come on." Fiona set off across the room, heading for the makeup area. She directed Ben to have a seat at one of the makeup stations and pulled a plastic bottle from her purse, handing it to him. It was filled with some sort of green goo. Fiona produced a straw and then gave him a handful of pills. Vitamins and minerals, I presumed. I had figured the models would eat the catering I'd ordered. I'd imagined Ben praising my choice of cheeses and exotic fruits. But I should have known Fiona was staking her claim, fawning all over him as usual.

He uncapped the drink and stuck in the straw, grimacing

as he took a large sip. The concoction looked brutal, whatever it was. The thick green liquid disappeared slowly as Ben
continued to suck it down, stopping only to pop pills in his
mouth between gulps.

My stomach twisted in revolt just watching him drink
that nasty stuff. I guess being beautiful took work.

Gunnar was chatting with the makeup artist beside us,
handing her various bottles of skincare products. "He breaks
out with anything oil-based. I'm having him try this new organic line. It's fucking fabulous."

The makeup artist accepted the bottles and added them
to the heap of products covering her workstation. Her expression was aloof—very much, *Let me do my damn job*. Gunnar
smiled sweetly and sauntered away.

I left Ben and Madeline to check on the set. I knew Fiona
would need a chair brought out to watch from, if those pumps
were any indication. After dragging a stool outside for her, everything was ready.

With only two models in the shoot today, the atmo-
sphere seemed low key and low stress. Once Ben and Madeline had finished with makeup and hair, they talked with
the photographer, getting comfortable with the backdrop
and each other. Both models looked impeccable. Madeline's
hair floated across her shoulders in a huge, wavy mass of
curls, and her makeup appeared dewy and fresh with a pop
of bright fuchsia lip stain. I couldn't even tell that Ben wore
any makeup—probably the point—because he just looked
beyond gorgeous. His hair had been smoothed down, parted

to one side, and slicked with pomade. The style worked quite well for him. And the growing moisture in my panties was a clear indication of *how* well. All the clothes seemed to hang off their bodies in a simply stunning way. Ben exuded cool sophistication and classic handsomeness in his tailored suit. The man just oozed *sexy*.

"He's almost too pretty, huh?"

I hadn't noticed Gunnar slide up beside me. "Oh, what?"

His eyes tracked Ben's movements. "Don't you dare pretend you didn't notice." His lips puckered in the most mocking way.

"Yeah, he's attractive; of course he is," I stammered.

Gunnar sighed dramatically. "Don't let those good looks fool you. That boy would be a hot mess without me, Fiona, and a pile of pills."

I had no idea what to make of his pill comment, but now wasn't the time to ask because Fiona was on a rampage, complaining loudly that Ben's shoes didn't fit. He needed a 12 and they'd brought an 11. I rushed to calm the situation, but before I could intervene Ben was at her side, speaking in hushed tones to soothe her.

He'd stuffed his feet into the shoes and pleaded with her, his arms out to his sides. "See. I'll survive for an hour."

Apparently mollified, Fiona merely nodded, and I released a deep exhale.

The photo shoot began, and watching Ben work was wonderful. He made it look so easy. It was clear that both he and Madeline were experienced professionals. They worked well together, posing, moving against each other to create interesting angles as the photographer clicked away.

I'd never get tired of looking at him. My body exploded as awareness, endorphins, and desire flooded my system. Remembering our secret conversation last night made it even hotter. His intense gaze landed on mine as he continued to pose for the photographer, and I swear, the look in his smoldering gaze was pure sex. Good Lord, I was going to need to change my panties soon. *Note to self: At the next photo shoot, pack Fiona flats and an extra pair of panties for me.*

When the shoot wrapped, Madeline immediately disappeared with her handler, and Ben and Fiona wandered back into the dressing area, seemingly in the middle of an intense conversation. I wondered what they could be discussing that was so serious, since his performance today seemed impeccable.

I busied myself packing everything up and even helped the photographer carry equipment to his car, but I could linger for only so long. Not to mention I was beginning to feel like an idiot for thinking that Ben and I actually shared something the previous night. He'd been bored, tired, drunk, or jet-lagged—who knows, maybe all of the above. I hated how desperate I was to get another look at him and made myself move on. *Big-girl panties, Em.*

I decided to walk back rather than take the Metro so that I could find a cute little sidewalk café at which to treat myself. Two glasses of red wine and one delicious *tarte au chocolat* later, I was en route to the hotel, stumbling along the uneven cobblestone streets, delightfully buzzed and carefree. Ben who? I could take on the world right now. Or just master this archaic elevator to get to my room. Either way, I was counting tonight as a win.

When I reached my hotel room I was lightheaded and buzzed—from the wine, the sugar, my beautiful surroundings, or probably all three, but I wasn't tired. After changing into my PJs, I fell into bed with my laptop. Perhaps some further stalking of Ben would relax me.

But before I could even open my browser, my inbox showed I had one new message.

The sender was Benjamin Riley Shaw.

My heart fluttered like a little idiot inside my chest as I waited for the message to load.

Ben: You disappeared today, Tennessee. Make it back to the hotel okay?

I hit reply, my breathing coming in fast pants.

Me: Back safe and sound. You looked great today, BTW.

The email notification blinked within seconds. So he was awake and at his computer, too, it seemed. My heartbeat thumped unevenly in my chest.

Ben: Thank you. It was fun today. I worked out after so I should be tired, but I'm not.

I worried why he seemed to have trouble sleeping. Perhaps it was the time zone change? And what about Gunnar's comments today? Another message popped up before I could respond.

Ben: Want to entertain me?

Holy shit. How did he make four little words sound so fucking hot? Especially since I heard his deep, masculine voice in my head as I read them. I took my time, thinking of a cheeky response before I replied.

Me: Hmm. What does that involve, Mr. Shaw? I should probably behave myself.

Ben: You don't have to behave.

If that wasn't an open invitation to flirt with him, I didn't know what was. I giggled to myself in the otherwise-silent room, wondering how to respond, when he sent another message through.

Ben: You want to text instead?

Me: Yes.

And by yes, I meant, God Bless America.

His phone number appeared in my inbox: 917 area code. How very New York City of him.

I crossed the room and grabbed my phone, typing in his number to compose a new text. One word—simple. It was my attempt at keeping things casual so I could see where he wanted to take this.

Me: Hi

His response came almost immediately.

Ben: Hi darlin'

Me: How do I know this isn't someone pretending to be you? I'm slightly worried I could be talking to a forty-year-old overweight creeper. ;)

Ben was silent for a moment. Then my phone blinked at me, informing me I had a new photo message. It took my trembling fingers three attempts to tap the correct button on the screen to open it.

Ben was leaning against the headboard wearing a white V-neck T-shirt. His hair, though still shiny and full of pomade from earlier, had been fussed with, like he'd run his hands through it several times, giving it a messy just-been-fucked look. He wasn't smiling, but he looked sexy as hell gazing thoughtfully into the camera. My heart pounded painfully hard. Seeing his photo made this all the more real.

Ben: Here's your forty-year-old creeper. ;)

Me: Cute.

Ben: Send me one of you.

I scrolled through the photos I already had on my phone. *Crap.* All of these were either me with Ellie, or with our dog Buck back home. I ran to the mirror, added some lip gloss, and fluffed my flat hair. I didn't want him to think I was taking too long or overthinking this, so I snapped a quick selfie and hit send. It wasn't my best picture, but it wasn't horrible either. The lighting in my room was soft and lent a sort of romantic feel to it.

Ben: You look like a girl I fucked once.

Holy crap! He did not just say that to me. His responses

floored me. He seemed so polite and well mannered one minute and then *BAM!* Filthy mouthed the next. I'd honestly wondered what he thought of my looks, and his comment, however crass, told me that perhaps I did measure up.

My phone pinged with a new message. That little ping was the sweetest sound.

Ben: What kind of panties are you wearing?

My pulse sped up. I wore full-bottomed undies, none of those damn dental-floss impersonating G-strings, thank you very much. Those blasted things felt like they were chaffing your ass like a piece of sandpaper. But dear Ben didn't need to know all that information. I thoughtfully typed out my response.

Me: Depends on the day's outfit. Right now I'm in pink lacy boy shorts.

Ben: It'd be better if they were around your ankles, but I approve.

Holy. Crap. Moisture dampened my panties. I fought to keep my thoughts under control and from jumping into the gutter. I ran through a mental list of nonsexy things: his schedule this week, the location of his next photo shoot, what he smelled like, his dick size. *Gah!* Where did that come from? I bit my lip. I knew I should keep it clean, but being naughty sounded like so much more fun. He was proving to be a terrible influence on me.

Me: Eager tonight, aren't we, Mr. Shaw?

Ben: Always, doll.

Me: Do you always text like this with Fiona's assistants?

Ben: No. They're usually men. And I told you, I like pussy.

God, anytime he used the p-word, I swear my lady parts clenched. Who knew I was such a glutton for a little dirty talk?

Me: How could I forget? You worded that so eloquently. Fine then, do you text like this w/ other girls often?

Ben: Depends on if I want to play with them or not.

I took a moment to compose myself and tried to decipher his words. He didn't deny it. But did that mean he was playing with me? Or that I was special because I was one of the few he wanted to play with? I felt a wine headache coming on and typed out the first thing I could think of.

Me: Are you seeing anyone right now?

After I hit send, I silently cursed myself. I didn't want to seem overly interested. He was probably just messing with me, anyway. Just bored and killing time. He couldn't really be interested in me. Could he?

Ben: I don't really date.

I could see that, I suppose. Being a model with a hectic travel schedule, it was probably hard for him to meet people, let alone quality women. My phone pinged again.

Ben: I don't like to be tied down.

Ha! So much for giving him the benefit of the doubt. He was practically admitting to being a player. Summoning my courage, I typed a response back.

Me: Spoken like a true manwhore.

Take that! That would put him in his place. There was a subtle difference between being flirty and being a bitch, and I wanted to stay on the correct side of it. But sheesh, someone had to call him out.

Ben: Not a manwhore, babe. Only three girls have gotten it.

It. My mouth went instantly dry. He was an exquisitely handsome man, quite obviously women threw themselves at him, yet only three lucky ladies had gotten the goods. That was rather curious information, if he was telling the truth. Maybe he had more restraint than I gave him credit for. Or maybe he'd had a long-term girlfriend somewhere along the way.

I wanted to type back and ask him why he was flirting with me when he could get anyone he wanted. I wondered if he even found me attractive. But of course I didn't write any of that. I needed to play it cool.

Ben: Emmy?

Wow. I liked that he used my real first name more than was even remotely normal. Breathe, Emmy. Breathe.

Me: Yes?

Ben: Do you have plans for tomorrow?

Breathing became secondary as I took a moment to squeal like a giddy schoolgirl. There wasn't a shoot tomorrow, and it would be one of the few days we had off, so Gunnar and I had planned to go to the Louvre.

Me: Not really. Probably going to do some sightseeing.

I was sooo canceling on Gunnar if the opportunity called for it. He would just have to deal with it. Our plans weren't set in stone, anyway.

Ben: I have plans with Fiona during the day, but if you want to meet up for a drink later.

His friendship with Fiona still confused me, but maybe that was one of the things I could ask him about tomorrow.

Perhaps she wasn't such a fire-breathing dragon once you got to know her. Who knew? And maybe I could discreetly pump Gunnar for information.

Me: Sure. I can meet you later.

Ben: Meet me in the lobby at eight. We can walk to the place I have in mind for drinks.

Me: Great. See you then.

And just like that, I had a date with Ben Freaking Shaw.

5

Ben

Fiona signaled the waiter for more wine. I took a piece of bread from the basket in the center of our table and Fiona frowned. She could shove it.

She rattled on about some up-and-coming French designer and a sample sale she wanted me to take her to. Oh, joy. I tuned her out and let my mind drift back to last night.

I couldn't stop thinking about Emmy's playful texts. I'd really just been messing around, feeling sort of lonely and, not gonna lie, horny. I didn't expect her to get naughty with me, yet she had. Even sent me a flirty pic of herself, softly lit, with bedroom eyes and pouty lips. I smiled at the memory.

I'd looked at the text first thing this morning, chuckling to myself. I was normally a really direct guy and told girls what I wanted. But I knew ordering her to come up to my room so I could fuck her wouldn't have gone over well. Something told me Emmy was different from most girls. I could tell she wasn't a one-night-stand kind of girl. She was smart and hardworking. And her sweet southern accent was pretty fucking adorable.

I had a vitamin consultant, a massage therapist, an aesthetician, a personal trainer, a dietitian, an herbal consultant, a fucking grooming companion, whatever that was, and Gunnar—my personal assistant. The only thing I didn't have here in Paris was a friend. Maybe Emmy could fill that role. Of course, I wanted to fuck her. Badly. And I doubted how friendly she'd feel toward me after that happened. And it would happen.

"What's that smile for?" Fiona asked, pulling me from my reverie.

I swallowed hard, letting my smile fade. "Nothing." Nothing she needed to know about, anyhow. I was looking forward to my plans with Emmy later.

Emmy

Pulling out the most recent stack of Post-its, I sat down on my bed with a cup of coffee to sort through them. I figured I would handle a few of Fiona's personal affairs before I went out sightseeing for the day. After booking her facial appointment and making dinner reservations for her and Ben early that Monday night, I decided some further Ben Shaw research was in order.

Relaxing on my duvet with my laptop, I typed his name into Google and hit enter, then I sat back to enjoy the view. Holy Mother, he was hot.

My brain screamed at me, *Abort! Abort!* I knew this was a bad idea, yet I couldn't help myself. I watched him go about his life: VIP parties, red-carpet events, black-tie charity functions with a beautiful model on his arm, and photos of him at the beach on his Instagram page. A sharp pain stabbed at my chest.

It was a decidedly baaad idea to crush on him, I knew that. But he was gorgeous, and he flirted with me. Clearly my fantasies knew no limit. I hoped that wouldn't come to a crashing end tonight when he realized I was so far out of his league that there were probably laws against us dating. Yet still, my stalking knew no bounds. Instagram, Facebook, and Twitter. I'd need a twelve-step program if I were to cut myself off from this. But he was so good-looking, I couldn't possibly be held accountable for my actions.

He seemed to communicate professionally and politely with fans online, but I liked that I secretly knew he had an absolutely filthy mouth.

Pulling myself away from my computer, I dressed in jeans and a T-shirt and grabbed my camera. Gunnar had hooked up with a French waiter last night and subsequently canceled on me since they were apparently still in bed. Regardless, the Louvre and I still had a hot date today. It was just the cultural and visual distraction, and I needed the diversion to keep my thoughts from diving into the gutter.

Deciding what to wear on a date with Ben Shaw was like trying to solve a Rubik's Cube in the dark. Damn near impossible. I tried on and abandoned nearly every article of clothing I brought. But soon, it was ten minutes to eight and I was forced to make a decision. A pair of dark-washed skinny jeans, ballet flats since he'd said we'd be walking, and a lacy black top with a camisole underneath.

There was just one question: Did I wear my Spanx to keep everything looking tucked in and in tip-top shape? Or did I hope for action later and forgo those awful things, knowing there was no sexy way to get them off? No, there would be no action later—that was silly. He was him. And I was me. Duh. It was a no-brainer. Still, I chose in favor of breathing and opted to leave the Spanx behind.

My hair was down and pin-straight and my makeup had cooperated for once. I'd managed to line my eyes with liquid eyeliner without stabbing myself in the retina even once. *Yay, me!*

Ben was already waiting in the lobby when I got downstairs. Since he hadn't yet looked up, I allowed my eyes to rake over him unashamedly, noting the way his black leather jacket stretched across his shoulders and hugged his biceps and his white V-neck T-shirt exposed his very kissable throat. His shirt was just snug enough to hint at how cut he was underneath. I could already envision the washboard abs hiding beneath the fabric. He could've just walked off a *GQ* shoot with the sexy charm he exuded. I didn't stand a chance. He was all man, but he was stylish as well and I suddenly felt a pang of nerves, realizing my clothes carried none of the designer labels his did. Did that type of thing matter to him?

Ben's eyes lifted to mine and a slow, sexy smile spread across his lips.

I stopped in front of him, fidgeting and knotting my fingers together. "Hi."

"Hi darlin'. You ready?" His mouth was still tugged up in a playful grin, and I couldn't help but smile like a lovesick fool at this sexy man.

"Ready." *As I'll ever be.*

He led me outside and across the street to the stone walkway along the Seine where we quickly fell into step together. I felt the warmth of his hand hover at my lower back, but he never made contact. It was sweet and innocent yet highly erotic at the same time. The promise of something more between us hung in the air, unspoken and unknown.

I enjoyed the endorphins that flooded my system. I felt alive. The stars were glittering like rhinestones in the darkened night sky. Paris at night was magical and seductive. It had a vibe—a casual sexiness that oozed from each little patisserie and brasserie we passed.

Ben glanced down, looked at my shoes, and gave me a smile. "I like that you wore flats. Girls never wear flats. Now we can actually walk."

Oh. I didn't know if that was a compliment or not. Of course the beautiful women he dated obviously wore the most exquisite shoes, but I went for comfort. Damn. *Fail.* Or win, depending on how you looked at it.

"Yeah, I knew we'd be walking," I quickly added. He didn't need to know that I always wore flats. Heels and I didn't get along. Wearing them had resulted in head trauma more than once, as I routinely fell on my face when I tried to walk in them.

At six feet three he had a full foot of height on me. No worries, though, because I would happily climb him like a freakin' jungle gym, if given the chance. I felt little next to him, and it was a decidedly nice feeling. Just being near him gave me a thrill. His presence alone held the power to captivate, titillate, and turn me on. In other words, I was doomed.

When we reached a very Parisian café at a charming intersection, Ben stopped and guided me forward, his fingers brushing my hip, sending a zip of heat through my belly. He spoke in flawless French—flawless to my untrained ears, at least—to the maître d'. Regardless of how busy the quaint little café appeared to be, authority radiated off him and we were quickly seated at a table for two out on the patio beside the bustling sidewalk. It was a perfect spot for people-watching. Ben pulled out my chair and I lowered myself in a ladylike fashion while he gently pushed it closer to the table. We had a view of the Eiffel Tower in the distance, lit up and glowing with brilliant yellow lights. It was spectacular. I loved everything about this date so far and it'd barely begun.

Ben's small, knowing smile remained in place as he passed me a drinks menu. "Thirsty, beautiful?"

I merely nodded and flipped open the menu. *Crap!* Everything was in French.

"Shall we order a bottle?" Ben asked. "And I should've asked earlier, are you hungry?"

First, there was no way I was eating in front of him. Second, bottle? Yes, please. I would need a couple of glasses to calm my nerves. "A bottle sounds good. Were you thinking white or red?"

"Red, but I can do either."

"Red is fine."

"The Château Saint Pierre is good—medium-bodied, creamy finish, and just a touch of sweetness."

"Sounds great." *Note to self—this man knows his wine.* That little fact only added to his hotness.

He smiled and folded his menu, setting his smartphone on the table in front of him. I couldn't help but notice the little blue light that flashed to indicate he had a new message. Ben ignored it, though, and when the waiter came back he spoke in the most mouthwateringly beautiful French and placed our order. Moments later, the waiter appeared to open our wine and fill two glasses. Just having something in my hands set me at ease.

Ben crossed his ankle over his knee and leaned back. The stem of his wineglass remained between his fingers and he thoughtfully swirled the ruby-colored liquid within the glass. His gaze met mine and that devilish, boyish charm that melted my resolve to stay away from him flashed in his eyes. "To our adventures in Paris."

"Yes." I met his glass with mine, a satisfying clink piercing the night air.

"So." His mouth turned up a playful smirk. "Tell me everything there is to know about Miss Emmy Clarke."

"Uh." I fumbled with the drinks menu, clumsily rearranging it on the table in front of us. "Let's see. I've been working for Fiona for a couple of weeks. I'm from Tennessee originally. Pretty standard stuff. What do you want to know?"

He shrugged.

I swallowed and shifted in my seat. Okay. Taking a deep breath, I continued, "In college I double majored in communications and fashion design."

A flicker of interest in his eyes revealed that he was impressed.

"I have a younger brother and two parents who are still very much in love." Someone shut me up. God, was I trying to put him to sleep? "Nothing really that exciting. Tell me more about you."

"What do you want to know?" His smile was playful, like he almost expected that I'd Googled him and assumed that I knew everything there was to know.

I did know a lot. His mom was retired supermodel Dakota Shaw, rumored to be quite a swinger. His dad appeared to be a mystery; possibly a politician or a rock star. But it didn't seem right to try to probe him for answers now. Instead, I simply asked, "Where did you grow up?"

His eyes drifted to his glass of wine, which he'd stopped swirling. I briefly wondered if I'd touched on a topic he didn't care to discuss. "All over, really. New York City, London, Barcelona, Prague, Rome, Brazil, everywhere. I want to hear more about you, though. Normal family. Tennessee. What else?" He grinned, taking a sip of his wine and licking those full lips.

The wine had started to get to me already, and it seemed surreal that Ben Shaw was sitting across from me. What was he even doing here with me? Was this a date? Two friends? Coworkers? My head was a wreck. I needed answers.

I set my glass down on the table and summoned my courage. "Ben." My tone came out too serious and his gaze flicked up to mine. "I'm sorry to disappoint you, but I'm probably a bit boring for your tastes."

Ben abandoned his casual posture and leaned in toward me. "I assure you; I'm anything but bored, Miss Clarke."

I twisted my fingers around the stem of my glass. "We both know I'm not a model. I'm not like the women you usually go out with."

"Emmy . . ." Ben set his glass down in front of him, his expression stern. "I don't only date models. I actually typically *don't* date models, so relax."

His little declaration did nothing to calm my anxieties. The fact that he only *sometimes* dated models was supposed to calm me? *Ha!* My insecurities were too deep rooted to vanish with that information.

He leaned closer, fixing me with an intense stare. "How about I admit to a little secret? Will that make you more comfortable?"

I stopped fidgeting at the table. I hated that I was being a girl, all self-conscious and nervous. "Yes," I admitted.

Ben took a sip from his glass. "Okay. Would it make you feel better if I told you I lost my virginity to a much older woman? My mom's friend, actually."

Whoa. I couldn't imagine losing my virginity to someone my dad's age. Creepy. My first time was with my high school boyfriend in the back of his Jeep my junior year. My life was shockingly normal in contrast to his. I could only imagine the cougar-turned-seductress must have persuaded him. "Were you . . . okay with that?"

"Yeah. She gave great head." He shrugged, giving me a megawatt, panty-dropping smile.

Okay then. No overanalyzing going on there. I guessed that was the difference between guys and girls. Girls were more emotional about sex, guys thought about the physical first. Good to know. I needed to remember that, keep my head about me.

"So, are you into older women or did she, like, seduce you?" I asked, unable to hide my curiosity at how things went down. No pun intended.

"It was one of my first overnight shoots and she was with me since my mom couldn't be bothered to come. She'd been sending me signals all day, touching my arm, rubbing my shoulders, stuff like that. I was eighteen and horny . . ." He chuckled. "I couldn't sleep, being away from home and all that, so that night I went up to her hotel room . . ."

Damn. That was bold. He just showed up on her doorstep expecting sex? But I supposed when you looked like him you'd earned the right to be bold. Lucky day for that cougar, whoever she was. I was slightly jealous. But I had the man sitting in front of me, all hard-toned muscle, golden skin, and lips built for kissing. All she had was the memory.

I couldn't envision many women rejecting him— something about his confidence, his penetrating eyes, and his blunt mouth. . . . He had a knack for getting what he wanted; of that, I was certain.

His little admission had done several things at once. Intrigued me, ignited a fire in my belly, and set me at complete ease. This man was good. Oh, he was damn good. "Bennn . . ." I whimpered.

"Yeah, beautiful?" His signature cocky smirk was firmly in place.

I squeezed my legs together. Ben using endearing nicknames was enough to undo me. I liked it a little too much.

"Nothing," I murmured. If I spoke just now, it wouldn't be pretty. I'd either admit to wanting him or mumble something incoherently dumb. Best to keep my trap shut. I was convinced I was about to do or say something stupid, so I sipped my wine instead. Zip it, crazy lady.

He refilled our wineglasses and continued to study me.

After several minutes, I found my courage again. "So how did you get into modeling?"

Ben met my eyes. "I grew up around it, but my mom wouldn't let me get involved. She didn't want me modeling, and wouldn't let me until I was seventeen. Then she didn't really have a choice, because I sent my photos off to a couple of agencies in New York. They all ended up being interested, so I started working right away."

"Why didn't she want you modeling?" That seemed curious to me, considering his mom was a world-renowned supermodel.

"She wanted more for me. She knew the downsides to the lifestyle—constant travel and invariably being judged on your appearance. She didn't always do well with it. I'm sure you've heard of her numerous rehab stays."

His gaze begged me to disagree. I had to look away. Of course I'd heard of Dakota Shaw's fall from grace.

"I'm sorry. Is she . . ."

"She's fine now. Living in Australia with a guy my age." He

shook his head like it was a thought he wanted to clear rather quickly.

"So you started working when you were seventeen? That's really young."

He nodded. "Yes. Fiona actually helped get me my start and I signed with her exclusively a short while later. We've been working together for several years now. She's helped make me what I am today."

I wanted to disagree, to tell him that he'd have made it on his own, but I guess I had no way of knowing. Already, I'd seen glimpses of just how cutthroat this industry was.

His phone buzzed again, rattling the glass tabletop until Ben reached down to quiet it. I couldn't help but notice Fiona's name flash across the screen.

I took a sip of my wine and noticed Ben was still staring down at his phone, lost in thought. "Do you need to get that?"

His gaze snapped up to mine. "No. It's Fiona. And I have nothing to say to her right now."

I still didn't understand the extent of their relationship. Was it just a close business partnership or something more? I brushed off the feelings of insecurity swimming inside me. My bitchy boss would most certainly not like me out with her golden boy right now, but I didn't care. She didn't own him.

I took another healthy swig of my wine, hoping that the alcohol would completely banish all thoughts of self-doubt inside me. That wouldn't happen, though. I was seated across from one of the world's most sought after male models. My head was an absolute wreck over that fact, not to mention my fluttering heart and damp panties.

"I'm sorry, but this is all new for me. I'm at a loss about what it is you want," I admitted, folding my hands in my lap.

All traces of seriousness disappeared from his face. His eyes danced on mine, possessive and hungry, and he leaned closer, sexy, boyish charm and playfulness radiating off him. "I think you know exactly what I want."

Heat crawled up my neck, staining my cheeks. The man certainly didn't mess around.

He chuckled, a rich warm sound that flooded my senses and sent me reeling, like there was some inside joke that only he and my pulse were privy to. "Let's get you to bed. I'm sure Fiona will have you up early for work tomorrow." Cool authority laced his voice, and I knew it'd be pointless to argue or probe further.

He rose and guided me from my chair, his hand resting against my back to assist my movement, leading me off into the night.

Ever the gentleman, Ben walked me to my door and pressed a kiss to my hand.

I leaned against the door, ready to collapse in a heap on the floor. My legs were done. My entire body was done. I was a limp noodle—turned on and humming for the past two hours spent with Ben. He was polite yet flirty. I hated that I didn't know if this was a date, but he did pay for the wine. Thank God for that, too, because I was pretty sure I didn't make that amount of euros in a week.

"Goodnight, Miss Clarke," he said, his voice low and sexy.

"Night." I breathed.

He leaned in close, giving me a chance to pull away. I let my eyes slip closed and seconds later felt Ben's full, sensuous mouth cover mine. One hand wound its way into my hair; the other curled around my waist. The warm weight of his hand anchored me, pulling me close until our bodies were pressed together. The hard length of his body against mine was a thing of bliss. His skilled lips made the other men I'd kissed look like boys.

His hand drifted from my waist, found my behind, and clutched me closer, pressing his hips against mine. His teeth caught my lip and grazed lightly against the flesh. My mouth opened in surprise, and Ben used the opportunity to stroke my tongue with his. I let out a soft groan and his kiss deepened, seemingly fueled by the small sound. My hands fumbled behind me for the door handle. Relieving me of the chore, Ben's hand swept the key past the reader and pushed open the door.

I tried to calm my fluttering heart to take stock of what I'd learned tonight. One: Fiona called Ben about every fifteen minutes, which he completely ignored. Two: Ben was fucking hot and the most incredible kisser. Three: I was falling for him. Hard. This information made me feel excited and depressed all at once. He was out of my league, but was that going to stop me? Nope. No, it wasn't. I'd gotten a taste, and there'd be no stopping me now.

6

Emmy

Once inside my room, we were tangled limbs fighting to get closer as we moved across the floor. Ben's big hands held my jaw so sweetly as his tongue made laps against mine. His commanding body forced my feet backward toward the bed.

My emotions were a combo of *Let's go make babies* to *Must. Stop. Kissing.* Shutting off my brain, I allowed my hormones to take over. I kicked off my shoes, crawled onto the bed, and tugged him down on top of me.

His warm weight pressed me into the mattress and his mouth was everywhere. He nibbled on my collarbone, nipped gentle bites at my neck, and used his tongue to sweep a damp path over the tender skin. Holy hell, did he know what he was doing.

Ben's rough hand was suddenly under my shirt, cupping my breast and rubbing his thumb along my nipple. A bolt of desire zipped through my body. My hips moved against his, pressing against the firm ridge there, and a broken plea tumbled from his lips and into my mouth. It was the sweetest sound. Desperate and wanting, exactly like I felt. I was glad I wasn't alone in that.

His palm found my ass again and squeezed, hauling me closer. I felt his thick erection press into my lower belly, and my insides went all molten.

"Do you have a condom?" His voice was low, raw with need.

"No," I choked out.

"I have some in my room." He continued moving his hips against mine.

I wanted this, I did. But my mind was reeling. Once he'd been inside me, there would be no turning back. My schoolgirl crush would be catapulted into outer space so far that I'd never come down. I needed to keep my wits about me. I just didn't sleep with men I wasn't dating.

"No," I managed.

"No?" His tone told me he wondered if I wanted him bare. And the hint of a smile on his lips told me this idea was a welcomed one.

"I'm not ready for all this. . . ." My body was in complete disagreement with my brain, my legs winding their way around his backside to press him closer.

Ben groaned at the contact. "Come on, baby, let me fuck you." He breathed against my neck. "I promise it'll feel good." He gripped my ass, pushing his erection against the damp spot between my legs, and I couldn't help the whimper that escaped my throat.

"That's not a good idea. We work together," I managed.

"Fuck work. Let me get you off."

His deep, sexy voice and the grinding of his hips were almost enough to convince me. Almost. "We can do some other things. But no sex." I didn't even know what I was saying, but I was certain which part of me was controlling my mouth. My throbbing sex. Ben had gotten me soaking wet and needy, and we'd barely rounded second base. Talk about playing out of my league.

His gaze met mine and he swept the hair back from my face. "I like other things."

"Yeah?" I was thankful he'd followed my line of thinking and didn't make me spell it out.

"Yes. And I think you'll find I excel at them. Particularly oral." His deep-set gaze was directed my way and that full, pouty mouth was just inches from mine. . . .

Holy. Crap. The look on his face. I was defenseless. "Umm . . . we'll see about that, Mr. Shaw."

He fixed me with an intense stare and leaned in close, his nose brushing past my jaw. I felt him inhale against my neck. "I wonder if you taste good." His low whisper caused heat to drift from my neck and pool at the base of my spine. His warm, wet tongue slid against my neck and I whimpered in response at the sudden, heated, longing ache between my thighs.

His hand slid down the front of my jeans and into my panties. "Fuck. You're soaking wet, baby." He kissed my throat, his breath tickling my ear. "I know you want me to fuck you. But we'll do things your way this time, okay?"

His fingers slid against me, massaging the slick, swollen tissue. Pleasure rocketed through me. I'd fantasized about his touch, and now that it was actually happening it was beyond any expectations I'd had. His skilled fingers massaged my clit with just enough pressure and a lazy rhythm that allowed the pleasure to build slowly.

"You're so soft," he whispered. He palmed one breast while his other hand remained buried in my panties.

I was soft, with extra padding on my hips, thighs, and breasts; my body was curvy and womanly, and though I would have thought this was a bad thing—especially for a toned and firm model like him—he seemed to like it.

He kissed a wet path across my neck as his hands explored. I should've stopped him but my mind was numb and my body was all kinds of lit up. I wanted more. I deserved more, didn't I? I'd been the good girl for so long.

He slid one long finger inside me and I whimpered, arching my back. "You're a little thing, aren't you?" He kissed my neck while his finger continued its slow progression, sliding in and out of me in a careful rhythm.

"Ben . . ." I groaned, frustrated by his measured strokes. I needed more.

"Tell me," he growled.

"I need it harder."

His mouth captured mine while his finger plunged deeper inside me, his bicep flexing with the motion. He added a second finger and pressed his thumb against the top of my sex.

I moaned loudly, rocking my hips against his hand. I didn't care that I looked like a horny mess. Hell, I *was* a horny mess.

He rhythmically fingered me in and out, his thick fingers filling an ache left untouched for too long. And now, Ben Shaw was in my bed. Holy hell.

Ben

She might have told me she didn't want this, but her body disagreed. She had sent me all kinds of signals. She liked this. A lot. Her breathing came in soft pants and her hips rocked closer. I didn't even think she realized she was doing it. She wanted me inside her, even if she wouldn't admit it. But I didn't want to ask her. I couldn't bear to hear her tell me to stop. I needed to touch this girl.

"That feel good, baby?" I needed to hear her say it did. I was naturally pretty aggressive and that had always served me well with girls, but something told me Emmy wouldn't like being told what to do. As much as I'd like to command her to strip naked, take off her panties, and stand before me, I wouldn't. She wasn't ready. She was too skittish around me. Too unsure.

"Mmm . . ." She let out a soft groan, her only signal that this felt good. She let her eyes slide closed and her head rested in the crook of my neck. That wouldn't do. I wanted to see her face when she came, but I let her remain there, feeling the soft pant of breath against my neck. It felt nice.

She was by far the classiest girl I'd been with. Double major in college. She was smart, hardworking, and articulate. She didn't sleep around. I could tell she was two seconds from pulling the plug on this whole thing, and I couldn't let that happen. I'd never wanted a girl more. Not that I was about to get all introspective and examine why that was. No. My goal was much simpler. I just wanted to get her naked and see her tits. From the first moment I'd seen her, we'd been headed toward this very moment.

I moved my hand against her, dragging my fingers slowly in and out of her. She was wet as fuck and it made my dick so hard. I wanted to be inside her. I needed it. But I wouldn't rush her. She felt amazing and she was literally soaking wet, now writhing against my hand. She went really tight and I could tell she was close. I could already read her body. I continued my measured strokes, unwilling to rush her to the finish line. I felt her begin to clench around my fingers as she started to unravel. Her eyes were a pretty gray-blue and clouded over with her pleasure. Still fucking her with my fingers, our eyes connected as she started to come.

Emmy

My orgasm built slowly then came rushing at me all at once, knocking the breath from my lungs and making me cry out. My world exploded around me. The climax hit me like a freight train, and I was in mindless ecstasy, clutching at Ben's biceps as I fought to hold on. He knew what he was doing; I'd certainly give him that.

Recovering slightly, I pulled in a shaky breath. I wondered how loud I'd been. Ben's smug smile of satisfaction confirmed he was pleased—with his performance, or mine, I didn't know. Didn't care. I needed to touch him. He removed his hand from my panties and planted a soft kiss on my mouth.

"Feel better, honey?" A smug smile was planted firmly on his lips. His reaction was cute. And yeah, that orgasm was a doozy. There was no denying that.

"Yes dear."

With my eyes watching his, my hands found his belt and worked to unlatch it. The moment felt highly erotic. We lay side by side on the bed, watching each other's eyes as I un-buttoned and unzipped his pants. We both knew what was coming, and the anticipation was thick between us. He kissed me softly on my lips and forehead while I slid my hand into the front of his boxers. I was rewarded with a rock-hard, thick cock pressing insistently against my palm. His skin was warm and taut and my sex muscles clenched in response. My hand curled tightly around his shaft and he groaned. The noise came from deep inside him and I loved that sound. Closing my hand around him, I began stroking. Ben dropped his head back against the pillow in complete surrender. I liked know-ing I did that to him. Not some supermodel. Me.

His hips rocked forward into my hand and his mouth momentarily stilled over mine as he released a low moan. "Emmy..."

The feel of Ben in my hand was amazing—a powerful rush surged through me. Even if it was just for this moment, he was mine.

"Fuuuck, that feels good." He watched me with a sexy half-lidded stare of awe, his breath coming fast through those pouty lips. "Faster baby, a little faster."

I could feel warm pre-cum already leaking from the tip. My hand gripped him tighter and I increased my speed, rub-bing along his hardened shaft and up over the head. A few more strokes and I was rewarded with a throaty groan and felt Ben come, warm jets of semen erupting against my hand and his stomach.

Neither of us had removed a single article of clothing,

but we'd each succeeded in finding release together. I was guessing I'd regret this in the morning, but the stupid feeling of bliss spreading through my chest wouldn't be dampened right now.

Ben dropped a kiss against my forehead then reached for the tissues on my nightstand. He quickly cleaned us both up then tucked his still hard cock back inside his pants.

Ben stood from the bed and leaned down to kiss my forehead. "Shall I tuck you in?"

I nodded drowsily.

He peeled back the covers and I shimmied out of my jeans, suddenly too tired to feel self-conscious. He chuckled at me and swept my hair back behind my ears.

"Sorry," I yawned. "I guess the wine hit me pretty hard."

Ben's lips curved upward. "Was it the wine or the orgasm?"

"Shh. Hush." I smiled.

"Night, darling."

"Night night."

Ben, still smiling, looked down at me. "Thanks for tonight. It was good to go out with someone who's not looking for me to be the guy they see in the pictures."

"I'm glad you felt comfortable enough to be yourself."

He brought his hand to my jawline and his thumb skittered along my cheek. "I did. Thank you."

"Sleep well."

He smiled softly. "We'll see. I'm not the best sleeper."

I frowned. What did that mean? Wasn't sleep a vital bodily function needed for survival? I knew it was pretty much one of my favorite things in the world. "Well, if you can't sleep, you know you can text me."

"Can I now?"

Captain fucking obvious. *Nice one, Emmy.* I simply nodded.

"I'll keep that in mind." His gaze lingered on mine for a moment, then he strode toward the door and left without another word. But really, what was there to say? Tonight had been nothing like I had expected.

After he left, I reluctantly left the warm cocoon of the bed to brush my teeth and change into my pajamas before crawling under the covers. I was nowhere near asleep when my phone chimed with a new message.

Ben: Are you awake?

Wasn't there some rule about texting a man back after midnight? I glanced at the clock. It was 12:20. I didn't care. I would break the rules for Ben.

Me: Yes. Hi

Ben: You sure it's wise to text me back when you're in bed, Miss Clarke? Now that I've got that visual in my head . . .

Me: Yes.

Ben: He misses you.

There was a dimly lit picture of Ben lying in bed. Just his chest, abs, and black boxer briefs, which were nicely filled out in the front.

I smiled to myself and shook my head. My exhaustion took a backseat if it meant flirting with Ben was an option. I liked that he'd texted me just moments after leaving. I liked the idea that he was still thinking of me. My brain refused to focus on anything else. I studied the picture more closely, imagining licking those grooves in his abs, working my way lower to bite his cock through the fabric of his boxers. Something about this man brought out my primal side.

Me: Are you hard again?

Ben: Nah

Me: He looks that good just being lazy?!

Who was this girl? And what had she done with careful, straight-laced Emmy? Ben turned me into a flirty version of myself I didn't quite recognize, but liked all the same. I giggled silently, my eyes glued to my phone and waiting for his response.

Ben: You can play with my cock any time.

Shit. Just as quickly as it had appeared, my smile faded. Panic flared through me. I couldn't be his booty call for the next three months. Could I? I was treading on dangerous ground here. He was so good-looking and charming; I knew I was already falling for him in a matter of days. He'd already told me he wasn't looking to be tied down. . . . I couldn't be his dirty little secret, wasn't cut out for that kind of frivolous relationship. My heart would never survive it.

Ben: That was fun.

Me: Yes it was.

I needed to find a way to tell him that wasn't happening again. I released a heavy exhale and my phone chimed again.

Ben: I want to fuck.

Me: Ben, I don't do the casual sex thing.

Ben: No worries, doll.

I had no clue how to interpret his last text. Should I not be worried because he didn't either . . . or because this was just harmless flirting? *Get a grip, Em!* God, we were coworkers. What had I been thinking shoving my hand down his pants tonight? I didn't want to sound like a dipstick, but I needed him to understand I was not some hussy he could have his way with.

Me: Tonight was fun, but we're coworkers, Ben. That can't happen again. Cool?

Ben: Whatever you want.

His message did nothing to calm my anxieties. What did I want? And why was I suddenly flooded with disappointment?

7

Emmy

By Thursday, I was ready to dropkick Fiona. We'd spent the week prepping for Ben's upcoming campaign. She had daily meetings to discuss budgeting, location scouting, styling, and storyboarding—all while weighing me down with heaps of Post-its.

I sat at the desk in her suite and she leaned over my shoulder, as if supervising my typing skills was a necessity. I was creating a new portfolio page for Ben that included a couple of his most recent shots. Fiona would share this with the fragrance company that was considering making him their spokesmodel. I opened the photo from his Calvin Klein shoot. Ben was in just his skivvies, a lucky pair of heather-gray boxer briefs that hugged him in all the right places. I reached for the mouse to click to the next photo but Fiona's talons caught my hand.

"Hold on." She leaned in closer to the screen.

I glanced at her from the corner of my eye. *Gosh, drool much??* It was Ben in his underpants, so I got it, but sheesh.

"This is a nice one," I commented, trying to keep my tone neutral.

A slow smile curled Fiona's mouth upward. "He's a big boy." Heat blossomed in my cheeks. Her words were confident, sure, and left me reeling. "Yes, let's use this one, the one from his Gucci shoot and the *GQ* cover."

Still speechless, I assembled all the photos into the document. Then I added his height, measurements, and the Status Models logo before printing several color copies. Fiona slid them into her leather portfolio and began packing up her things for her meeting.

I scrubbed a hand across my face. I hadn't heard from Ben since our encounter in my hotel room and our subsequent texting when I told him that that was a one-time thing. I didn't know if that was good or bad. Supermodels probably weren't used to the word *no*.

My last text to him ran through my head on repeat. He seemed to have taken it to heart, but what did I expect? Did I want him to argue with me? *Hold me down and make love to me?* The visual made me shiver.

I checked my phone for messages. Nothing. It was time to get ready for tonight's cocktail mixer, anyway. I excused myself from Fiona's room and made my way downstairs to shower, fighting off the feelings of disappointment and hurt.

Ben

I stood under the rough spray of water, letting it wash away the makeup from the shoot. It had been a tiring day. Henri, the photographer, was known for favoring a jumping style in his shoots. He liked to capture his subjects midjump to evoke a sense of movement, so I'd spent several hours leaping into the air, pushing my body into various positions and angles while keeping my face neutral and making sure the clothes and my hair remained in place. Fun times.

The streaming hot water beat against my back, relaxing me, and my thoughts wandered to Emmy. She was proving to be quite the contradiction.

Some girls were model-fuckers—willing to drop their panties as soon as they heard my profession. Others were intimidated and self-conscious, assuming they'd never be good enough to be with a model. Both types annoyed me.

Emmy was neither. Her self-confidence wasn't as robust as it probably should be; I sensed some of that was from Fiona's hurled insults. But, mostly, I was attracted to her uncanny ability to keep me guessing.

Since I was pretty sure that fucking me wasn't number one on her agenda, her behavior confused me. She was flirty and sexy through text, polite and professional at work. Distant, even.

If I had to put my finger on it, I'd say she was most interested in being friends. And while I might have thought having her as a friend was a good idea initially, I didn't really *have* friends. Certainly not friends I wanted to fuck. Badly.

I'd never had to work to get a girl in my bed. The thought was almost laughable. Almost. If my balls weren't fucking aching at the thought of waiting, it would be funny. That wouldn't do. I needed to have her.

After several long minutes, I reluctantly shut off the water and climbed out of the glass-enclosed shower. I wrapped a towel around my hips, tossing another across my shoulders. Emerging into the bedroom, I rubbed the towel across my face but the feeling that I wasn't alone caused me to pull the towel away. Fiona sat on the edge of my bed with a wide, cocky grin.

"You were brilliant today." Her eyes traveled down my naked chest before coming to rest on mine.

"Thank you."

Crossing the room to the bureau, I grabbed a pair of boxers, a T-shirt, and jeans. The sound of Fiona's soft laughter filled the silence. I pulled the shirt over my head and turned away from her, letting the towel drop to the floor. It wasn't like Fiona hadn't seen my bare ass before. I pulled on the boxer briefs and heard her softly padding across the room to stand behind me. Her hands came around my middle, encircling my waist as she pressed her breasts into my back.

"Love," she whispered. Her voice was a desperate plea, full of longing.

"I'm tired, Fiona." I removed her hands from where they'd been caressing my abs and turned to face her.

The clouded look in her eyes fell away as she snapped her gaze to mine. "Of course. You worked hard today. Dinner's on the way and then I can give you a massage after. We'll see if we can get you to sleep tonight." She offered a weak smile.

I merely nodded. I'd been hoping to text with Emmy again tonight. Maybe even pay her a visit, see if I could get beyond that exterior she tried to put up. A quick glance past Fiona to the clock told me it was only eight. She should still be up for a while.

A knock at the door broke our eye contact. Fiona let in the room service while I pulled on my jeans.

We sat on my bed and dined, as we had so many times before in cities around the globe. Even the meal was familiar— grilled fish and vegetables, wine and sparkling water. God forbid there be fat or carbs involved.

Fiona's mouth moved sensually while she ate, gliding over the tines of her fork. Her eyes stayed on mine. She was an attractive woman; despite our sixteen-year age difference, I found her appealing. Then again, I found things to appreciate about all women. Their frilly panties, their little manicured toes, the curve of a lower back, their scent. Yes, I loved women. Just looking at them, admiring them. Maybe it was because of my chosen profession that I was aware of all their beauty.

I'd spent countless hours with my mom's old issues of *Vogue* and *InStyle*. We'd sit in her big canopied bed on Sunday morning, have breakfast in bed, and flip through every page. As a mom-son bonding experience, it was odd. But it was the one we'd had. She was usually too hung over for breakfast, but she'd sip her coffee and watch me eat and we'd comment on all the looks.

Brunette, blonde, redhead, olive skinned, or freckled, I found beauty in it all. And I didn't discriminate. Sure, most of my female companions were models, but I attracted more than my fair share of attention from other girls, too. I'd messed around with girls in my teen years, at first a little shy and fumbling, but as I learned their bodies, I grew confident. And after I lost my virginity at eighteen, my sexual appetite increased dramatically. Much to Fiona's dismay. She regularly reminded me how much my interest in other girls displeased her. And since she was more than just my boss—she was a family friend—I tried my best to keep her happy. I think I'd been blown on every continent as a result. Quick indiscretions were easier. Plus, there was no girl to try to get out of my hotel room later on.

Of course, now just twenty-two, almost twenty-three, I already felt jaded. Being alone was just easier. I'd never had a girlfriend, never really wanted one. And it was clear Fiona wouldn't take well to the idea. Not that it should bother me, but it did somehow.

We finished our meal and Fiona removed the dishes, setting them outside the door to be picked up later. "Shall I get your pills?" she asked.

"Sure."

She returned a moment later with the few bottles, shaking the pills out into my hand. No matter how much trouble she was, she really was good to me. I dutifully swallowed down the handful.

"I can rub your back if you like," Fiona said.

A massage sounded heavenly, but I had other plans tonight. "No, that's okay." I didn't want to straight up ask her to leave, but I wasn't above doing it if she didn't take my subtle hints.

Fiona frowned and shifted a step toward the door. "Well, I guess I'll go then."

I nodded and walked her to the door. "Night, and thank you for dinner."

"Of course."

She kissed both my cheeks before heading out.

It was almost ten and I wondered if Emmy was asleep. She'd said before that I could text her if I couldn't sleep. I wondered if that offer still stood, since she also told me we needed to keep things professional from now on. Too bad I had no plans of letting that happen.

A few minutes later, I'd brushed and flossed and crawled between the sheets with my phone. Flipping off the bedside lamp, the bluish glow from my phone illuminated the keypad enough to type.

Me: Hey sexy

I hit send and set the phone on my stomach, laying back to stare at the ceiling. I wondered if she'd be bold and return my text. Or if I'd be able to get to sleep tonight. Several long seconds later my phone chimed. The sound made me smile. She wasn't immune to me, despite what she'd said.

Emmy: Hiiii

I grinned. Already I felt better. I could just hear her sweet southern accent drawing out the greeting. It was crazy how one simple word with several extra vowels could make me so happy.

Me: You're still up?

Emmy: Nope. Sound asleep. ;)

Smartass. This girl made me smile. She didn't tiptoe around me because of who I was and I liked that.

Emmy: Can't sleep?

Me: Not tired yet

Emmy: Did you need something? ;)

I smirked. Oh yeah, she wanted it. She might try to deny it and act uninterested, but I knew the truth. I could read her like a book.

Me: Yeah, send me a pic of your tits.

I knew it was crass, but something in me liked taunting her, wanted to see how she'd react. To my surprise, several seconds later a dark, grainy photo appeared. Emmy was dressed in a white tank top that was pulled low on her chest, exposing several inches of creamy smooth cleavage. I wanted to stick my face in between those beauties and smother them with kisses.

Me: Beautiful girl. Looks like you're lying in bed. Why aren't you sleeping?

Emmy: I was thinking about you, actually.

Me: Oh really? ;)

I needed to keep the upper hand, get her talking without giving too much away.

Emmy: Yes, and about the other night.

Me: Go on . . .

Emmy: You're a good kisser.

Me: You're sexy when you come.

Emmy: Ben . . .

Me: Yes darling?

Emmy: :)

Me: What's your favorite sexual position?

Emmy: I like to be on top.

Me: Like it deep?

Emmy: Bennn . . .

I could practically hear the whimper in her tone, the way she'd moan my name. I liked it.

Emmy: Are you okay with girl on top?

Me: Yes. As long as you're facing me so I can look into your eyes while I fuck you.

It'd be more fun to see her reactions in person, to watch her cheeks blossom in pink. To see if she'd look down shyly or be daring and watch me with those pretty gray eyes. Her eyes

were so expressive, so open. I'd love to watch the desire overtake her features, to see just how much my words affected her.
But for now, I'd have to settle for knowing she was a few floors
below me, alone in her hotel room, her heartbeat elevated,
and her panties damp.

Emmy: We shouldn't do this.

Me: No?

Emmy: What's your favorite?

I actually laughed out loud. One second she was telling
me we shouldn't do this, and the next she was asking for my
favorite sexual position. I loved how unsure she was. It was
actually a turn-on to think I'd have to coax this girl out of her
shell. Somehow I knew she'd be worth the effort.

*Me: Probably cowgirl, too. That way I can see all of the girl
and control her body on me. Also it's also easier for her to go as
deep as she can take.*

Emmy: Oh . . .

Me: Are you getting wet baby?

Emmy: Yes.

Fuck, that was sexy. Part of me wanted to tell her to rub
herself, to get nice and wet for me, but I didn't want to push
her too hard, too fast. I couldn't have her shutting down on
me again.

While I considered what to type next my phone chimed
again.

Emmy: You get me soaking wet so fast. Are you hard?

Me: I'm getting there . . .

It wasn't a lie. She was getting me there. Just the thought of getting in her panties again, touching her soft curves.

Emmy: I wanna see . . .

Me: :)

I trusted her, but the last thing I needed was a cock shot ending up online. That'd be a publicity nightmare I didn't need.

Emmy

I guess he had to be cautious with photos like that. He was a public figure after all, and could probably get in trouble. He was smart. I probably shouldn't have been so willing to send him dirty pics, but something in me liked being naughty, liked knowing that I was turning him on.

Emmy: Hmm, too bad because I was going to send you a pic...

Ben: Emmyyy... don't tease, baby. Send me one.

Emmy: What do you want to see?

Ben: Your ass in a sexy pair of panties.

I nearly giggled to myself. He was an ass man. I had that in spades, so we were a good match there. I turned to pose in front of the full-length mirror, capturing a photo on my camera phone. It was just my lower half, my butt in a pair of black lacy panties, legs, and bare feet. It didn't look half bad. I hit send and hopped back onto the bed to await his response.

Ben: Mmm I like that.

I felt proud, like I'd really affected him. He had no witty

comeback, just raw honesty in his reaction. Satisfaction bubbled up inside me. *I am woman, hear me roar!*

Ben: That ass is perfect.

Emmy: You sure you can't send me a pic?

Ben: You're killin' me, girl.

Like a peacock strutting around shaking its tail feathers, I paced my hotel room, suddenly too anxious to sit still.

Ben: Behave or I'll have to spank that sexy ass.

Texting with Ben was made even hotter knowing that his room was only a few floors up, and he could ask me to come upstairs if things got too heated. What would I say then? How would I respond? I would say no, of course. I had morals. I wouldn't be someone's middle-of-the-night secret. Not even Ben Shaw's. Because I knew already it wouldn't be that simple. It wouldn't be the no-strings physical relationship he was probably looking for. My pesky heart was already in the game, sporting a jersey with his name on the back. I was firmly on Team Ben. Shit, I could be the team captain.

His witty banter, sense of humor, dirty mouth . . . all of it was adding up to trouble. I needed to keep my head on straight. Ben was never going to be my boyfriend. We were coworkers. Well, I guess that wasn't entirely accurate. He was a god. I was a lowly assistant.

Emmy: Maybe next time . . .

Ben: Mmm . . . next time, yes.

My heart raced and my skin was warm and flushed all over. There was no denying how turned on Ben got me. Of course, the brain was the largest sex organ, and all this mental stimulation was like foreplay. My nipples puckered and rasped against my shirt, feeling extra sensitive. The cotton panties I wore were thoroughly drenched and annoyingly bunched against my skin. I was too turned on. I needed relief. Slipping one hand inside my panties, I held the image of Ben in my mind: his chiseled jawline, his full mouth, those dark eyelashes and intense hazel eyes.

I soothed the pad of my middle finger over my swollen clit, a soft moan tumbling from my lips. Using the warm, slick fluid, I rubbed in small circles, quickly building toward orgasm, my body primed and ready. I pushed my tank top up with my free hand and palmed my breasts, rubbing my nipples as I imagined Ben would do. All too soon, waves of pleasure crashed against me, a blind sensation ricocheting through my womb, causing it to clench violently with the need for something to fill it. With a ragged breath, I moaned out Ben's name as I came.

I squirmed under the weight of Fiona's exasperated stare. I had tried the best I could, buying an expensive but basic black cocktail dress from a department store, thinking I could make it work for a variety of occasions. Wrong again. The blocky straps and slit in the back had already earned me generous critiques from Fiona, and we were only fifteen minutes into the welcome party being hosted in Ben's honor at a local nightclub. He was being paid generous sums of money to make an appearance but hadn't even shown yet.

Fiona was on her third glass of champagne and was flirting with a few of the execs from the advertisers Ben would be modeling for in the coming weeks.

I inconspicuously watched the door for Ben to arrive. Moments later, I got my wish. He came strolling in, the epitome of tall, dark, and handsome. Black Gucci suit, crisp white shirt, thin black tie. His jaw was unshaven, and his hair was pushed up in a playful swoop in the front. His eyes scanned the room as those long, sexy legs carried him in purposeful strides toward our table. He crossed the room like he owned it, like he was walking a runway. It was captivating.

He turned his body fully toward mine and treated me to direct eye contact for several long seconds. His eyes were so expressive, so intense that my blood pumped faster, my heart working harder just from his attention. It was startling.

My eyes fell to my lap, but I could still feel him watching me. My skin erupted into flames and my heart kicked up a notch remembering the way his mouth felt on mine, how his fingers pumped into me until I came. I gripped the table in front of me just to keep from falling from my seat.

Fiona stood to greet him, kissing both cheeks in her customary way, and then introduced him to the executives who were there to meet the man behind the pictures. I could already tell there would be some serious wooing tonight. They wanted him. And were practically salivating just from meeting him. I was sure Fiona would be in a happy mood, realizing they'd likely book him for several more large campaigns this season and next. I could almost see the dollar signs in her eyes as she introduced Ben around. He smiled and shook hands, but I could tell something was wrong. He bit down, his jaw clenching as he quietly slipped into the seat next to Fiona.

What was supposed to be a casual night out Fiona had turned into a promotional opportunity to sell Ben. She pulled a stack of the new comp cards and passed them across the table. Ben smiled and fielded questions, turning up the charm like Fiona expected. But I could tell he wasn't happy. I found myself wondering if he ever got a day off, just time to himself—time to not be the model everyone clamored for.

I knew I shouldn't, but I felt bad for him. He was gorgeous, wealthy, well traveled, multilingual—yet I did. A tiny piece of me felt bad that he probably didn't know the simple pleasures of being utterly carefree, able to eat whatever he wanted. Hell, eating enough comfort food to ensure a breakout and an increased pants size were practically the norm after a good breakup. Ben had probably never had that luxury.

He pulled out his phone, checking his schedule as they discussed the upcoming campaigns. Had he known tonight was going to be about work, I'm guessing he would have brought along Gunnar.

Fiona leaned across and whispered in Ben's ear. She tried to keep her features relaxed, glancing up nervously at their guests, but Ben made no apologies for his pissed-off look.

Fiona thrust her camera at me. "Take a group shot of us, will you?"

I accepted the camera and stood, heading around the front of the table. "Squeeze in a little."

Fiona threw one arm around Ben, the other around the French executive on her left, and proudly beamed.

"We'll get the waitress to take it. Emmy should be in the photo, too," Ben said.

The look Fiona shot him was pure venom. He should know better than to try to stick up for me. "Not wearing that, she's not. Pierre, if you sign us up, you may have to throw in a new dress for this one."

She waved a dismissive hand in my direction. All their eyes found me, and the wave of laughter at Fiona's joke hit me like a smack to the face. I swallowed hard and kept my chin up. I counted to three and snapped the photo, mentally high-fiving myself that Fiona's eyes were half closed in the picture. She looked like a stroke victim. I inwardly giggled. *Take that, bitch!*

"It's perfect." I turned the camera off and passed it back to her. Then I excused myself.

I tried not to get emotional, not to let Fiona bother me. But I was PMSing. Bad. And I knew that wasn't a promise I could keep. I made it to the restroom and ducked into a stall, blinking against the stupid tears filling my eyes. This was supposed to be a great adventure—working for the elite Status Models agency, living abroad, making something of myself. But it was times like this that I missed home. I missed the smell of Tennessee and fresh-cut grass, lazy Sundays watching football with my dad, and the fact that the guys at home weren't supermodels. They drove mud-encrusted trucks and wore holey jeans. And they didn't send me into a near panic attack with their sexiness, either.

I sucked a cleansing breath into my lungs. I wouldn't let Fiona win. And things with Ben were . . . confusing . . . but fine. Yes, everything would be fine. I smoothed the dress that I now despised over my hips and studied myself in the mirror. My brown hair had gone flat. My eyes were tinged in red and I looked pale. Screw it. I exited the bathroom, needing this night to end. Stat.

Ben

Tonight was supposed to be a relaxing night out—not some circus where I felt the need to sell myself to these douche bag executives. And Fiona commenting on Emmy's dress like that was utter bullshit. I fought to keep my anger under control. "Fiona, can I have a word?"

She nodded tightly and rose, following me from the table.

I took a deep breath. I could handle myself and whatever tasks Fiona threw my way. But I was bothered by how she treated Emmy. We paused in the corridor, facing each other. "Take it easy on Emmy, all right? She's not used to this world."

Her mouth pulled into a frown. "I don't want you distracted by some country bumpkin."

Biting down, my jaw tensed. I shook my head. I knew I needed to handle this the right way. Things with Fiona were delicate. Always had been. And our past was complicated, to say the least. I reached out toward her, smoothing a hand up and down her arm. Her lips quirked up at the contact. I knew just how to make her putty in my hands. "I've got this."

"Okay, love."

I should have been thrilled with the amount of work Fiona had lined up for me this season. I was set to appear in all the major campaigns, walk in several big shows, and make a slew of money. Yet, all I wanted to do was go back to the hotel, hang out with Emmy, and maybe take her to Luxembourg Gardens. I wanted to see how her pretty pink skin looked in the afternoon sun. I used to go there with my mother when we'd briefly lived in Paris. Emmy and I could walk to a café, sip wine, and I could hear all about her growing up in Tennessee. Surely, her childhood had been much different from mine.

I had never let anything get in the way of my work. I didn't know what it was about this girl, but I liked her. I wanted to get to know her more. And I wouldn't mind getting her naked. Her skin was so soft, her body a thing of wonder. She had curves. Real curves. Not like the models I was used to. Her tits were full and heavy. Fuck, I wanted to suckle those babies. I wouldn't mind kissing her all over, for that matter.

I shook away the thought, focusing on Fiona again. She was discussing my campaign. I'd show up and do whatever she wanted me to. We both knew that. And Gunnar, or Emmy, would make sure I got where I needed to be.

"I mean it, Fiona. Relax, okay?" I turned without waiting for her response and strolled into the men's room. Sooner or later I would need to make a break from her.

Emmy

Exiting the restroom, I ran smack into something hard. Ben.

"S-sorry." I stumbled back a step, smoothing shaky hands down his lapels. He was standing in the hallway, leaning against the wall. Was he waiting for me?

"Everything okay?" His eyes saw too much. When he looked at me like that, I felt it deep inside my body. I ached to know the intensity that lurked behind those hazel eyes.

"Fine," I bit out.

The enormity of everything hit me. I was thousands of miles from home, my boss hated me, and I was in over my head with Ben. Tears welled in my eyes. I hated that I was about to cry in front of him. It all hit me in that moment, and there was no stopping my tears now. I was half a world away and out of my depth. A lone teardrop rolled down my cheek.

"It's all right." He reached a hand out for me and I took a step back, quickly wiping my cheek.

"I think I'm going to head out." My voice sounded surprisingly composed. Thank God for that. Small miracle considering my emotional state. Damn PMS.

"It's not true, you know." His voice in comparison was thick, husky, and rolled over me in the most sensual way.

"What?"

"What Fiona said." His gaze lowered, sliding over my curves.

I felt squirmy when he looked at me like that—all dark and hungry. My tears dried and a new wave of emotions hit me. The way his eyes wandered made me remember his kiss, his warm tongue gliding against mine, one hand buried in my hair to pull me closer, his dirty texts last night. It was all too much.

"The dress *is* a cheap knockoff. She was right, Ben." I hated how dejected my voice sounded, but I could do little to control it.

Ben shook his head. "Trust me."

I wanted to assure him he was wrong, but I suddenly found that under his hot, intense stare, with his lean body so close to mine, I'd forgotten the finer points of my argument. Hell, I'd forgotten my damn name. His eyes slid lower, caressing my breasts, and a smile curved over his lips. My breasts had never felt so full and achy, so ready to be touched, licked, and kissed.

Lazily making his eyes return to mine, Ben said, "Let me walk you back. I'm done with Fiona's shit show, anyway."

I nodded and allowed Ben to guide me back to the table. We said our good-byes, and Fiona shot me a dark, icy stare. I kept my eyes downcast, knowing she was fuming. Awesome. I'd have that to deal with tomorrow.

Once we reached the hotel elevator, Ben hesitated. The way his eyes traveled over me . . . I just knew he didn't see an unfashionable dress or an unpolished assistant. He saw me—a girl from Tennessee who wore her heart on her sleeve. I felt fully present with him. Not because I was relaxed—that wasn't it—I was hyperaware of every sensation, overanalyzing every emotion when he was near. When he looked at me, it felt like he'd always known me. And he accepted me just how I was.

His hand at my wrist stopped me from pressing the button for my floor. "Come to my room. Have a drink with me." His brilliant eyes sparked playfully on mine. He placed his big warm hand against the small of my back and suddenly I felt normal. His touch grounded me more than it should. "Emmy?"

I wouldn't argue with him. Not now. "After the night I had—yes please." I knew I was probably asking for trouble being alone with him again, but I felt powerless to say no.

He took my hand, tucking it in the crook of his arm so it rested against his ribs. He was warm and whole, and my body responded with a tiny shudder at the contact. It had been far too long since I'd been with someone. My body was merely confused—responding to the simple contact from a man. Okay, a hot man. A hot man who brought me to orgasm with only his hand in a matter of minutes. A man I had fantasized about . . .

He punched the button for the top floor and grinned slightly as the elevator carried us higher.

Ben slid the key into the card reader and pushed open the door. I entered the darkened room, noticing it smelled like him: crisp soap and the musk of spicy cologne. He flicked on the light, illuminating a large room with a king-sized bed, a desk, and a chair in front of a large picture window. His room was bigger than mine.

"Nice view," I said, walking toward the window. Gauzy white curtains framed the picturesque twinkling lights below.

I heard the rattle of glass and looked back to watch him carry two glasses and a few little bottles over to the bed. Dumping everything onto the nightstand, he surveyed our options. "We can go super-sophisticated tonight and I can offer you an exclusive mix of cheap vodka and Perrier. Flat, of course."

"And warm?" I giggled, noting the lack of ice.

He tossed a sexy smile over one shoulder. "I'm classy like that."

"I'm in."

He chuckled again and I decided I liked hearing him laugh. I needed to hear more of that sound.

I crossed the room, slipped off my heels, and sat on the edge of the bed. Ben sat next to me and handed me a glass. He filled it with vodka and then topped it with the no-longer-sparkling water.

Raising his glass, his eyes met mine. "To vodka. My second favorite V-word."

My smile faltered. I wondered if our flirty-playful banter was permitted only through text messaging since we'd yet to actually flirt in person. Was this allowed?

I took a sip and grimaced at the bitter concoction burning a path down my throat. "Mmm, vodka and water."

Ben shrugged, taking a much more poised sip of his own. "At least it's low-cal."

That made me sad. Don't get me wrong, I appreciated his flawless physique, but I wanted to give this boy a cheeseburger, stat. Maybe a big cupcake and a sugary daiquiri, too. But I supposed vodka would do the trick. And Lord knew my waistline could use a break. My daily chocolate croissants and café au laits with frothy whole milk had started to add up. I looked up and saw Ben surveying me, his playful smile lifting on one side, just for me. This man watched me with definite interest, and in an instant the shitty, insecure feelings inside me vanished.

He took another sip, continuing to appraise me over the rim of his glass. It was times like this, when he turned all thoughtful and quiet, that I'd kill to know what was running through his mind. Especially where I was concerned.

"What's your angle?" he asked, finally.

"I'm sorry?" My what?

"I'm just confused about what you want—your motivations. Everyone's got an angle with me, Emmy. I've seen and heard it all—bossy photographers trying to manipulate me into showing more skin, girls who just want to say they've fucked a model. Forgive me if I sound like a dick, but people usually hang around for my looks, money, fame, connections, or the VIP events I can take them to."

"I'm not interested in those things."

"I know. Which is why I'm confused." He swirled the liquor in his glass, taking another sip.

Working alongside Fiona for all these years had messed with his head. Just like the executives tonight, everyone wanted a piece of him—a piece of this godlike man.

"You're sweet to me . . . so giving . . . it's unexpected . . ." He rubbed the back of his neck, looking lost.

"Ben, when I see you on set and you're tired or hungry or have low blood sugar—my momma raised me better than that. I can't let a man go hungry."

"So you're a bit of a food peddler." He smirked.

"I suppose that's an inherited gene." I returned his uneasy smile.

"I'm sorry." He shook his head. "I tend to be skeptical about girls wanting to hang around me. You'll tell me if there's something you want? Autographed photos for your friends, maybe? Tell me what you want from me, Emmy."

I blushed irrationally. I knew he couldn't read my thoughts, or see the dirty video of me and him replaying inside my head. "Well, I don't have an angle." I didn't know how to answer him, and I certainly couldn't admit my feelings, so I did the only thing I could. I picked up the book sitting on his pillow. "*The Prince*, huh? He's more than just a pretty face. I'm impressed." My awkward attempt at a topic change was cringe-worthy.

Ben seemed to go with it, however, a smug smile tugging at his mouth. "I can read. Let's calm down," he said dryly, plucking the book from my hands.

"Sorry, I didn't mean to sound so surprised, but honestly, you have to know models aren't usually known for their intelligence." Regret instantly followed my little rant.

Ben's jaw twitched. "Fair. Annoying. But fair. Nothing's worse than showing up for a shoot, only to have a photographer speak to me like a small child."

"They do that?"

"You wouldn't believe how often. Half of them are just arrogant and rude, and the other half act like they want to get in my pants."

I giggled. "Asshats."

"Precisely. Can I top you off?"

My sick little sex-deprived mind thought we were jumping into the dirty talk—until I realized he was opening another minibottle of vodka and was awaiting my response. "Oh, sure. Can I just hit the little girl's room first?"

"I only have a boy's room, but it's all yours."

I strolled to the bathroom, closing the door behind me. A line of men's upscale grooming products littered the marble countertop, and a fancy electronic toothbrush sat cradled in its charger. If all that wasn't enough to tell me that this man was different from the boys back home, the pair of black Armani Exchange boxer briefs that lay discarded on the floor should have. Part of me liked seeing that he was still just a guy—a messy, toilet-seat-left-up-and-everything guy.

I couldn't explain to him, let alone myself, what I was doing here, other than simply giving in to the pull to be near him. He was gorgeous and funny and made me feel all kinds of alive. Okay, I suppose that was reason enough. I glanced in the mirror as I washed my hands. This man dated supermodels. The girl in the mirror was no supermodel. I wasn't delusional enough to think I could compare with the women he was exposed to. Straight brown hair, big bluish-gray eyes, a funny mouth that often curled into a smile for no reason at all. I was typically described as cute. Not that I'd ever minded that before. But being around models all the time made me wish I was six feet tall with legs up to my armpits and looks best described as exotic. Sadly, that wasn't in the cards. I finger-combed my loose brown waves. The girl staring back at me was a mess of nerves. What was the real reason that Ben asked me up here? I wondered if Fiona ever felt this insecure. Not likely with her thousand-dollar Louboutins, designer clothes, and the male attention she garnered with a simple smile. I gave up and tucked my unruly locks behind my ears.

Ben was sexy, rich, and probably had girls dropping their panties left and right. Yes, I was sure he got more ass than a toilet seat, yada yada yada. Three girls—as if. *Shut up, Emmy*. I was smart, hardworking, and a good cook. If that was all I had to offer, it would either be enough or it wouldn't. I was the girl he'd invited back to his room, dammit.

I lifted the hand towel from the counter and stopped cold. Two bottles of prescription medications were sitting underneath. Three more pill bottles sat on the glass shelf under the vanity. I wondered what they were for. He didn't seem sick, but he had more pills than a pharmacy. Seriously, was he sick or dying? That could be the only probable reason for all these bottles. Otherwise, he had a major problem. Gunnar's words rang in my head. Something about Ben being a mess without a pile of pills. It couldn't be true. Ben didn't seem that way at all. My hand shook as I lifted the bottle from the counter. The name of the medication was something foreign to me. No chance of pronouncing that.

Ben knocked on the door. "You okay in there?"

"Fine!" I called. My heart jumped into my throat, like he was going to somehow know I had snooped. It wasn't *really* snooping since everything was sitting out in the open, but still. I buried the bottles back under the towel and wiped the confused scowl from my face before rejoining him.

"There she is. Thought I was going to have to send in a search party." Ben had removed his dress shirt and was now in black slacks and a white V-neck T-shirt that sharply contrasted with his tanned skin.

"Nope. I'm here." I smiled, tension falling from my shoulders.

Ben watched me with guarded eyes, and I wondered if he knew that I'd seen his pill collection. Then again, he could have been watching for my reaction, because when I saw what was on his bed, my breath caught in my throat.

He chuckled softly. "That excited, huh?"

I stumbled to a halt. His bed held an array of sex toys—whips, cuffs, dildos, vibrators, weird little rubbery things I had no name for, and a large box sat discarded nearby. "W-what's all this?"

Ben chuckled at my innocent response. "Gunnar goes through my fan mail and only gives me what he thinks might be interesting. This came from a sex-toy company. They want me to be a spokesmodel."

"Oh." My pulse accelerated. "And are you going to?"

"Not planning on it, no. The girl I'm with wouldn't need any toys, so I wouldn't make a very good advocate for their products." He patted the bed beside him. "Come sit. I just thought it'd be fun to look."

"Right." I joined him on the bed, arranging myself politely next to him. There sure were a lot of kinky toys.

"And if you wanted anything . . ." He trailed off, leaving the second half of the sentence unspoken but seductive all the same. Was he asking if I wanted any sex toys? I fought to keep my breathing under control, but I could feel the heat crawling up my neck, my chest rising and falling with shallow pants. *Sex. Ben.* And to think, I'd only just gotten my mind out of the gutter.

"Ben . . . I know things got heated between us the other night . . . but I don't want to give you the wrong impression. I'm not that girl. I've never had a one-night stand. I'm more of a committed relationship, one-boyfriend-at-a-time type." Thankful my voice sounded calm, I pulled in a breath and met his eyes. "This isn't going to work for me. I'm sorry."

He watched me with an amused expression. He leaned

down to whisper near my ear, his breath warm against my skin. "When I want something, I can be very persuasive."

"What do you want?" I whispered, barely recognizing my own voice. It was breathless and much too high.

He rubbed his lips against my jaw, our mouths so close that I could feel the strain in his jaw as he fought the urge to kiss me. "I want to fuck, Emmy."

"Who?" Heat flooded my cheeks, and I struggled to maintain deep, even breaths.

"You." Ben's dark eyes roamed over me, and his fingertips caressed my jaw. "Stop playing games with me. I want you. You're not like other girls."

I knew he could see my pulse flutter violently against my neck. I was achy and distracted and completely thrown off center. I'd told him no, convinced him that this couldn't happen, yet it was all I could think about. All I wanted. I wanted to feel his big, warm hands on my body, feel him press those full, sensuous lips to my skin. I wanted his thick length to invade my body while he whispered filthy things in my ear.

I still hadn't answered him, and he was waiting. Still watching me. I knew I was frustrating him, and I didn't mean to. I was leaving us both unsatisfied, but I couldn't let myself take that leap, could I? Could this really be just sex? Maybe I'd be stupid to deny myself this. It wasn't every day a girl got to spend a few months living and working in Paris and having a fling with a supermodel. I almost giggled at my predicament. Almost. But Ben's hungry gaze was still locked on me.

"I want to be clear." His voice dropped lower. "My past is complicated, my future is uncertain—I travel all the time, I move every few months. But we have this. Here. Now. Don't deny me, baby."

Part of me couldn't even believe I was questioning this. There were people with real problems in the world. Disease. World hunger. And my biggest dilemma was whether or not to give in to exquisite supermodel Ben Shaw. I should've slapped myself for worrying about this so much. Just once I wanted to do what I wanted, to listen to my body, to act on my hidden desires rather than be the good, responsible girl my parents raised. I wanted hot, sweaty sex. No strings attached. I wanted to let this man have his way with me, dominate my body, show me all the ways he could pleasure me.

Everything about this man oozed sex appeal. His strong jaw, the curve of his mouth, the set of his posture, his possessive eyes. His smile had disappeared and he was watching me intently.

Ben dropped his hand from my jawline and pulled in a sharp breath. "Any of these interest you?" His hand swept across the bed, indicating the array of oversized toys.

I chuckled nervously. "A lady never tells."

"And a gentleman never asks, but I'm neither, so spill it, darling."

Don't let him see how rattled you are. Be confident. Pushing my shoulders back to conceal the flash of heat that traveled through my core, I pointed to a modest purple glittery toy. "That would do the trick."

"Hmm." He thoughtfully looked over the toy I'd indicated. "We'll have to work up to this then." He placed the largest one next to my hip—a long, flesh-colored member, thick as all get-out.

"Ha, aren't you funny." I shifted uncomfortably on the bed. The damn thing was nudging my hip. "Nooo, I don't need all that."

"I wasn't talking about the toy, sweetheart." His stare cut straight into mine. He picked up a little silver vibrator, holding it in his large, masculine palm. "You can borrow this one. It won't do me any good." His voice had dropped even lower and sent a rush of desire through me.

I didn't have the heart to tell him I had the upgraded model down in my room. My heart kicked up a notch, stuttering inside my chest. My resolve to keep things professional vanished. The alcohol had left me gloriously relaxed. And slightly turned on.

Ben turned on the toy, running it along my knee. The gentle buzz against the bare skin made my entire leg tingle. I swallowed roughly. I clamped my knees together, my breathing shallow and much too fast. The gentle hum from the toy sent little jolts up my leg as Ben lazily traced it against my skin. My panties were soaking wet and my breasts felt so full and heavy, they heaved with each breath I drew.

He placed the toy against my knee. I started to quiver.

"Ben?" My voice was a soft murmur but I meant it as a warning.

He ignored me, moving the little buzzing toy in a slow progression up my thigh.

"Shh. Let me make you feel good." He pushed the fabric of my dress up, exposing my white panties, and lightly pressed the toy against the already damp fabric. I gripped his biceps for support as pleasure rocketed through me.

I knew things could go further if I wanted. And I wanted to give in. So bad. But I knew that despite only knowing him such a short time, this wouldn't be just a physical act. My heart was already engaged. I sucked so hard at casual sex.

"We can't do this." I found my voice, however shaky it sounded.

"Let me make you come." His voice was raw with need.

He touched my panties with the toy, rubbing it in circles along my sensitive flesh. "Isn't this what you want?"

I pulled my bottom lip into my mouth and bit down. Oh God, yes. I wanted to come. I needed that release.

Without waiting for my response, his warm mouth closed over mine. His lips were full and soft and at the same time demanding. He kissed my lips, my neck, before pulling back to watch me. He took his time, barely brushing my lips with his, letting the anticipation build while our breath mingled.

His lips pressed lightly against mine, not taking but seeking. The answer was yes, God, help me. Yes to anything he wanted. To this. To us. Even if it was only one night of passion, I was defenseless against this man. The toy hummed against me, bringing me closer and closer.

He nibbled my bottom lip and I let out a weak murmur of protest or encouragement; I wasn't entirely sure which. Ben read it as desire for more because his tongue suddenly caressed my bottom lip where his teeth had just been. My hands moved against the back of his neck and I pulled him closer. His tongue entered my mouth, flirting, sliding gloriously against mine. The stolen moments inside my hotel room came rushing back. His kisses were addictive and desire pooled between my thighs.

The powerful sensations spiraled through me, and I exhaled in a whimper. He didn't kiss me. He just watched my expression as he moved the toy against me. I was going to come. With him watching me. My fingers curled around his wrist and I let out a breathy moan. I was so close. My legs parted and my hips shifted, allowing him to reach the spot I needed. Ben groaned and, using his free hand, shifted the erection tenting his slacks. I looked down and watched him massage the toy against me, and my world exploded into a million tiny pieces. My body clenched wildly, needing something to fill it.

Still reeling from my intense orgasm, I moaned, "Ben, fuck me."

He turned off the toy and roughly pulled my damp panties down my legs, kissing my inner thigh as he stripped the fabric away. Our hands were suddenly everywhere at once. He unzipped my dress while I pulled his shirt over his head.

He stripped his pants and boxers away in one brief movement, leaving him nude and fully erect in front of me. Now I understood what he meant about the large toy and working up to it. To him. A rock-hard chest and defined abs led the way to a heavy erection. He was big. Bigger than any of the guys I'd been with before. And he was beautiful down there. All man. Long, straight, and thick. I had the strongest desire to curl my hand around him, to touch him and see if he was real. But this moment seemed real. I could see his chest expanding with his slow, certain breaths and smell the masculine scent of his skin.

He leaned down over me, forcing me to lie back against the bed. His body covered mine, pressing me into the mattress. I felt one of the toys press into my lower back, which only made the moment more erotic. My legs moved around his back, tugging him closer. He let out a breathless groan against my neck, causing my sex muscles to clench uncomfortably.

We tumbled together on the bed, kissing deeply. Only my bra remained in place. Ben reached into the drawer of the nightstand and withdrew a package of condoms. He leaned in to kiss me while he rolled one on.

"Come on top, cowgirl." He lifted me over him so my knees were on either side of his hips. I looked between us to where his long length lay on his belly, nearly reaching his belly button. I swallowed a wave of nerves while a smirk tugged up one corner of his mouth. "Only take what you can handle."

Sweet baby Jesus, I was already out of my depth. I thought of our sexy texts and a hot shiver raced down my spine. No one could turn me on the way this man could.

He nudged against me and I suddenly worried if he would fit. I lowered myself onto him and sank down slowly. Inch by agonizing inch as he stretched me. I was completely overtaken by the sudden feeling of fullness. Sucking in a sharp breath, I closed my eyes and gripped his shoulders as he slowly but completely filled me. Ben's large hand on my hip guided, encouraged, and his dark eyes watched mine. His hips moved up off the bed, filling me and retreating so his thick cock dragged slowly in and out of me. The sensation was incredible. Too much, yet not enough at the same time.

I sat up straight, rotating my hips in tiny circles, unable to stop the whimpers tumbling from my lips. I increased my movements, sliding up and down, and his eyes dropped closed. A surge of pride swelled within me. Each time I sank lower and was completely filled, the pleasure burst into a new sensation. Raw need consumed me and my rhythm increased against him.

"Bennn . . ." His name was perfect for moaning and I used it to my advantage, repeating it like a mantra each time he hit the right spot.

His hands reached behind me, unclasping my bra, and removing it from my arms as I moved against him. He sat up to take my breast in his mouth, licking and sucking as I bounced with our movement.

I was only faintly aware that the lights burned brightly overhead, and while it should have made me self-conscious, it didn't. I wanted to watch this beautiful man. With him I felt alive. There was no room for self-consciousness to creep in around the edges. I let go of all inhibitions and moved against him, crying out his name in a litany of mumbled whimpers.

"Enough." He sat up and moved me under him in one quick

motion. The man had strength to him. The edge to his voice and his serious expression made me wonder if I'd done something wrong. "No more playing. I need to fuck you hard now."

Oh.

He moved my legs, arranged them so I was completely open for his perusal, and then he pushed forward, sinking into me, invading my body with his. My breath caught in my throat and I struggled for air.

"Fuck, Emmy. You feel good." His eyes were dark, his lips parted, and his breathing was fast. This man who was always in perfect control was losing it. For me. I arched my back as the pleasure coursed through me.

There was always a delicate guessing game the first time I was intimate with someone new: wondering how long he would last, if he would warn me before he came, if he'd be loud about it, or completely silent. With Ben, I didn't have to guess.

"This tight little pussy's going to make me come too fast." His pace slowed, dragging his length in and out of me slowly. He moved his hand between us and pressed his thumb firmly to my clit. I cried out loudly, moving my hips.

I loved how he knew to slow to an almost stop for me to completely enjoy the sensations blossoming inside me. My tight walls clung to him, pulsing and gripping as pleasure exploded deep inside.

"Bennn . . ." I breathed.

His hand pulled away and his strokes slowed, milking the second orgasm from my body.

Once I quieted, his pace picked up and he pumped into me several times hard and fast. He buried his face in my neck, kissing me softly as he came. "Emmy."

The deep, broken quality of his voice against my neck undid me. I was falling for him. He could own me completely, use me for his plaything, and I wouldn't care. That realization sent panic racing through me.

What was I even doing? This wasn't me.

I pulled away from the warm cocoon of his body. "Ben, we can't do this. . . . Fiona will fire me. . . ."

His brow drew together. "Who I fuck is none of Fiona's business."

"That's good." *Actually it stung like hell.* "Because she hates me, and I wouldn't want anything to affect your bookings."

He smiled at me like I was a small child. "I can handle Fiona."

All of this was too much. I needed out of this room. "I should probably go." I leapt from the bed, gathering my clothes.

He sat up, confusion apparent in his features. His lips, always full and sensual, were swollen and slightly pink, his breathing still too fast. I almost felt bad leaving him like this. Almost. Until I realized I was in just as ragged a state. My heart was fucking pounding and I was woozy, not from the alcohol but from him. He was intoxicating. And apparently there was nothing between us but the physical act. It wasn't enough. I stepped into my still damp panties and slid them up my legs.

"Okay." He didn't try to stop me, and I wasn't sure what

that meant, but a pang of disappointment settled in my chest. I pulled my dress into place and tucked my hair behind my ears. He rose from the bed and walked me to the door. Slipping into my shoes, I rushed through the open door.

"Emmy." His low voice washed over me in a way that was both familiar and intoxicating.

I spun to face him.

His expression had softened, turned more serious. "Are you okay?"

"I'm good. I'll see you in the morning. Your call time is eight thirty," I mumbled, still weak and shaky from our erotic encounter.

Frown lines settled around that sensuous mouth. "I know. Gunnar told me."

"Well, good night." I disappeared down the hall, trying to forget the look on his face that couldn't have possibly been disappointment.

When I reached my room, my heart and head were at war with my body. My body knew exactly what it wanted—Ben. My head knew I should draw a professional line between us and maintain it. My heart fluttered, a giddy fool at the thought of him. That was bad. I paced my hotel room, my legs still jelly from the thorough fucking he'd given me. There was no way I'd be able to sleep yet. I was still tipsy from the vodka, and my hormones were raging.

I needed Ellie. She'd know what to do.

We hadn't been in touch since I'd arrived. I'd left her emails unanswered and knew it was time to give her an update before she called in a rescue squad. I felt a little guilty, realizing I never even called her when I'd landed. This phone call was long over-due. She could help me sort out this mess. Ellie never had any trouble in the guy department. Her looks were dark and exotic and she exuded enough sexy confidence to capture any man's attention. I felt like a fish out of water when it came to men. Especially a man like Ben. I prayed she'd have some answers for me. If I was to survive the next three months, I needed help.

Glancing at the clock, I realized it was afternoon in New York. Ellie was likely at work. But with any luck, I could catch her.

I paced my hotel room as the phone rang. Other than calling my mom when I'd arrived, it was the first time I put my international calling plan to work.

"Emmy!" she answered after several rings.

I laughed despite myself. "Hey, Ellie."

"How's Paree? How's the megabitch? I miss you! The new roommate's a nightmare."

My shoulders relaxed at the familiar sound of her voice and I sunk onto the bed. "Everything's good. God, girl, I miss you. I need some girl time, bad."

"What's his name, sweetheart?"

I released a deep sigh. *Was it that obvious?* "Ben."

"Name sounds harmless enough. So what's the story with this *Ben*?"

"He's the reason we're here all season. Ben Shaw. Just Google him. He's way out of my league."

"So, what, you want to know how to get him to notice you?" I could hear Ellie typing—at work, no doubt.

"No. We've hung out a couple of times, but God, Ellie, he's a freaking supermodel. I like him, but seriously, what chance do I have?"

"Hush, you're as cute as they come. Okay, please hold, I'm Google-stalking him now. I need a visual."

I swallowed nervously and lay back against the bed, waiting for her to confirm I had no business crushing on this man.

"Fuck me running, he's hot. I'd peel those Calvin Kleins off with my teeth. Nibble on that package."

I laughed. Sadly, I knew the exact photo she was looking at. It was one of the first images that came up on Google when you typed in his name. "Told you."

"Seriously, I'd bite that firm cock right through the fabric. Just gnaw on it."

There was no beating around the bush with Ellie. She always said exactly what was on her mind. Which is why I knew her advice would be perfect.

"Is he really that hot in person? Without the perfect lighting and camera angles?" she asked.

"Hotter," I confirmed. Something about the deep tone of his voice, the confident way he carried himself, his intelligence. He was the complete package.

"Damn honey. So . . . you guys have hung out. . . ." Ellie urged me to continue.

"Yes, grabbing drinks, stuff like that, and of course I've

seen him on set. He's sent me a couple of naughty texts." I smiled at the memory.

"Ohhh, a hot boy who knows the value of dirty sexting. I approve." I could hear the smile in her voice.

"Yeah, but I just feel so out of my element. I'm torn between keeping things professional and dropping my panties every time I see him."

She laughed that deep, throaty chuckle I missed. "My vote is panties off."

"Well . . . about that . . ." I hesitated.

"Have you slept with him?"

"No." The lie slipped easily off my tongue. "Just a little messing around." *With his penis in my vagina. Thirty minutes ago.*

"Okay, well, if you really like him . . . make him wait for sex. Guys like the chase. Don't give up the P right away."

"Right." *Shit. Fuck.* I dragged a hand through my tangled hair.

"Seriously, just have fun, girl. Don't overthink this. Even if he is a model, he's still just a guy."

"Ellie, he's dated supermodels. And I'm sure he's used to girls throwing themselves at him left and right."

"Yes, exactly, but that's exactly what you're not going to do. Don't be one of his groupies following him around like a lost puppy. Be Emmy. You're funny, cool, and real. If he likes you, he likes you."

"True. Thanks, hon." She made it sound so simple. I knew I could count on Ellie.

"Okay, well, I've gotta get back to work. Keep me posted. Oh, and Em . . . don't fall in love with him."

Asking me not to fall in love with Ben was like asking a meth dealer not to let you get addicted. Not possible. "Thanks for your advice. Bye, hon."

I ended the call and curled onto my side, hugging a pillow to my chest. The scent of Ben was still on my skin. I could recall in perfect detail the way he felt deep inside me, his hard body moving above mine. And I wanted more.

8

Emmy

With Ellie's words still ringing in my head, I got ready for work, faking a confidence I didn't feel. The combo of six hours of sleep and a vodka haze didn't help, either. Anticipating seeing Ben on set was a special kind of torture. My cheeks were lit up like a Christmas tree and I could do little to hide it. The memories of last night flooded my senses. Ben rubbing the toy along my panties. Pushing his big cock inside me. Stretching me, filling me almost to the point of pain. Kissing me while his throaty groans punctuated the silence. I remembered how he lost control, moaning my name when he came. It wasn't a memory I would soon forget. If ever.

He was by far the best lover I'd ever had. He was confident and sure. Extremely in tune with both his body and mine. There would be no forgetting last night. And that was what I was most afraid of. I'd be forever comparing every man to Ben. Which was exactly why I shouldn't have let last night happen. I silently cursed myself. How could I work around this man all season?

I could hear Ben's voice and I mustered the courage to enter the makeup area. I didn't know where we stood after last night. I begged him to fuck me and then promptly ran out of his room. I felt like an idiot. That was exactly what I didn't want to happen—an awkward morning-after run-in. We had to work together in close proximity for the next few months. I needed to keep my head on straight. I pushed my shoulders back and headed behind the curtained off makeup area.

As soon as I saw him, all my sexual thoughts were obliterated. He looked like hell. Dark circles lined his eyes, his hair was a mess, and he was slouched over in his seat. My heart squeezed in my chest.

"Don't play with your breakfast," Fiona scolded, standing over him.

Ben looked up, almost as if he sensed my presence. He had arranged his pills into a smiley face on the table in front of him.

His green smoothie from hell sat untouched beside him. I wondered if he woke feeling the effects of the vodka like I had. Poor guy. No way could I stomach a handful of pills or that drink. Why the hell did he let Fiona do that to him?

Thankfully, my upbringing kicked in and I didn't even have to think. He needed taking care of. He was hung over. Too much vodka last night. And by the looks of it, too little sleep. I jumped into southern hospitality mode and strode to the catering table, returning with a plate of toast and a cup of steaming black coffee. It was the exact thing that had cured my hangover a few hours before.

I moved his green drink aside and set down the plate and mug. "You need to eat something."

His tortured gaze met mine and he smiled weakly. "Thank you."

Fiona huffed and walked away, muttering something under her breath about processed carbs.

Whatever. She could bite me. I was raised better than that. My momma would have a fit if she saw what they were feeding this man. Pills and blended vegetables were not a proper meal.

Ben lifted the slice of buttered toast to his mouth. "I'm not supposed to have this, you know."

"Eat up. It'll make you feel better."

His eyes danced on mine, communicating so much. He clearly wasn't used to people taking care of him. Just him as a person and not as a model. His eyes slipped closed as he took a sip of the strong coffee, and he let out a soft moan of bliss. I knew that would do the trick. The man was human, after all. And no human should be forced to endure pureed spinach and kale on a hung-over stomach. I studied the pills spread before him in the shape of a smiley face. The eyes were two golden caplets, vitamin E I assumed, and the rest appeared to be vitamins, too, leaving me to wonder about all those prescription bottles I saw in his room. Did he only take those in private? What were they for?

"You're trouble, you know that?" he asked, finishing the coffee and toast.

"You like it," I flirted.

He cracked a smile. "I know."

He watched me refill his coffee, and I couldn't help but notice there was a softness there I hadn't seen before. That softness was every bit as seductive as his hard body.

Little by little, Ben was letting me in. I could sense that the real him was just a regular guy, looking for a connection. The thought tugged at me. Everyone took from him. No one gave. They wanted photos, autographs, endorsements; girls wanted to sleep with him, Gunnar was dying to turn him gay—but no one was signing up to selflessly give him the simple acceptance he craved. I wasn't sure why, but my taking care of him this morning was a bigger gesture to him than getting naked in his bed last night.

He wanted to just be . . . not be *the* Ben Shaw, the man, the legend. That must have been what he was trying to tell me last night. Maybe I had a shot with him after all. Or I'd had one too many vodka-waters and believed what I wanted to.

Momma would love nothing more than for me to settle down with a nice guy. She reminded me of that each time we talked. What she didn't understand was that all the nice guys I'd dated were just so boring. It made me want to try something different, something new and exciting. Nice guys never sent my pulse racing with a sexy text, or used a toy on me until I was begging to be fucked. The memories of last night refused to fade. Would never fade, I was sure. Visions of us moving together against his sheets danced through my mind as I tried to distract myself from staring at Ben.

Just act normal, Emmy. Riffling through my purse, I handed him two new pills to add to his collection. Pain reliever. "Here. Take these. Then go make pretty pictures."

He smiled. "Okay."

I looked down, unable to handle the full force of that megawatt smile he used just for me. I forced myself to find something to do while Ben was shuffled off to hair and makeup.

Thirty minutes later, my body was instantly aware when he entered the set.

Seemingly recovered—with a little more color in his cheeks—Ben looked amazing. He stood in the center of the studio against a white backdrop while two stylists fussed over him. One played with his hair, which was styled into a perfect mess. Bedroom hair. Another tucked his shirt halfway into the designer jeans to show off the impressive bulge in front. She said something to him and he chuckled softly, then stuck one hand down his pants and adjusted himself. Holy crap. Did she just tell him to adjust his junk? I almost laughed, if it wasn't for the overwhelming memory of that beautiful, large cock. The fact that I now knew it intimately . . .

Ben's gaze flicked to mine and my cheeks blossomed in heat. I felt like I'd been caught with my hand in the cookie jar. But I guess he'd been the one with his hand there. He said something to the stylists and then strode purposefully toward me.

His penetrating gaze remained on mine. Warm honey

with flecks of mossy green. "Can we talk?" His voice was low and laced with concern.

I nodded. "Of course."

His hand captured my wrist and he towed me around the corner, out of sight from the crew. I caught Fiona's eyes, which zeroed in on Ben's hand on me and narrowed.

Following Ben behind the large drop-clothed set, we stood just inches apart. His hand remained on my wrist, his fingers lightly pressing into the skin. My pulse was thrumming at the contact, my body instantly responding.

Ben looked cool and in control. "Thank you for taking care of me."

"That green concoction didn't look very appetizing."

"It's not." He chuckled lightly.

"Well, you're welcome, but it was nothing."

His voice softened, "I appreciate it." Ben took a step closer and heat raced down my spine. "Emmy, about last night . . ."

"I'm sorry about that. . . ."

His jaw clenched. "Sorry you ran out on me or sorry that it happened?"

"Ben, we work together. We shouldn't . . ."

He stroked my cheek lightly with his free hand. "Things like this happen on the road, Emmy. It doesn't make you a bad person."

Now I felt like an even bigger idiot. I'd drunkenly slept with the man one time, and suddenly I was acting like we were dating. Get a grip. "It was fun, right?" I attempted a more lighthearted stance.

He smiled his panty-dropping smile that I'd grown so fond of. His brilliant hazel eyes burned brightly, flecks of deep green glinting in the light. "Tell me what you really want."

"Ben," I managed, my voice just a whisper. I couldn't admit what I really wanted.

He stepped in closer, his fingertips dropping away from my jaw as he studied me closely. I was terrified he'd see how I really felt. This wasn't some fun fling—fuck buddies due to the convenience of a close living situation, like he'd implied. I was developing real feelings. I wanted to get to know him, the real him. I wanted to go on romantic strolls around the city, to lounge in bed in his arms, to learn all about the many sides of this man.

Fiona appeared around the corner, obviously curious about what business Ben and I could possibly have together. Her gaze darted back and forth between us. "The photographer is ready, love," she drawled in her perfect British accent. Her eyes moved again between Ben's playful expression and my stiff posture. "Everything okay?"

Ben dropped his hand from my wrist. "Of course. I was just thanking Emmy for her concern earlier."

Fiona's mouth clamped closed, her jaw working. "Brilliant. Good thinking, Emerson."

I nodded. "It was nothing."

The three of us made our way back to the set by silent agreement. The photographer was waiting for Ben, a DSLR that likely cost more than a small car hanging around his neck. He motioned Ben over.

I watched him converse with the photographer about his vision and review the storyboards and inspiration shots. Ben took his work seriously, he managed to be commanding—all testosterone, edgy yet cool, and playful all at once. He was mesmerizing.

Despite his fame in this industry, he had a way of setting people at ease. Everyone from the set designers, to makeup artists, to executives who lingered just off set. Which was good, because Fiona usually put everyone in a fucking tizzy. I know she did me. But I watched Ben work, discussing the specifics of the shoot with this famed photographer, and I instantly calmed again. He had the strangest effect on me. One minute he was winding me impossibly tight, and the next captivating me with just his presence.

Ben got into position in the center of the set and was fussed over again briefly by the stylists, hair and makeup people, but honestly he looked perfect. I felt like slapping their hands away. Can't mess with perfection.

The photographer took a few shots then called for lighting adjustments. A big, white umbrella-looking thing and a silver reflector were adjusted at different angles.

Once they were ready again, the photographer prompted Ben very little. He knew how to move on camera, holding each pose for a few clicks then turning, tilting his jaw just slightly, pouting his mouth, placing his hands on his hips, in his hair. He knew how to work the camera. The one thing that remained constant despite his movements was his death stare, looking straight into the camera. Those hazel eyes burning so intensely. A shiver raced up my spine remembering how dark and hungry his eyes looked when he rubbed the toy against my panties last night.

The photographer clicked away in obvious joy at getting to work with such a talent. "Chin up," he directed. "Beautiful." Click, click. "Relax your shoulders." Click. "Stunning. Just like that." Click, click.

The ads for the designer jeans hugging Ben in all the right places would be on billboards and in magazines in the fall. I felt like a cool kid that I got to sneak a peek at the behind-the-scenes action.

"Great, now look off camera. Pick something to focus on," the photographer told Ben.

His eyes found mine.

"Good, stay there," the photographer said.

Ben's pouty lips parted and his gaze slipped lower, settling over my chest. His jaw twitched. Desire raced through my system. My breasts felt so full and heavy, they practically throbbed for his touch.

Every tilt of his jaw, each flex of his arms, felt sexual to me, a silent beckoning. I suppressed a hot shiver. The things he could do to my body without laying a finger on me scared me. This man was devastating to my system.

"Smoldering!" the photographer called out, continuing to click away.

If he only knew . . . my panties were about to ignite. Honest to God, I was a fire hazard. Ben needed to stop looking at me like that. His eyes wandered the length of my body, and

I lost any interest I had in keeping us apart. My body wanted this too bad. Craved it. Like a junkie needing a fix.

I became aware of Fiona beside me, her posture stiff and foreboding. She knew Ben was watching me. "Don't drool, darling," she warned, her voice dripping with sarcasm.

I snapped my mouth closed. Oops. I guess I had been staring open mouthed at him, and my breathing was much too fast. I was thankful she couldn't possibly know the thoughts racing through my mind, the blood pumping south, making my lady parts throb.

"He's doing great," I commented instead. Even my voice betrayed me, sounding husky.

Fiona's thin lips curled into a practiced smile. "Ben's very good at what he does. Don't let him fool you, though; he's a complicated man. With a very complicated past. I've been with him since he was eighteen. Trust me when I say girls come and go. He needs to focus on his career, not get hand-fed by some southern housewife type. I know what's best for him."

I nodded. Her warning was ridiculous. Wasn't it? She couldn't really think that Ben was interested in me, could she? But Fiona obviously knew him well, working alongside him for the past five years.

The photographer captured his final shot and Ben's gaze reluctantly dropped from mine and landed on Fiona. I fled to the makeup area, needing to find something to do with my shaking hands.

9

Emmy

Gunnar and I had rescheduled our outing and spent the day silently roaming the massive Notre Dame Cathedral. Afterward, we headed to a little sidewalk café to grab some wine and appetizers.

I listened to him complain about the latest guy he was seeing while nibbling on still-warm, crusty bread slathered with generous amounts of butter.

We were on our second glass of wine and I still wasn't sure how to pump him for information about Ben. I didn't want to give away anything—didn't want him to know I'd begun seeing him on the down-low.

"What's on your mind?" He grinned at me. "You look like the cat who caught the mouse, honey. Spill it."

Okay. So much for being inconspicuous. Was I that obvious? "It's nothing. I just . . . I've begun sort of seeing someone. It's still really new."

"Oh, that wonderfully fun, exciting new stage. New sex! Cheers!" He lifted his wineglass to mine. "Who's the lucky guy? A local? They're not circumcised here, you know."

I nearly spit my wine. I knew that circumcisions weren't common in European men, but geez. Was this really our lunchtime conversation? "He's been . . . uh . . . never mind." I smiled politely. I was *not* telling him that Ben was circumcised. *Lord.*

Gunnar chuckled. "He's been cut . . . hmm, so he's not a local." He leaned forward on his elbows, his eyes widening. "Holy shit, it's not one of our boys, is it?"

Heaven knew I couldn't tell a lie to save my life. "No comment."

"Ha! He's a Status model, isn't he?"

Shit. This wasn't good. There were only a few models traveling with us in Paris. "Maybe."

Gunnar grinned. "Emmy. Stop being cute. I know it's Ben."

"How?" I blurted.

He laughed easily, tipping his head back. "One, you just admitted it. Two, he's straight, unfortunately for me. And three, I've seen the way you look at him."

Damn. Was I that obvious? "Don't say anything, Gunnar. This is still new, and I don't know where it's heading." Disaster City, that's where.

He took another thoughtful sip of his wine. "I don't like it, Emmy." He frowned.

"It's all in good fun, Gunnar. Seriously, it's not a big deal." My dreams of pumping him for information vanished. Gunnar was not in support of this, and I wasn't even sure why.

He reached across the table and took my hand. "You're a sweet, wholesome girl and he's got more issues than *Vogue,* honey."

My stomach turned, the wine I'd consumed churning. How could this possibly end well? Maybe Gunnar was right. I needed to be careful, keep my wits about me. Of course, all I wanted to do was crawl right back into Ben's bed. *Crap.*

Four: the number of days since I'd seen Ben.

Seven: the number of times I'd allowed myself to read our thread of naughty texts.

One: the number of times I'd made myself come while moaning his name. That would be a dangerous habit to get into. I couldn't have him running circles through my head all day and owning all my orgasms. I needed something within my control.

I crawled into bed, flipping off the lamp and resting my phone on the pillow beside me, just in case. I hadn't heard from him, but I hadn't reached out to him, either. I knew the past few days he'd been busy meeting with casting directors and designers for the upcoming Paris Fashion Week. He had been cast in a slew of shows, according to Fiona. I should've felt proud of him, excited for the agency I worked for, but instead I just felt lonely. I wanted the man, not the model.

There was nothing quite so lonely as crawling into bed

alone four thousand miles from home. My legs were restless under the sheets, my limbs aching with the need to do something. A good mattress workout would do the trick.

Ben beneath me.

Come on top, cowgirl.

I remembered the way he lifted me by the hips, moving me over him, positioning himself at my entrance . . . controlling both our pleasure.

A hot shiver ripped through my body, making me crave him more. I was so wrapped up in him, my emotions twisted and raw, my body hot with desire, that I briefly considered just quitting—flying back to New York and looking for a regular job. One without supermodels and bitchy British cougars. I was a wreck.

I kicked the covers off my restless legs, suddenly too warm. Several days without hearing from Ben, especially now that we'd been intimate, seemed like a lifetime. At least Fiona and I were getting along okay. Thankfully, she didn't suspect that I'd hooked up with her prized possession. Otherwise, the shit would hit the fan. Hard. I'd kept things professional with her this week and tried my best not to let her cryptic comments cut into me. But during the quiet times, and especially at night, I couldn't help my mind from drifting to thoughts of Ben. I wondered what he was doing. If he was sleeping okay. What all those pill bottles were for. I know I should just let it go, but something inside me couldn't.

I needed some girl talk. I grabbed my phone and checked the time before dialing Ellie.

We caught up briefly while she got ready for work. Mostly she complained about the new roommate drinking all her soy milk. I took a deep breath and decided to tell her about things heating up with Ben.

"I will spazz if you tell me you've slept with him," she said.

I chuckled. "Initiate spazzing."

"WHAT?!" She screamed into the phone, making me laugh harder. "Holy shit, Emmy. Details, stat."

"Well he's amazing. Honestly. The best ever. Amazing kisser, sweet and tender, yet takes control in the bedroom."

"Wowza. Big dick, too?"

"Ellie!" I laughed again.

"What? Inquiring minds want to know. What's that boy workin' with? A teeny peeny or hung like a hippo?"

"Um . . . hippo." I couldn't keep the smile from my face. God, I missed Ellie. I was seriously overdue for some girl time.

"So what's the problem?"

I took a deep breath. "It's just . . . he's repeatedly told me he doesn't want a relationship. I think I'm in over my head."

"Babe. His dong rivals a Subway foot long. Enjoy it. What the fuck is there to think about?"

I let out a sigh. She made it sound so easy. "He's hard not to fall for, Ellie. He's gorgeous, smart, funny, considerate, amazing in bed. . . ." The list went on. *Oh, and apparently he has more issues than* Vogue—*according to Gunnar.*

"Ah. I see. Well listen, baby girl. There's no reason you can't be the one in control. This isn't about love, or being tied down. Do you think any man on the planet would think twice about engaging in some no-strings sex with a supermodel? Of course not. Any man would go for it. Hit it and quit it. Think like a man, Emmy. Think with your dick."

I laughed again at her choice of words. Fuck buddies with Ben Shaw, I could do that.

After Ellie's pep talk, I felt a little more encouraged and in control about my relationship with Ben.

"I've gotta get to work," she reminded me.

"'Kay. And I've got to get some sleep. Talk soon."

"Mwah!" Ellie said, ending the call.

I curled up on my side, hugging the pillow beside me, and was just about asleep when my phone chimed beside me. My hands scrambled for it in the dark. Just that little chime made me think of Ben, which in turn made me horny. I was like a trained Pavlov dog for that sound.

Ben: It's my birthday . . . in four minutes

I glanced at the clock. Almost midnight. I hadn't known it was his birthday tomorrow, today, whatever. I smiled at the image of him lying in bed alone, several floors up, feeling alone and just needing someone to know it was his birthday. I liked that I was the person he reached out to. I waited until the clock changed to midnight then texted him back.

Me: Happy Birthday

Ben: Thanks, beautiful. You should come to my birthday dinner tomorrow night.

I replied that I would be there, and Ben provided the name of the restaurant. I hadn't known there was a birthday dinner for him. Surely Fiona had planned it. Normally, she made me handle everything—from sending her clothes out to be laundered, to booking her monthly bikini waxes. My only conclusion was that she'd wanted to keep this from me. Tomorrow night should be interesting.

10

Emmy

I stood naked in front of the full-length mirror while the bathtub filled. Lazy heat vapors drifted toward the ceiling as I inspected myself in the mirror. My thighs jiggled when I walked, my breasts, while still high, would sag with their weight as I aged. It was just gravity. I pressed my hands into my fleshy hips, willing them to shrink. I'd never been so aware of my body in my entire life. It turned out getting naked with a supermodel would do that to you. I remembered Ben's hoarse whisper, the desire in his voice when he said I was soft. But maybe I was only remembering it the way I wanted to. Maybe he'd prefer I had a six-pack, or a tiny, firm little butt.

Once the tub was filled, I stepped into the steaming hot water and sank down, submerging myself in the fragrant bubbles. I lathered every part of my body, exfoliated every inch, and shaved every bit of hair until I was bare. I shampooed and conditioned my hair, and made sure all of me was scrubbed clean. As much as I'd told myself that I couldn't be with Ben again, I didn't trust my body not to betray me.

I emerged pruned and boneless. But I felt wonderful. After wrapping myself in the fluffy robe from the wardrobe, I worked the callouses from my heel and trimmed, filed, and painted my fingernails and toenails. I plucked stray eyebrows in the magnifying mirror in the full sunlight pouring through my window where I could see every speck of everything. After every pore was extracted and spotless, I expertly applied my makeup and styled my hair. I slathered lotion on my skin, mixing in several droplets of baby oil. I was soft and glowing when I was done. I knew I couldn't compete with the women Ben attracted, but my self-confidence had tripled in the last hour. I needed this. I wanted to feel sexy tonight. Powerful and in control. Ellie would be proud.

I slipped into my black skinny jeans, ballet flats, and a gauzy cream top that fell off one shoulder. I added a few chunky necklaces and fluffed my hair one last time. Ready as I'd ever be.

The dinner was being held at a swanky restaurant on the river. I found it strange that Fiona had booked the reservation for Ben's birthday herself. I hoped she wasn't going to shit a brick at the sight of me. I arrived a few minutes after eight and learned our party was still having drinks at the bar.

I took a moment to gather myself and scope out my surroundings. Deep beats of house music played in the background; glittering dim lighting from crystal chandeliers and beautiful people mingling at the high-top tables completed the ambience. I was glad I'd taken the time to make myself presentable.

Fiona's shrill wave of accented laughter caught my attention. She, Ben, and a few others I didn't recognize were at the far end of the bar. Ben looked scrumptious in tailored dark-gray trousers and a button-down shirt rolled to his elbows, showing off those thick, sexy forearms coursing with veins. His shirt was open at the collar and memories of inhaling the skin at his neck danced through my mind. Fiona spotted me across the bar and her mouth pulled into a tight line. Ben's smile fell at Fiona's sudden change in mood and his gaze lifted to meet mine.

"Hi," I mumbled weakly, suddenly regretting my decision to come.

Ben pulled me close, wrapping his arms around me, and all the fears I had fell away. He wanted me here. Fiona could shove it.

"You came," he whispered against my hair, breathing me in.

"Happy birthday." I smiled up at him as he released me.

Ben grinned. One little tug of his mouth and my heart was beating like a drum. I could tell he'd already had a few drinks. His normally penetrating stare was relaxed and happy. And he was holding a glass of amber-colored liquor. The strong stuff.

"Hi, Fiona." I gave her a cordial smile. I knew she wasn't my biggest fan, but we could at least try to be civil about things.

"Emerson." She tipped her head and turned her focus back to Ben.

I sensed the mood shift in the little group when I arrived, like they'd been in the middle of a story. But a strange hushed silence fell over the group as their eyes moved back and forth between me and Ben. I hated being the center of attention. I hated feeling scrutinized.

Stepping away, I murmured, "I'm going to grab a drink."

I recognized one of the photographers from an earlier shoot and Madeline. I said hello, but she didn't seem to recognize me even though I'd just met her a few days before. The few others were new faces.

Approaching the bar, I ordered a beer. You could take the girl out of the country but you'd never take the country out of the girl. The bartender filled a pint glass with amber-colored goodness and slid it toward me. Grabbing it with shaky hands, I took a long, icy sip.

When I rejoined the group, Fiona slyly smiled at me. "You know how many calories are in that, dear?"

Soft laughter erupted nervously across the group. They could sense the catfight brewing. Stupid industry people sipping their stupid skinny cocktails.

Ben stood across from me looking troubled. I didn't like being responsible for that look. I didn't want to be a source of tension between him and the head of the agency—our boss. I didn't think she'd do anything foolish, like stop booking him for jobs—he was too valuable for that. But she could fire me. And something told me if I got too close to Ben, that's exactly what she might do. I could handle her snarky comments about my clothing and calorie consumption. I didn't want to blow this out of proportion, so I merely smiled and nodded and took another sip of my carbohydrates-rich drink.

"Fiona, can I have a word?" Ben asked.

"Of course, love."

Fiona followed him around the corner and out of sight.

I knew I shouldn't, but I slipped away from the group and trailed after them. In what universe was this okay? I must have been dropped as a baby. But if this was about me, I needed to know.

They stood at the far end of the hall in an alcove near the restrooms. I remained just out of sight, hidden around the corner, but near enough that I could hear their low, murmured conversation.

"We're not curing cancer, Fiona; stop being so serious," Ben said.

"I'm always serious where you're concerned," Fiona returned, her voice tense.

"Why don't you tell me what this is really about?"

Fiona let out a heavy sigh. "I think you know." She hesitated a moment, silence falling over them as my pulse thrummed in my ears. "You haven't come by to see me lately. . . . Is this about her?" Her voice took on a whiny plea.

"I told you that was done. That has nothing to do with Emmy."

Holy shit. What did this conversation have to do with me? And why was my spine tingling like there was something big I was missing here?

"Just be civil," Ben added.

"Then don't shag my assistant," Fiona hissed.

"Calm down, pussycat," Ben chuckled. "It is my birthday, after all."

"Love, if you want birthday sex, all you have to do is ask," Fiona's sultry, accented voice whispered.

"Fiona . . ." Ben warned, letting the rest of the statement hang in the air.

All the oxygen was sucked from my lungs. Had they slept together? I didn't doubt that Fiona would be interested, but would Ben do that? Damn, this situation was far more complicated than I'd imagined.

"Do you have plans for a girl later?" Fiona asked.

"No girls, Fiona, I told you. You can relax."

My legs felt shaky, but I pushed them into action, disappearing back down the hall before I was discovered. Rejoining the group, I stood on trembling legs, sucking down mouthfuls of the icy-cold drink until my temples throbbed. Ben and Fiona rounded the corner and he crossed the room to stand next to me, letting his hand rest at the small of my lower back. The contact made me jump and I sloshed a bit of the beer from the rim of my glass.

"You okay?" Ben murmured beside me.

"I'm fine."

He took a deep breath and reached for my hand. "Our table's ready. Come on."

Ben sat between me and Fiona, which was good because I wasn't above flicking a booger in her food, given the chance. Lord knows she'd deserve it. She leaned over him, reading the menu and pointing out things he would like, which annoyed me to no end. He ordered the salade Niçoise. I wondered if he ever got to actually eat what he liked. It seemed like a birthday was the one day you should be entitled to do so. I sure as heck wouldn't order a salad on my birthday.

I switched to sparkling water toward the end of dinner. I wanted to be clearheaded for later. I didn't know if I'd get any alone time with Ben. But if I did, I wanted to be thinking clearly. I needed to know what was happening between us. Clouding my head with alcohol probably wouldn't help any. And I didn't want to see Fiona have a coronary at the table if I ordered another beer.

The guests chatted with Ben throughout much of the meal. I quickly learned the others in our party were more executives for luxury brands that Fiona was trying to book. I was so frustrated, I couldn't even look at her fake smile. Tonight was supposed to be a relaxing, low-key night for him, but of course she had turned it into a job interview. Ben politely fielded all their questions, acting like none of it bothered him, but I could tell it did. I nibbled on my food and stayed quiet for the most part, but Ben glanced my way several times and once squeezed my hand under the table.

The drinks continued flowing after dinner, and Fiona told story after story about Ben, designed to either impress our guests or scare me away. She painted him as quite the playboy, and my dinner churned in my stomach with each new bit of information.

"We were in Singapore, what was it, two years ago, love?"

Ben nodded.

"We were on set for Versace, and he was all sour and mardy."

Ben grimaced, like he knew the story she was about to tell.

"He hadn't been sleeping well—jet lag, and all that."

"Fiona," he warned, his voice dropping lower.

"Oh, hush; it's funny, love." Fiona waved a hand in his direction then turned back to the group. "It was a brilliant set, beautiful clothes, and our gorgeous model here was pissy— in need of a good shag. I knew he needed to take the edge off before we started shooting." A few of the business executives leaned forward in interest and Madeline's cheeks grew pink. Ben was growing increasingly agitated. He removed the napkin from his lap and balled it on the table beside his plate.

Fiona continued, "So I found this little assistant in the back, asked if her duties extended to oral, and shoved her at Ben. She took one look at him and nodded, pulling him into an empty broom closet. I don't know what happened next; all I know is that when he emerged fifteen minutes later, there was a smile on his face."

The table erupted in soft laughter. A lump lodged in my throat and I had to take a drink of water to get my windpipe working again.

Fiona's story demonstrated that Ben was in an entirely different category of men. He'd lived and worked all over the world, and apparently got blow jobs from assistants at the drop of a hat. Did he even remember her name? Was that what I was to him? A plaything to take the edge off? That was exactly why I wasn't cut out for this. Sex meant more to me. There was no way to separate the physical connection from the emotional in my mind. Ellie was right. I never should've slept with him. But I also knew if he asked me to bed again, I probably wouldn't say no. Part of me wished I was stronger; part of me was dreaming up ways to get him alone later.

Fiona carried over a large bag filled with wrapped gifts, taking each one out and placing them in front of Ben.

He smiled and tried to act humbled, opening each one and thanking the giver. An Hermès scarf, Cartier watch, Balenciaga satchel, men's grooming kit—some luxury brand I didn't recognize but was surely out of my price range.

I did get him something, or rather made him something. It was in poor taste to show up to a birthday party empty-handed, but there was no way I was going to embarrass myself by whipping out a homemade gift among this extravagance. It would stay tucked in my purse. Thank you very much.

Fiona packed the gifts back in the bag and asked the restaurant if a concierge could have them delivered to the hotel. It was amazing to see she was actually capable of making her own arrangements.

After dinner, coffee was poured but there was no dessert. What was a birthday party without cake? Ben looked bored to tears. I needed to rescue him. I leaned in closer. "No cake on your birthday? That's practically a crime."

He shrugged. "I'm not allowed to have cake."

"Allowed?" I wasn't gluten free, all organic, dairy free,

or vegan. I liked food. I often ate too much of it. Sue me. "We need cake." I pushed my chair back from the table and grabbed my handbag. "Thank you for dinner," I said to Fiona. Then I grabbed Ben's hand. "Come on."

His eyes widened and darted up to mine, and after a second of hesitation he rose to his feet. "Fiona." He bent to press a kiss to her cheek.

She smiled, fake as all get-out. "Off so soon?"

He shrugged. "Yes, if that's okay with you all." He directed the statement to the table.

Everyone nodded and smiled, no one willing to disagree with him.

Genius.

Fiona couldn't say anything. Everyone else had already agreed. I could've kissed him. But I would save that for later.

Once we were safely outside the restaurant, Ben gripped my hand, lacing his fingers between mine, his mouth twitching in a smile. "Phew. Thank you for rescuing me."

I beamed up at him, feeling like an utter genius, and squeezed his hand.

We ventured to the bar/restaurant inside the lobby of our hotel, slid into a secluded booth, and ordered two glasses of fizzy champagne.

When the server came back, I ordered the biggest slice of chocolate cake they had.

"Really?" Ben grinned at me. "Sure you can handle all that, sweetheart?"

I nodded enthusiastically. "Bring it on."

When the server delivered the cake, it was with a little Parisian smirk. It was towering off the plate.

"I didn't expect it to be so large," I commented.

Ben's eyebrows raised suggestively. He handed me a spoon. "Ladies first."

I was about to argue that it was his birthday and he should do the honors, but his stern expression left no room for discussion. I accepted the proffered spoon and dug into the dense cake. My favorite bite, the little triangle piece right from the tip. Ben's eyes followed my movements, watching as my mouth closed around the spoon.

"Mmm," I moaned, dropping my head back. His eyes widened and he visibly swallowed.

Ben dug in, joining me in chocolate bliss. "I haven't had cake in . . . years." He took a bite and his eyes slipped closed as he chewed. "Holy shit."

I laughed. These calories were sooo worth it. So was watching Ben's expression. He clearly enjoyed himself. Ben leaned back against the booth, crossing his arms and observing me. I took another bite, licking the chocolate frosting from my spoon. As my tongue darted out, his breathing hitched, his chest rising and falling systematically. I liked that I was having an effect on him. Lord knows he affected me. My entire body hummed in arousal when he was near. And forget it when he swept that deep hazel gaze fringed with dark lashes over my curves. I mentally parted my knees, ready and waiting.

"Hope it's been a good birthday." I lifted my champagne glass and clinked it against his.

"It is now."

I smiled at the compliment, glad I'd had the courage to save him. "I got you something, well, *made* you something."

"You made me something? What is it?"

"It's nothing big; I just felt dumb giving it to you at the restaurant."

He leaned back in his seat, studying me. "I like that you waited." Ben's gaze followed my movement as I reached into my purse to retrieve the gift.

I handed him a flat package wrapped in brown paper, suddenly feeling like an idiot. *This isn't sixth grade, Emmy.*

Ben looked down at the gift, his eyes wide and filled with disbelief. "You made this for me?"

I nodded sheepishly.

"I've never gotten a homemade gift." He held it with reverence as if it were something priceless and important, rather than a CD—a playlist I'd burned just for him.

"It's nothing. Open it." Homemade gifts and cards were pretty much the norm in my family. Growing up, we didn't have much extra money and we tended to get creative.

Ben tore away the paper and smiled when he saw the silver disk with my messy writing scrawled in black marker: *Birthday Boy.* I picked out a bunch of sexy jams, songs I was hoping he hadn't heard before from the eclectic mix of music on my laptop.

"Thank you, this is awesome. The best gift I got all night." His smile was genuine for the first time tonight, reaching his eyes and crinkling the corners.

My heart pounded in a strange rhythm, knowing he was watching me. These simple acts—the cake, the homemade gift—I don't know why, but he acted as if these gestures meant more to him than the thousand-dollar dinner and extravagant gifts he had just received.

"You're welcome," I murmured. Why my voice had gone all husky and low, I didn't know.

"Let's get out of here." His tone left little room for argument. But wasn't this what I wanted? I wanted to feel desired and sexy, to lose myself in this man.

The glass of fizzy champagne had gone straight to my head, and I clutched Ben's arms as we made our way to the elevator. He was unusually quiet and intense, and I wondered what was going on inside his head.

Once inside the elevator, Ben left no doubt where we were headed. He punched the button for his floor then turned to face me, caging me in with his arms against the wall. He dipped his head to inhale the scent of my neck, sending a rush of pleasure tingling down my body.

"Come upstairs with me," he growled, his warm breath washing over the curve of my jaw. My pulse drummed in my throat where his lips hovered.

I didn't answer—couldn't. My body wanted this. My brain wasn't so sure. Whatever was between him and Fiona was a definite concern. Once he was done with me, it would be like a Taylor Swift song—heartbreak city. No amount of ice cream or vodka would cheer me up. Would I lose my job, too?

Ben pulled back and met my eyes, his fingertips grazing the thinking lines etched into my forehead. "Hey," his voice went all soft and sweet. "Stop fighting this."

Easy for him to say. I swallowed the lump lodged in my throat. "I don't do the casual sex thing."

"Who said that's what I wanted?" I remembered his earlier comment that only three girls had gotten it. I guess that made me lucky number four. "You're the one who ran out of my room the other night."

Why had I done that? I'd been tipsy from the alcohol, and humiliated that I let things go that far. I knew my heart was already engaged, and it was safer and easier to flee than face an awkward postsex discussion. "Ben, what am I supposed to think? You're you . . . and I'm me . . ."

Confusion fixed across his features and his mouth pulled into a tight line, but he stayed silent.

The elevator stopped, and he motioned for me to exit as the doors slid open. We walked to his room in silence.

When we reached his room, Ben, still watching me quietly, let me inside.

"I'm sorry I left," I said.

He nodded and lifted my hand to his mouth. "Spend the night with me."

Raw need blossomed inside me. I was powerless against his charms. "Like a sleepover?"

"Yes. With playtime," Ben confirmed, a smirk tugging his lips.

My pulse thundered in my ears. "I like playtime."

His hands circled my waist, hauling me closer. "Good girl. And this time I get to taste that sweet pussy."

I turned bright pink and my knees trembled. I braced my hands against his shoulders, needing something sturdy to grasp on to. I nodded, completely lost and falling. Falling for this beautiful man whose deep hazel eyes were watching mine.

"I want you. It's simple. Don't make it complicated," he whispered.

My eyes slipped closed. "This isn't just sex, Ben."

Soft fingertips stroked my jaw. "I know, beautiful. Stop assuming you know what I want. I've never had a girl like you. Soft . . ." His thumb caressed my cheek. "Sweet . . ." His lips pressed over mine. "And southern . . ." His hand found my backside and he squeezed, pulling me closer. "Let me do this. Let me have you, Emmy."

I opened my eyes and nodded. He could have anything he wanted, so long as he touched me soon. My knees were jelly and my nipples were hard and tingling. "Only if I can have you, too."

"You can have anything you want." His tone was so solemn, so sincere, I believed him.

With a sudden burst of confidence that I could have this man, I dropped to my knees in front of him. I needed to consume him, to own him. I fought with his belt and button then tugged open his zipper. His hands remained at his sides, and when my eyes fluttered up to watch his, a playful smirk was tugging his lips. The growing bulge in his trousers proved he wasn't as calm and in control as his expression demonstrated.

Seeing him up close and personal was so intimate; I nuzzled my nose and mouth against his flesh, breathing in his scent. He smelled so good. A trace of soap and musk. All man. I wanted more. Moving lower, I pressed tender kisses along his length and heard him suck in a breath.

I could feel him watching me. Knowing he was looking down at me only fueled my desire and I licked and suckled as I tried to take him deeper. His hips pushed forward as he invaded my mouth, and my hands scrambled to stroke his engorged shaft.

It was a powerful thing, pleasing him like this, being in control of his pleasure. I thrust my mouth down around his cock, taking him all the way to the back of my throat. His large length hit my tonsils and I gagged, salivating around him. Ben moaned and his knees went stiff. I knew I had done something right. I loved learning what he liked. If he wasn't going to tell me, it was up to me to find out. And, apparently, he liked it deep. I continued my ministrations, not stopping until he bumped against the back of my throat with each thrust.

"Yeah baby, fuck." His fingertips threaded through my hair, tugging me closer. A low whimper escaped the back of his throat, the sound raw and primal. A rush of endorphins hit my bloodstream and I tightened my grasp around him, needing him closer, wanting him inside me. I let his cock fall free from my mouth and rose on shaky feet. His big hands cradled my jaw, and he kissed me deeply, his tongue flirting with mine.

"Ben . . ."

"Anything you want . . ." he breathed against my mouth.

I had no idea how to ask for what I wanted, so instead I kissed him again, the one thing I felt confident with. His breathing was accelerated, just like mine, so I at least felt comforted that I wasn't alone in the craziness overtaking my system.

He tugged at the button on my jeans, popping it open while he kissed me. "Take off your panties, baby. I need to be inside you."

His deep, sexy voice sent shivers racing down my spine as I fought for control. His fingers skimmed across my belly, lighting up my nerve endings and making my pulse race.

"I don't want to use a condom. I want to feel you. I'm clean. Are you on the pill?"

I nodded and it was all the information he needed. He captured my mouth in a hungry kiss and his hands found mine. He helped me pull my jeans and panties down my legs until I was bare from the waist down.

Ben suddenly lifted me, and I wrapped my legs around his waist. He walked us backward until my back hit the wall, forcing a breath from my lungs. I groaned at the sensation of his thick erection pressing against me. I ground my hips against his. But Ben, always in control, made no move to join our bodies and continued kissing me deeply. I craved him, I needed him.

"Ben . . ." I whimpered, breaking free from the kiss.

"Tell me what you want." His lips rubbed against mine as he spoke, our foreheads resting together.

Was he serious? I could feel his erection nudging me. "Please."

"Beg for it, baby."

"Bennn . . . I need you . . . deep inside me . . ."

His guttural moan sent a new wave of wetness rushing against his hardened flesh. He was teasing me, running his slickened manhood along me, making me whimper.

"You want me to fuck that beautiful pussy, baby?" Ben pressed his hard tip against me without entering.

"Yes please. Ben, fuck me." How I always seemed to end up begging for him I had no idea, but this man made me crazy with desire. I'd never been this way before—this out of control and desperate. He pushed against me, sliding inside slowly, letting his body invade mine until he was deeply buried within me. The pleasure/pain combo sent a groan tumbling from my throat. I gripped his shoulders and he held my ass in his hands, lifting me up and down, fucking me hard and without mercy.

My back bumped against the wall with each thrust, but I didn't care if I had bruises tomorrow. I wanted it hard. Needed it. I needed him to claim me and show me I was his. Watching Ben lose control was a thing of beauty. His face remained impassive, but his pulse thrummed in his neck and his muscles tensed and quivered as he held my weight.

Never normally vocal during sex, I mumbled his name and moaned with each stroke. Sex had never been so intimate before. This was more than sharing in bodily pleasure. Ben's gaze stayed locked on mine as he read my every cue, responded to my every need. I braced my hand on the wall behind my head. Ben's hand cradled the back of my head in his hand.

"Is this hurting you?" Without waiting for my answer, he walked us across the room and tossed me down on the bed.

The physical separation was abrupt and unwelcome. I instantly missed him. His erection hung heavily between us and I couldn't resist the urge to lean forward on the bed and plant a damp kiss against his tip. His hands moved to my hair and arranged it away from my face.

His eyes were dark, his pupils dilated as he watched me. "Fuck, girl. You're too good."

I smiled up at him, and Ben's hand cupped my cheek, stroking lovingly as his eyes met mine. I felt beautiful. Desirable. Tugging him by the hand, I pulled him onto the bed. I needed him closer.

Once he'd successfully rid me of my shirt and bra, Ben pressed against me again, easing inside me slowly. I wrapped my legs around his waist and held on as he rocked into me, slowly at first, letting me adjust, then with an urgent rhythm.

He felt incredible. Big. Almost too big, but pleasurably so. I lost myself in the sensations: the roughness of his stubbled jaw rubbing my cheek, his fingertips biting into my hips, his broad chest rasping against mine as he moved over me.

Losing all control, his body pounded against mine ruthlessly, bringing us closer and closer to release. I wanted to make it last, to savor everything he had to offer, but all too soon the pressure built inside me. Ben read my body and slowed his thrusts, dragging himself almost all of the way out of me and sinking in again slowly. My back arched and I tilted my pelvis to meet him, letting the sensations overtake me. I came loudly, groaning his name in a litany of murmured whispers. Ben pressed his mouth to my neck, lightly biting me as he found his release. His body shuddered against mine as hot jets of semen exploded within me.

Refusing to move, we lay together in bed, a heap of sweaty, tangled limbs and sheets strewn about. I was glad to see there was no postsex awkwardness. Why had I been so desperate to flee last time? Ben was proving to be nothing like I would have imagined. He wasn't the overconfident, self-absorbed model my worst fears had made him out to be. He was sweet and caring and apparently liked to cuddle. He pulled me close, his arms circling my waist in a tight embrace.

Once our breathing had returned to normal, Ben lifted up on one elbow to look down on me. "Hi."

"Hi." I smiled. I liked the easy playfulness between us.

"I have an extra toothbrush, pajamas, whatever you want." He leaned down and kissed my forehead then removed himself from the bed. I got a peek at his tight backside before he slipped back into his discarded boxer briefs. He removed a white T-shirt from his wardrobe and tossed it on the bed for me before heading into the bathroom. He left the door open and I could hear the water running and the soft hum of his electric toothbrush.

I stretched in the bed, taking my time before moving. Slipping the T-shirt over my head, I joined him in the bathroom. I guessed he was serious about this being a sleepover. With toothpaste bubbles on his bottom lip, he smiled lazily and surveyed me from head to toe. Messy bedroom hair, smudged makeup, and an oversized T-shirt that fell to midthigh. By the look on his face, you'd think he'd never seen me look more gorgeous.

He leaned in to kiss me, leaving a dot of toothpaste on my top lip. "I like you in my clothes." Ben handed me a spare toothbrush, still wrapped in plastic, and leaned down to rinse his mouth.

This felt very comfortable and domestic, sharing a sink with him. I liked it. I couldn't help but notice his bottles of pills were neatly lined up on the counter. I wanted to ask him about them, but Ben wiped his mouth and headed out, giving me some privacy. All types of special creams and serums lined his bathroom vanity, but I liked that he seemed to be low maintenance. I didn't think I could handle a guy who had a more involved bathroom regimen than me.

When I returned to the bedroom, Ben had turned off the lights so just the dim glow of the bedside lamp illuminated my path to the bed. He lifted the covers and I crawled in beside him. He wasted no time pulling me closer so that we lay spooned together.

"You feel so good," he mumbled against my neck. "So soft. So warm."

I relished the feel of his arms around me. I felt safe. And warm. And feminine. His hard body pressed against mine. The few times I'd spent the night with my college boyfriend, he'd rolled over, facing away from me to sleep, his large back looming like an impenetrable wall. And when I tried to hug him from behind, he'd shrug me off, saying he was too hot.

This was different . . . and nice. Our own little warm cocoon, away from the prying eyes of the world. He didn't have to be the man everyone expected, and I wasn't the meek little assistant, out of her element. I was just Emmy. I felt at peace.

Ben pulled me closer, wrapping his arms around my waist and pulling me in until my back was pressed against his front. "Sleep, baby."

I couldn't forget the pills I'd seen in his bathroom. I knew now might not be the best time to ask, but . . . "Ben?" I whispered.

"Hmm?"

I couldn't resist asking the question burning a hole in my brain. "Those pills in your bathroom . . . I know I shouldn't pry, but . . ."

He released a heavy breath.

"Tell me." I rolled over to face him, his features barely visible in the soft moonlight. "Are you okay? Are you sick?"

"I'm okay, Emmy," he whispered.

"That's a lot of pills, Ben. I'm just worried."

His warm hand captured mine and squeezed. "I don't want to hide anything from you."

"So don't," I whispered.

He was quiet for a moment, just the sounds of our breathing in the silent room. "But I also don't want to scare you away."

My heart rate kicked up a notch. Did he have a pill-popping addiction? Was he sick? I braced for the worst. "You won't. I'm here."

"Just don't go anywhere."

I squeezed his hand back. "I'm not planning on it." I was here for the next three months, or however long this thing between us lasted. He was quickly getting under my skin.

"I will tell you. But it's a conversation for another time."

"Okay." I wasn't going to lie. I was a little disappointed. Now seemed like a fine time, we were safe and warm, and it was dark. But Ben wasn't ready. I guess I had to respect that.

"Rest, baby." He clutched me tighter, like he was truly afraid I was going to leave.

I closed my eyes, curling into his warm body, and tried not to worry about what the future might hold.

Within a few minutes he was breathing deeply against the skin on the back of my neck, his heavy exhales signaling he'd already fallen asleep. I couldn't help remembering all the times he said he had trouble sleeping, and a smile overtook my mouth. He was asleep. My baby. I curled my legs up, getting comfortable, and let him hold me.

11

Emmy

In the morning, Ben woke me with a trail of soft kisses down my thigh. I blinked my eyes open to find him leaning over my lower half. He lifted my leg to his mouth, kissing along my calf muscle, my ankle, the arch of my foot.

"Morning," I whispered, stretching my arms above my head. His scent still clung to my skin and I was deliciously sore.

"You're fucking sexy in the morning," he growled in a sleep-roughened voice.

I laughed, watching him press soft kisses along the top of my foot, my toes. It was a lovely way to be woken up. I felt worshipped, pretty, and very much wanted.

He kept his gaze on mine, the hungry look in his eyes making my belly flutter. His teeth grazed my instep and the laughter died on my lips, need filling my system almost instantly. Memories of last night danced through my mind, watching Ben's mouth move over my skin. He kissed a path up my lower leg, hovering briefly at the skin on the back of my knee. His breath tickled and I squirmed in the bed, already anticipating where he was heading.

He gently bit the flesh inside my thigh and my sex clenched. Pushing my T-shirt up, his fingers hooked into my panties and he dragged them down my legs. I pulled the shirt over my head and tossed it beside the bed while Ben shoved off his boxers. I noticed the clock read ten after seven. He had a fitting at eight.

"You have to be at the Versace offices at eight."

"Yes, but first I need breakfast, and this little pussy has been begging me to taste it." He resumed nibbling along my inner thigh and my protests died. He pressed a tender kiss on the top of my pubic bone and began kissing his way lower. I had never felt so cherished, so thoroughly worshipped. The feeling was addictive. I could sense his warm breath, his unshaven jaw scratching my inner thighs. Completely unrushed, Ben continued lightly kissing me all over. I squirmed against the mattress, ready to have his mouth cover me. He gripped my hips, holding me in place, and softly chuckled against my skin.

"Lie still, you naughty little thing."

His tongue made lazy strokes against me, tasting me, torturing me with his unrushed exploration. I whimpered and threaded my fingers in his hair, fighting the urge to pull him closer.

Ben delivered on the promise that he excelled at oral. His

warm mouth covered me, sucking lightly, swirling his tongue against my sensitive flesh in a hypnotic pattern. Within minutes, my world exploded in pleasure and I thrashed against him, clutching the sheets in my fists as I came.

He rose on his knees, his lips pink and swollen from his assault on my lady parts. He was fucking sexy. His hand caught his eager erection and he stroked himself slowly, continuing to watch me. My body was still trembling from the intense orgasm when Ben positioned himself against me and pressed forward. I dug my heels into his ass, and arched my back, forcing him deeper. His thick length invaded me, parting me, making me whimper.

A low growl murmured in his throat. "Fuck, your body feels good. I'll never get tired of this."

My walls clenched around him and I clung to his shoulders. Ben pounded into me, not holding back as he sent us both closer to release. He captured my wrists and held my hands above my head as our lower bodies joined in a frantic rhythm. He released one hand to grip my bottom, lifting me to meet his thrusts, and drove into me with wild abandon, his eyes slipping closed, and his forehead resting against mine. Our mouths brushed, lips parted with heavy breaths.

For only knowing each other a short time, we were closer than two people had a right to be. But I didn't care, didn't want to overanalyze why I'd fallen so deeply. I only knew I had. And that Ben seemed to be falling for me, too.

"Emmy..." he groaned, releasing a sigh. "I can't last, baby."

"Inside me." I breathed. "Come inside me..."

He clutched my ass, capturing my mouth with his, and kissed me deeply as he exploded inside me.

"Shit. You're too much, beautiful girl." Ben kissed my forehead then moved to lay beside me.

My galloping heart soared at his words. I constantly wondered what he thought of me, of my looks, always nervous that I didn't measure up, but his little declaration did a lot to ease my worries. It was a small thing, but hearing him call me beautiful made everything okay. His hand rested against my hip, and as much as I wanted to turn and snuggle into his warm, broad body, I knew we were running late and didn't have the luxury of cuddle time. I sat up and tugged the sheet to cover my breasts. I wasn't completely comfortable with Ben seeing my body, especially in the stark morning light.

He watched me, his eyes sweeping over the bare skin of my shoulder, with a dark, hungry look that my body already seemed to know. My stomach chose that exact moment to rumble loudly, interrupting the silence.

Ben smiled lightly. "I'm sorry I don't have time to take you out for a proper breakfast."

I smirked. "Your idea of breakfast or mine? I'm craving my momma's cooking. Biscuits and gravy, eggs, and homemade pecan pancakes."

He laughed. "Hmm. I'll have to see where you come from sometime. I can't say I've ever had a true southern breakfast."

I liked the idea of taking Ben to Tennessee. "Yes, well, vitamins and a green smoothie hardly count as a proper breakfast where I come from."

Ben chuckled. "Fiona means well, Emmy. She really does."

My quirked-up eyebrow told him I disagreed.

"I've been with her a long time. I want to make sure you guys get along."

"I'm pretty sure she hates me," I mumbled.

"Hmm." He thought it over, not disagreeing. "She's just protective of me." He rubbed the back of his neck. "And things certainly won't get easier once she knows I'm seeing you."

Oh, I was *seeing* Ben Shaw now. Whatever happened to going on actual dates, knowing where you stood, who you were dating—if you were exclusive? Ellie and I complained about that often. Nowadays, you had guys you were *talking to, seeing,* or *hanging out with casually,* or in the case of Ben and me, *having mind-blowing sex with.* But I didn't dare inquire about what this was between us. Because let's be serious, if this was all he had to offer, I would take it. No questions asked. Already, I was in too deep. I couldn't hold back.

Men like Ben didn't do traditional relationships. For all my Googling, I'd never once turned up a past girlfriend. Maybe he kept his private life private; but still, jetting around the globe was hardly conducive for maintaining a healthy relationship. Not to mention he had girls throwing themselves at his feet on a daily basis. Why would he need to bother dating? He could get regular sex whenever he wanted it, without any strings, any hassles. Getting the milk for free, my momma would say.

I wasn't like him. I knew I'd want more. I wanted it all—a committed boyfriend, monogamy, eventual marriage, two kids, and a house in Tennessee, hopefully near my parents. But I could enjoy this with Ben and worry about my future later. I was choosing to live in the here and now. And I had a very tempting half-naked man in front of me. It was no question. All doubts and insecurities fled my brain.

"Ben, we should just keep this between us. Fiona doesn't need to know."

He watched me thoughtfully, stroking my thigh with his fingertips.

I could only imagine how she'd treat me if she found out about me and Ben.

He ran a hand through his wildly misbehaving hair, cursing softly. "You might be right." At least he wasn't so fooled by Fiona that he couldn't see that. "But I don't want to have to sneak around. I'll find a way to talk to her."

I wanted to tell him not to bother, but I liked that he'd be willing to tell her about us—this, whatever this was. But maybe I was reading too much into it. It wasn't some chivalrous act, some romantic gesture. He just didn't want to have to sneak around for the next three months.

Ben pushed the loose strands of hair back from my face. "And about what you asked me last night . . . we'll talk about that tonight, okay?" Ben's big, warm palm cupped my cheek. "I didn't forget."

Our whispered conversation in the darkness last night came rushing back: his raw emotional state, the bathroom cabinet full of prescription bottles, Gunnar's warning, Fiona's possessiveness. All of it hit me like a wave. I was headed for an early nervous breakdown at this rate. But I was powerless to stop the crazy train carrying me straight for destruction. In fact, I wanted an express ticket. I nodded, pulling my shirt over my head and letting the sheet drop away once I was covered.

I knew he'd be busy all day with fittings and meetings. "Go," I shooed him from the bed, knowing he was already late. "I'll let myself out."

He dropped a light kiss on my lips then rose from the bed. I stepped into my panties and jeans while Ben headed into the shower. Back to reality.

12

Emmy

After a hot shower back in my room and my usual coffee and croissant, I logged into my email. The benefit of Fiona having a separate room meant her usual mode of communication—Post-it notes—was reduced to email. There was just one message, sent at one in the morning. *Crap.*

I sipped my coffee and stared at the offending message without opening it. I wondered if she'd commented on last night. It'd been a bold move even showing up at Ben's birthday dinner, and then stealing the guest of honor right from under her nose. What had I been thinking? Fiona was my boss. She could fire me and send me packing at her discretion. And then what would I tell my mom? I'd gotten fired for sleeping with one of the models. God, could you imagine? I shuddered.

Opening Fiona's email, I breathed a sigh of relief. Her note instructed me to meet her at 11 a.m. at the Yves Saint

Laurent offices in the 8th arrondissement near the Champs-Élysées.

I knew Paris Fashion Week was just a few weeks away, which meant our schedule was about to get crazy.

When I arrived at the limestone building, a beautiful young receptionist sat at the sleek, marble-topped desk. Her lips were painted YSL red, her dark hair tucked into a sleek chignon.

"Bonjour," she greeted me in a perfectly pretty and feminine accent. Great. Even the receptionist had me feeling insecure.

"Bonjour," I returned, stopping in front of her desk. "Um, I'm with Status Model Management. I'm supposed to meet Fiona Stone," I muttered, hoping to God she spoke English.

"Yes, this way." She rose on precariously high black patent leather pumps—how very chic—and showed me down the hall.

The hallway was lined with guys looking to be cast in the show. Some sat on the floor, others stood, many played with their phones, while others talked quietly to the guys near them.

I pushed open the heavy door as the receptionist retreated back to the lobby. Aside from the row of chairs facing the front of the stark white room, it was empty. I spotted Fiona right away, seated with a small cluster of stylists. I approached them carefully, cursing myself for not dressing better. I was in simple khakis, sensible flats, and a white button-down shirt paired with a navy cardigan. Basically, Fiona was going to have a stroke when she saw me. But I didn't care. I had a job to do, and I was comfortable.

I inched my way toward my boss. A male model came out

from behind the curtain slung across the front of the room and began walking for the stylists. With his classic death stare in place, he strutted forward. His walk was perfect—cold and calculating, without blinking. He paused, then turned and headed back behind the curtain. Today was casting for our guys, as well as fittings for the ones who had already been chosen for the show. I slid down into the chair behind Fiona. She instantly turned and looked me over with a critical sigh, shaking her head and frowning. *Off to a great start, Emmy.*

We watched several more guys come out and walk for the group of Yves Saint Laurent executives. I did my best to quickly pass Fiona the comp cards as each guy was announced. I'd printed off the portfolios that morning and arranged them in a binder, choosing our younger guys with dark features and intense looks, a favorite of YSL. As much as I complained about Fiona, I enjoyed my job and took pride in what I did.

John Paul from our agency, just nineteen years old and starting his career in this crazy business, came out next, dressed to kill in a beautifully tailored pin-striped suit that appeared made just for him.

"Street walk, darling," Fiona drawled, correcting him.

His walk had been too exaggerated, too much swish in his hips. I'd come to learn street walk meant walk as naturally as you would down the street, no posing, no hands on hips. Each designer preferred a different walk. Versace was known for wanting lots of swagger and attitude, but apparently the classy folks at YSL were looking for the understated. John Paul straightened his shoulders and walked naturally down the center of the room before turning on his heel and heading back behind the curtain.

The stylist seated next to Fiona jotted notes into her iPad. I wondered if he'd made the show or not. Little things like the way your hips moved when you walked mattered so greatly in this field. It was a cutthroat business. While the models' walks set the mood for the show, it was all about the clothes. Then fashion editors would write about the next big trends, orders would be placed, and the next year we'd all be wearing remnants inspired by these shows. It was fascinating, really.

I wasn't expecting Ben to be here, but the production assistant announced "Ben Shaw" in the most adorable French accent. My eyes snapped up to the front.

Ben walked out from behind the curtain like he owned the room and strutted down the walkway. He looked straight ahead and didn't make eye contact with anyone. A smile tugged at my lips. He was devastatingly handsome, outfitted from head to toe in the designer clothing. A cropped gray wool coat for fall, paired with fitted black trousers. Oh wow. He was sex on a stick. I couldn't believe this was the same man I'd just shared a bed with. The same man who'd sleepily offered to take me to breakfast. He was absolute perfection. Ben was a professional, his walk sure and strong, his gaze cast forward, undistracted and certain. Unlike the guys who were nervous or scattered, their gazes darting to check for reactions as they walked, Ben was utter confidence, staring straight ahead and letting nothing stand in his way. Commanding. And sexy as hell.

His eyes caught mine and a lazy smile lit up his face. My body temperature ratcheted up several degrees.

Moments later, Ben turned and disappeared back behind the white curtain concealing the small changing area. My phone vibrated in my pocket, and though I knew I shouldn't let it distract me from work, I pulled it out to see who was texting me.

To my surprise, it was Ben.

Ben: I can't stop thinking about how good you taste.

My cheeks flamed bright red as I shielded my phone and peeked around me. No one was paying any attention to me, but that was beside the point. He couldn't just text me things like that. We were at work.

Ben: Come back here, babe. I want that pretty pussy.

Holy shit! Was he crazy?

Me: No way! You'll get us both in trouble. Go change into your next outfit.

Ben: Just a little taste.

I should have typed back *no*, been firm and resolute, but instead I just replied: *Later.*

My heart hammered away at my ribs as I watched my phone, waiting for his reply. I was astounded by the things he wrote me. He normally seemed so polite and well mannered. But I secretly liked that he had a filthy fucking mouth. Thankfully, my phone stayed silent for the time being.

A moment later, Fiona dug her smartphone from her purse, answering it loudly, interrupting the poor model walking for her and the YSL reps. Fiona cupped a hand over the mouthpiece of her phone and tried to speak privately in the not-at-all-private room. "I can't come back there right now, love." She sighed heavily. "Did you sleep last night? Hmm . . . are you coming down with something?" She listened for a moment then added, "Hang tight. I'll send in Emmy."

Fiona turned to me, shoving the phone back in her giant bag. "It's Ben. He's feeling flat knackered. Early mornings are not his thing."

I didn't mention that it was already after 11 a.m.; I merely nodded.

"Go bring him a pain reliever and some water, dear." She shooed me with a dismissive wave of her hand.

"Sure." I hopped from my chair, grabbed my purse, and headed back behind the curtain, ready to give him a piece of my mind. This was some little ploy to get me back here, and he was using Fiona to do it. He was going to get us both in trouble. I didn't know whether to be mad, nervous, excited, or horny.

When I spotted him, he was standing casually near the back, his eyes already pinned on mine. His eyebrow quirked up and he raked his gaze boldly down my body, stopping at my chest. He smiled just slightly. My sex muscles clenched. That cleared up the horny part. But geez, we couldn't do this now. Was he crazy?

Approaching him, I stopped at arm's length. "We can't do this, Ben. Fiona will fire me so fast, I'll be on the next plane out of here. . . ."

"Never going to happen." The cool authority in his voice made my stomach flip.

Ben

Emmy looked all proper in her pressed khaki pants and button-down shirt. It made me want to mess her up and leave her looking thoroughly fucked. Claimed. It was twisted, I know.

I never really thought I could get a normal girl. They all wanted me for my persona—what they saw on the outside. The supermodel they thought I was. I didn't feel like that guy. Which is why I liked that Emmy seemed to see beyond it all. Part of it was because I'd let her in—told her things about me I rarely told anyone. Things only Fiona knew. I'd been around enough women to know that the way Emmy affected me was different.

Sure, I had physical needs that I satisfied but I was never stupid enough to believe it was love when they looked at me. Some would profess their devotion, swear they loved me, but I wondered if they could even see past the designer-labeled clothes. Emmy saw through all that and directly into the real me. She leveled me with her humanity, her realness. She'd pushed me to be more open, taken care of me on and off set, been my advocate simply because it was the right thing to do. She had an open-faced belief that the world was a good place and that people could be trusted. It was refreshing, especially in this business. She wouldn't be changed simply because she'd gotten a job in an industry where looks were everything. From what I'd seen, she was the type to stay true to herself. I realized with absolute clarity, I respected the hell out of her.

I stepped toward her, closing the distance she'd purposefully left between us. "Do you trust me?" I could still remember her smell, her taste, the little whimpering sounds she made last night. She was fucking delicious and I wanted more.

She swallowed, visibly shaken, but gave a tiny nod. It was enough. I took her hand and pulled her behind the partition that separated off a small area for changing. There was a dude behind there buttoning up a shirt. I tossed him a look that he accurately read as *Get the fuck out*. He made a hasty retreat. Smart guy. Because I was three seconds away from having Emmy's panties around her ankles, and no one was going to see her bare little pussy but me. I wanted to smell her, taste her, devour her. Never had a girl gotten under my skin so completely. I had to have her.

The expression on her face was a mix of panic and curiosity. She bit down, burying her teeth in her bottom lip, and met my eyes. She did trust me. I saw that. And she was worried how far I'd push her.

Fuck.

I wouldn't betray her trust by doing something she wasn't

sure about. She took her job seriously, and now I'd lured her back here for sex. Shit. My hard-on would have to wait. *Sorry, buddy.*

"Later, okay? You're mine."

She looked up into my eyes, her face awash with relief. "Yes," she confirmed. "Later."

The promise of later would have to be enough to get me through the next few hours.

13

Emmy

It was eight o'clock when I made it back to the hotel, and I was exhausted. My body was fighting this European schedule, and Fiona's ridiculous demands kept me running. But Ben's text said to come straight to his room and to come hungry.

When I arrived at his door, he planted a tender kiss on my lips and pulled me inside.

"I listened to the CD you made me."

"And?"

"I loved it. Thank you." He pressed a soft kiss to my forehead, his expression truly grateful.

I sensed this was a new side of him, a softer, sweeter Ben, and I liked it. I didn't know what had changed between us but he was clearly letting me into his world.

I noticed a room service cart with various platters covered with silver domes. "Breakfast in bed okay?" he asked.

"Breakfast? For dinner?" I loved the idea, but it was a little unusual.

"Since I didn't get to take you out to breakfast like you wanted this morning."

I didn't realize it before, but now that I could smell the food, I was ravenous. Ben lifted the domes from the plates, and my mouth began to water. Golden waffles dusted with powdered sugar and topped with a mixed-berry compote, fluffy omelets with goat cheese and mushrooms drizzled with truffle oil, thick cuts of ham and a green salad on the side. It was anything but a country breakfast, almost too pretty and elegant to eat, but it was perfect.

"This is lovely, thank you."

"Dig in."

"You didn't have to do all this. . . ." I wanted to remind him he'd said this was just sex between us, but I didn't. Couldn't.

"I need you fueled up for what I want to do to you to-night." His eyes lingered on mine.

Oh. So it wasn't some romantic gesture. It was about sex. I helped myself to the food. I might as well enjoy the meal.

We made our plates, taking a little of everything, and then settled on the bed. Ben flipped on the TV to some French news program for background noise while we ate. It was re-laxing and so ordinary. And perfect.

We chatted casually throughout the meal, and Ben asked me questions about college. He seemed genuinely interested and admitted he'd always wanted to go to college, but Fiona thought it would slow down his career. Money and exposure now, college later. Even if I could see her reasoning, it made me sad for him.

The conversation I really wanted to have—about his prescriptions—remained just out of reach. I'd already asked about them once; I didn't want to push him. He'd tell me when he was ready. I had to believe that.

Ben cleared away the dishes then stretched out on the bed next to me. I was comfortable and full and relaxed into the fluffy white bedding. Ben lifted my bare feet into his lap and began lazily rubbing them. It felt amazing. I let my eyes slip closed, allowing the food coma to set in.

"Thank you for breakfast. It wasn't anything like the home cooking where I'm from, but . . ." I smiled. "It was delicious. Maybe you'll have to come to Tennessee with me sometime."

His brow crinkled.

Ben

"I want to be upfront with you."

Her eyes lifted to mine. God, she was so sweet, it almost made me feel bad. Almost. But I knew what I wanted and the pleasures I could show her. I wouldn't let anything complicate that. If she was talking about taking me home to Tennessee, clearly we weren't on the same page about what this was.

"Emmy, I'm not looking for a relationship. I've been on my own too long; I've gotten too good at it."

"That doesn't mean that's how it has to be." Her voice was small and she looked down. She wanted to challenge me on this, but seemed reluctant to push me. She wanted it to be my choice. But I knew what I wanted.

Using two fingers, I lifted her chin, forcing her eyes up to mine. "I know. But it's how I like it. Having to only worry about myself."

Emmy waited, her eyes on mine, waiting to see what else I'd say.

If I was smart, I'd push her away right now. I'd spill my history, my twisted past, all the many ways I'd fucked up. That would send her running. But something in me wouldn't do that. Refused. I wanted her too badly. This sweet, soft-spoken girl who was far too normal and nice for me. I wanted her. And it wasn't just about sex, either. I couldn't lie, being buried balls deep in her sweet body sounded fucking amazing, though that wasn't all I wanted if I was being honest. But, unwilling to let myself fuck with both her body and her mind, I needed to re-mind her this was only about sex.

I pushed on, needing to kill her hope for more. "Is what we have right now so bad?" I asked, one side of my mouth lifting in a playful grin.

She merely blinked up at me, like she wanted to disagree, to tell me I was wrong, that this could work if I would only try. But she deserved better—a proper boyfriend who'd cherish her, not hide her from the world in a hotel room.

"Ben . . ." she started.

My finger over her lips silenced her. "I'm just not capable of giving you everything you need."

She took my hand and squeezed it in hers, as if saying, "You're wrong."

My chest throbbed. She looked at me like I was good and whole and someone she wanted to take care of. I wouldn't push her away, as long as she knew what she was getting and not getting. "I don't know where I'll be living a few months from now. There's constant temptation in this business. Don't complicate this, Emmy. It's two and a half months. Let me have you."

She hesitated.

"Baby, you're on my mind constantly. There's no one else. Come on . . . let me have you how I want you. I promise you won't regret it."

Emmy

Let me have you. Ben's words rang in my head while his soulful eyes remained locked on mine. Could I do that? Could I hand him the keys to my body and not my heart? I realized with shocking clarity that this was who he was—how he grew up. He had watched his mom with a constant parade of men, and that was the norm. Moving all the time, relying only on himself. He learned to meet his physical needs with whomever was there with him, never getting too attached, knowing he'd eventually move on.

In contrast, my parents were high school sweethearts. I was pretty sure they'd been intimate only with each other—yet I knew they regretted nothing. They were still deeply in love after all these years.

The resolute look in his eyes, his belief that he was better off alone, broke my heart.

I tried not to read too much into it. He said it was two and a half more months—just sex. But every time he said or did something sweet, like this breakfast, or opening up to me, or insisting I spend the night in his bed, my heart got confused. I knew it was stupid, wishful thinking, but maybe we could be more. Maybe I could change his mind about commitment. It was probably stupid, but my brain latched on anyway. Didn't every girl want the fairy-tale romance with Prince Charming? Maybe this was my chance. I couldn't give up on him.

"Thank you for dinner," I murmured, determined to relax and enjoy myself, despite his disappointing attitude on relationships.

"Anytime, beautiful."

Each time he called me *beautiful* my heart skipped a beat. He made me feel all squirmy, like I was fifteen again, trying to attract the cute guy's attention. Luckily, I seemed to have somehow captured his complete attention and adoration. His thumbs stroked my instep and his eyes stayed locked on mine.

"Does this feel good?" he asked, pressing his knuckles firmly into the bottom of my foot.

Good wasn't a strong enough word. After walking all day in unsupportive flats that pinched my feet, this was heaven. "I fucking love it. Actually I *flove* it."

He raised an eyebrow. "Inventing new words, Miss Clarke?"

I smiled and nodded shyly.

"I'll call *Webster's*," he said. "Have it added to the dictionary."

His playfulness should have lightened the tone, but I could tell something more was on his mind. He continued rubbing my feet for several minutes in silence before laying them gingerly at the end of the bed to join me, leaning against the headboard. He didn't meet my eyes, just continued staring straight ahead.

"I take meds for anxiety and insomnia, and a couple different prescription sleep aids. I've had trouble sleeping since I was a kid. And the anxiety meds help with that. I don't like taking the sleep aids. They make me feel like a zombie."

I waited, nodding slightly, urging him to continue.

"I didn't have the most traditional upbringing."

That was the understatement of the year. His mom was a celebrity and they'd lived all over the world. I knew instead of going to school he'd had a private tutor that traveled with them.

"I used to stay up late at night, baby-sitting my mom while she partied. Used to force my eyelids to stay open, trying my hardest to stay awake. I was convinced something bad would happen if I fell asleep. It was a stupid childhood fear, really. But I used to find her in the morning and regret not staying up to take care of her."

His childhood had been so different from mine. Instead of days filled with climbing trees and catching frogs, and nights spent making pillow-forts, Ben watched over his mom. It broke my heart. I now understood the intensity in his eyes was due in part to his life experiences, the wariness to open himself up for a relationship. But it had to mean something that he was sharing this with me.

Ben took a deep breath and released it slowly. I gave his hand a gentle squeeze, urging him onward.

"I'd find her in the morning, sick, hung over, vomit in her hair, mascara smudged under her eyes, or worse, unconscious on the floor. Sleep was the enemy. And even now, I don't know why that stayed with me all these years—the hectic travel schedule, time zone changes, stress from work, you name it. I guess old habits die hard, because I still can't sleep for shit."

I thought about the times I'd seen Ben on set, the hardened intensity in his eyes. His steely look had nothing to do with hours of practice in front of a mirror, but instead had everything to do with a sad, lonely life devoid of love. How had no one made this beautiful man feel loved and cared for?

He shrugged, looking down. "I'm probably not the guy you thought I was."

I grabbed his hands and gave them a squeeze. "No." His eyes lifted to meet mine. "You're better. You're sweet and giving and insanely good at dirty texts." And a boy that loved his momma was something I could relate to.

He laughed, a deep, rumbling belly laugh that was like music to my ears. "The crazy thing is that last night, I curled right up with you and fell asleep. I never do that. Every night I lie awake for hours. You're like a magic cure."

I remembered the way he'd held me against his chest, his breathing growing deep and even as he'd fallen right to sleep. It was sweet to think I was some type of cure to his insomnia.

He leaned toward me and kissed me softly. "Thank you."

Ben

Her gaze was so sincere, so humble, so caring, I had no choice but to open up and tell her the whole sordid truth. Even if it was too much for her to handle, and she got up and fled the room, that would have been okay, too. I'd repeatedly told her this wasn't anything more than two people enjoying each other. But the idea of her leaving sent an ache racing through my chest. I didn't want to watch her walk away again.

I was glad she hadn't. She'd simply grabbed my hand and squeezed.

Emmy was caring and warm. She was the make-you-soup-when-you're-sick type. She'd bring you a pain reliever and palm your forehead to see if you had a temperature. She had natural motherly instincts. Not that I would know much about that. No, I didn't have that type of mother. I had the party-till-4 a.m.–red-carpet–jet-setting–yacht-gracing–actor-dating type of mom who barely managed to stay out of the tabloids.

Emmy's sweet, simple lifestyle and outlook was a nice

change of pace. It was shockingly normal, and I found that great. Sometimes I craved normal. Especially since my life was anything but.

I'd envied those families in the sitcoms I watched growing up—with a mom and a dad who went to jobs and came home each night, threw the ball around in the yard. I'd never known anything like that growing up. I was willing to bet Emmy had.

She'd listened to me speak without interrupting, a little line creasing her forehead. She didn't judge me, didn't look at me like I was some damaged asshole. Then after we'd been intimate, she'd changed into one of my T-shirts while we got ready for bed. I loved seeing her wearing one of my old shirts. She looked a fuck of a lot better in them than I did. Her soft, curvy body and chest filled out the front nicely.

Climbing into bed, Emmy turned to face me, looking up at me. The way she looked at me wasn't like I was used to. She gazed deep into my eyes in a sort of mesmerized way while I brushed the long strands of hair back from her face. The moment meant something. I'd told her it was just physical, yet even I couldn't deny that this felt deeper than two people sharing a blissful postsex moment. I didn't quite understand it, but I couldn't look away, either. Her pretty gray eyes were wide and continued watching mine. Her skin was pink and glowing, and a calm relaxation spread across her features. I liked knowing I put that look there.

I just liked being around her—even without the sex. It was a strange realization. I didn't have girlfriends. Shit, I rarely hung out with *friends,* period. My travel schedule didn't allow it. I had fellow models I hung out with and girls I fucked. But Emmy was more than that; I didn't know how or even what that meant; she just was.

Everything about her was special and beautiful. I didn't know what was happening between us, but this was definitely some type of moment. The way her eyes saw everything—looked straight into me—was too much. I pulled her down to my chest, feeling her heart thumping wildly against mine.

"Rest, baby." I just wanted to hold her. Normally I wanted girls gone as soon as I came. But not Emmy. She could stick around. She was warm and soft, and she smelled nice. And she didn't feel the need to fill the silence with mindless chatter, a quality I definitely appreciated. This was nice. Just the beating of our two hearts and her soft breathing. It provided the perfect backdrop to fall asleep to. Something I never thought I'd say. But this girl seemed to be a cure to my insomnia.

Emmy

I woke in the night, too warm, with a heavy weight pressing against me. Ben's arm was flung over my middle, locking me in place beside him. I tore the covers off my legs, separating myself from the death grip Ben had me in. I rolled away from him, the cool sheets feeling like heaven against my overheated skin.

Waking slightly, Ben whispered my name and I could tell something was bothering him. The distressed tone of his voice was like a knife to my heart. He bore some great burden and I was the key to freeing him. I moved closer, and forgetting all about how warm I had been, held him tight, running my hands up and down his back to soothe him back to sleep. If he needed me, I was there.

He breathed my name once more before dozing off again. I wanted him to feel safe and comforted. To not have to take those pills again.

His story about his mother ripped at my heart. Ben was

like no one I'd ever met. I could feel something pulling us together in my very soul. We were the same: This man who wanted more had desperately tried to win his mother's love and approval. I wanted more—better—for myself, too. I wanted to make my parents proud. I wasn't trying to win their approval, but wanted to show them all their hard work was for a reason, that I could make something of myself. We were each driven by that basic need to please our parents. I guess it was true what they said—you never really escaped your childhood. The desire to soothe his fears was an overwhelming urge. I wrapped my arms around him and held on tight.

After last night, I was eager to get to the hotel to see Ben. It felt like we were moving in the right direction. He'd opened up to me and I could see us spending passionate nights together in his bed becoming a regular thing. Something that would be just fine with me.

Once inside my room, I shucked off my shoes and tossed my purse on the chair, then retrieved my phone to call Ben. Glancing at the clock, I realized he should be back from his shoot.

He answered on the third ring, sounding breathless. "Hello?"

"Hi sexy. It's me."

"Uh . . . hi." His tone was short and slightly frustrated.

"Is now a bad time?"

"One sec." I heard him say something to someone in the

background and a female voice answered. The voice had a British accent.

My stomach knotted. "Where are you?"

"My room. Can I call you back in a few?"

"Sure." I put the phone down with shaky hands. He said he'd call me back later, but he was in his room with Fiona and something about that didn't sit right with me. I didn't trust Fiona, didn't know if I trusted the two of them alone together.

I made my way to his room, some unknown force propelling me forward. I knocked on the door, my heart pounding, and my expression determined.

A few moments later, Ben answered, his face flushed, his pulse thrumming in his neck.

"Emmy . . ."

He was dressed in jeans and a T-shirt but his hair was damp, like he'd just come from the shower. Had he showered with Fiona? My stomach cramped violently at the thought.

Ben's hand moved to the doorframe, blocking me from entering. "I'm discussing something with Fiona. Now's not a good time." His voice was low and his posture tense. I'd definitely interrupted something.

Glancing behind him, I spotted Fiona sitting on his bed, her heels kicked off and her purse spilled open beside her.

I'd always figured Fiona was emotionally indestructible, yet here she was, eyes red and swollen with tears freely streaming down her cheeks. She hastily wiped her face with the back of her hand. Ben cleared his throat and my eyes swung back to him. The mood was tense and it was clear I was intruding.

"I'll call you in a bit," he said, speaking in hushed tones as he watched me with sorrowful eyes.

I nodded and swallowed the lump in my throat. Ben closed the door, leaving me standing alone in the hall.

Holy. Shit.

Ben

Fiona had thrown me for a fucking loop. Showing up at my door, crying like I'd never seen her do. I'd listened and held her while she cried and told me all about her failed attempts to have a baby. I'd never taken Fiona for the motherly type. But at thirty-eight, she was apparently desperate to have a baby, with or without a man in her life. It was admirable of her—her desire to be a parent. Of course there was little I could do to help other than hold her and try to quiet her sobs. But then when she'd dumped the contents of her purse out onto my bed, revealing the syringe filled with fertility drugs she wanted me to inject her with, I quickly learned why she'd come to me.

She said she didn't want anyone to know in case it didn't work. And she was too scared to give herself the shot.

Just as she was walking me through the instructions, a knock at the door had startled us both.

I couldn't tell Emmy about this. I respected Fiona's desires to keep it private. Hopefully she would get pregnant with her next scheduled artificial insemination, and no one would ever need to know about her struggles.

Fiona's puckered mouth told me she wasn't naïve—she was all too aware of Emmy's evening visit to my room.

"You're getting too close to my assistant," she said after a full minute of silence.

"Emmy?" I played dumb.

"Yes, Emerson. And don't act surprised. I can see there's something between you two." I stayed quiet, unpacking the syringe and alcohol wipes on the bed beside us.

"Ben, I'm serious. I don't like it. When I told you not to shag my assistant, I meant it."

"Relax, Fiona. You can't be tensed up for what I'm about to do."

She pulled in a deep breath, trying to calm herself. "Okay, but you realize if there's something going on, I could fire her and send her home." My jaw tensed, but I didn't tell her that if she fired Emmy, I'd just move her into my room and have her remain here with me.

"You wouldn't do that. You want me to continue helping you, don't you?" I uncapped the syringe and Fiona nodded meekly. We both knew I had the upper hand here.

She walked me through the instructions the nurse had given her, how to swab a spot near her belly button with an alcohol wipe then pinch the skin before swiftly jabbing in the needle.

After I administered Fiona's shot and sent her on her way, I made myself a stiff drink.

Now with one vodka tonic under my belt, I sent Emmy a text message and waited for her response. I was considering pouring another drink when my phone vibrated against the nightstand.

Emmy: Are you still with her?

I could tell she was pissed. She didn't even want to say Fiona's name. I guess I couldn't blame her. I sensed they had some strange female jealousy thing happening and it wasn't something I wanted to encourage.

Me: No, she's gone. Have you eaten?

Emmy: Not hungry

Me: Come back up. Let me make you a drink.

It took her several minutes to reply.

Emmy: Okay

Her response was less than enthusiastic but she was coming. A few minutes later, just as I'd returned from filling the ice bucket, she knocked softly at my door. I pulled it open and tugged her inside, kissing her gently on the mouth.

Emmy was tense at first, but as my hands curled around her waist and slid down to cup her ass, I felt her relax against me. God, her ass felt amazing in my hands. I knew I owed her some type of explanation, but damn if my body didn't jump to attention when she was near. There'd be time for talking later. I wanted her. I deepened the kiss, hauling her even closer, until her chest was pressed flat against me, and her tongue softly flickered against mine. She was perfect. "I need to be inside you, baby."

Emmy let out a whimper and my dick jumped. I loved her

soft, feminine sounds. Backing her across the room while my tongue flirted with hers, I gave Emmy a playful shove onto the bed. She laid back, a little grin tugging up her lips.

Her eyes danced on mine while her smile grew even wider. I loved seeing her honest reactions to me. The flush of her skin, the way she bit into her bottom lip. She was beautiful, natural. And something inside me loved that. Maybe it was this overly critical, overly judgmental business I was in, but I admired her simplicity. Maybe it was her country upbringing—hell, maybe it was just her. But whatever it was, Emmy Clarke was quickly becoming a habit.

As I stood in front of her, her eyes wandered from mine, down my chest, and rested on the erection tenting my slacks. She bit her lip again.

"Come here." I extended a hand toward her, and she accepted, placed her small palm against mine, and crawled across the bed toward me.

Emmy knelt in front of me, those large blue-gray eyes watching my movements as I freed my belt buckle.

She licked her lips as I unbuttoned my pants and then slowly tugged down my zipper. Leaning up on her knees, Emmy's hands reached forward to help. I clasped her hands in mine, placing them firmly by her sides. "Behave."

Her eyes widened at my warning, but she obeyed. She was naturally feisty yet so submissive in the bedroom. It was a big fucking turn-on. I pushed my jeans and boxers down my legs and then gripped my length. Her pulse fluttered erratically in her neck and her eyes zeroed in on my cock. I lazily stroked my length, slowly drawing my hand from base to tip. The desire in her eyes made me rock fucking hard.

I cupped Emmy's cheek. "Come here, pretty girl."

Looking up at me with complete lust, Emmy leaned forward and opened her mouth.

Fuckkk.

The warm caress of her tongue was fucking bliss. Emmy opened wider, her eyes still locked on mine as I pushed forward, filling her. When the head of my cock hit the back of her throat, she gagged slightly and I retreated, reluctantly dragging myself out. Still covered in her saliva, Emmy stroked me, her little hands massaging and caressing me. It felt amazing. I didn't want to stop her but she still had far too many clothes on. I wanted to see her beautiful tits, to kiss her all over, to make her come, to fuck her senseless.

Grabbing the hem of her shirt, I lifted and she obediently raised her arms above her head, allowing me to remove it. She wore a lavender lace bra I hadn't seen before. I liked that there were so many things to discover still. It was a pretty, frilly thing, but I wanted it the fuck off her body. Reaching behind her to free the clasp, the bra dropped down her arms and I removed it slowly while leaning down to kiss her full mouth. I didn't think I could ever get tired of kissing her mouth. The little breathy sounds she made, the way her hands restlessly tugged me, trying to get closer. She was so sexual and sweet at the same time. It was heaven.

Emmy

Several weeks passed and Ben and I continued seeing each other regularly. I knew I was being delusional, I knew we weren't dating. You didn't date a man like Ben Shaw. He couldn't be tamed. He was like Clooney. But we'd been having regular sex, enjoying meals together, and talking; he shared things with me, as I did with him. I had no idea what all that added up to. The question was, did it matter? A man like Ben had the potential to destroy me. I knew this from that first time he'd been inside me, moving above me, his stubble scraping against my neck, his warm breath on my shoulder. We were closer than I'd been with anyone. My body was addicted, my heart was engaged, but my head knew this would probably end badly.

I had a weakness where he was concerned. I couldn't stay away. His relationship with Fiona still worried me. We'd never spoken about that teary moment in his hotel room. Ben didn't offer up the information about what Fiona was doing there that night, and I never asked.

Whatever their history, I wasn't sure, but he was her golden boy and I was her country-bumpkin assistant. She freaked if he overlooked taking his vitamins. She'd no doubt think me touching him tainted him in some way.

Ben had casting calls and fittings during the day, which was fine, because Fiona kept me running. He sent me unexpected sweet texts while I was at work to let me know he was thinking of me. In one he grumbled about an outfit a designer had put him in. After some prodding, he'd sent me a funny picture. The outfit looked like a lampshade. But he still looked hot. My lampshade hottie.

Paris Fashion Week was coming up and I knew Ben was going to walk in several designers' shows. I was excited to see him on the catwalk, with all eyes glued to him and knowing he was mine. I felt like Cinderella who'd somehow captured Prince Charming's attention.

I glanced down at my watch; I couldn't wait to get back to the hotel and see him. It was ridiculous how attached I had become to him.

Ben waved an airline ticket at me. "Milan tomorrow. Wanna come?"

Fiona hadn't mentioned anything about Milan, which I took to mean I wasn't invited. "I can't just go to Milan with you. I have to work."

He crossed the hotel room, his warm hand coming around

me to cup my backside. "Oh, I'll put you to work." His hand caressed my bottom, pulling me closer so he could plant a soft kiss on my lips.

Pulling back before I got lost in his kisses, I placed a hand on his chest. "Fiona won't just let me go with you guys for the fun of it."

"She's not coming. It's just me. And you, if you'll join me. It's only one night."

I looked at him skeptically. She wasn't coming?

"She has doctor appointments. Don't worry, I'll take care of Fiona," he said.

The fact that he was willing to discuss me with Fiona was a big deal. He planted a soft kiss against my forehead before stepping away and pulling his phone from his pocket. He dialed and resumed packing a small brown leather bag that sat open on his bed.

"Hey. It's me," he said into the phone. "Fine, and you?" He continued shoving items into the bag while I paced the room. Fiona was going to freak. "I'd like Emmy to join me in Milan. Can you do without her for a night?"

He paused, listening, while I held my breath.

"Thank you, that'd be great."

He ended the call and tossed the phone on the bed. "Go pack, babe."

I stood there, dumbfounded. "She said yes?"

He flashed me a gorgeous smile. "She's calling the airline now to get you a ticket."

Fiona was calling to arrange my ticket? Had I entered an

alternate universe? Clearly Ben had powers of persuasion with her. Something about the blind way she obeyed him didn't sit well with me, but I nodded and ventured to my room.

When we arrived at the airline ticket counter Ben's cheerful mood disappeared. The agent told him my ticket had been booked in coach, back of the plane, middle seat. With him sitting in first class, we wouldn't be sitting together. It looked like Fiona had exacted her revenge.

Ben began conversing with the woman in French while I stood uselessly beside him. His jaw tensed while she clicked away at her keyboard.

I tugged on his arm. "It's okay if we're not together. It's a quick flight."

"I'm seeing if I can get you a seat in first class with me, and if not, I'm getting moved to coach."

"Ben, no, that's silly. I'm fine in coach." It was Fiona's way of pointing out my place.

He and the agent exchanged a few more tense words and then he pulled out his wallet and handed her his credit card.

"You don't have to do this; first class is expensive."

"I want to, baby. Let me do this." His hand found mine and he laced our fingers together.

I nodded, seeing that he wasn't going to be deterred. It did feel nice to be looked after like this, though. And I'd never sat in first class before.

Soon we were seated in the wide, leather seats of the plane's first row, sipping champagne from crystal stemware. First class blew my expectations out of the water. Instead of having a cramped, smelly seat with someone bumping my arm and stealing my armrest, Ben and I lounged and chatted, sipped champagne, and nibbled on salted almonds. Before I knew it, we were deplaning and en route to our hotel.

"There's someone I want to introduce you to," Ben said, kicking off his shoes.

I'd envisioned a romantic candlelit dinner in the heart of Milan, but I nodded. "Okay."

"Angelo and Rosa own a winery just outside the city. I haven't seen them in years. We'll have a tour and dinner, if that sounds okay to you."

"Yes. Of course. I just need to shower."

He nodded. "Will an hour work? I'll call ahead."

"An hour's fine." I'd have to hustle; I needed to shave, too.

Fifty-seven minutes later, I emerged from the marble bathroom showered and made up, dressed in a black pencil skirt, strappy heels, and a silver beaded tank top. Ben was lounging across the bed, reading a novel he'd picked up at the airport. I grabbed my little diamond-studded earrings left to me by my grandmother and stood in front of the bureau mirror to put them on. Ben rose from the bed, coming up behind me to sweep my hair over one shoulder, and planted soft kisses against the back of my neck.

"Mmm, that feels nice." I dropped my head to rest against his shoulder and his arms came around me.

"You look beautiful."

Our reflections staring back at me were a study in contrasts. Ben was a foot taller than me and strikingly handsome. The plain brunette I saw with him wasn't beautiful to me, but I was glad he thought so.

Ben slipped on his loafers. His two-minute getting-ready ritual left him looking amazing, as usual. He was dressed in dark chinos and a polo shirt rolled up at the sleeves. He looked casual yet still gorgeous.

We hailed a cab and were en route to the countryside, holding hands in the backseat. Homes and buildings dotted the rolling hills, which soon turned into an expanse of leafy green trees unlike any we had back home.

"So how do you know Angelo and Rosa?" I asked.

"Rosa is a friend of my mom's from a long time ago. They used to model together during Milan Fashion Week. And now she runs a winery with her brother. I usually try to visit when I'm in town."

I turned to face him. "She's not the one you . . . lost your virginity to, is she?"

Ben laughed loudly, catching the attention of our cab-driver in the mirror. "No."

I wasn't sure what was so funny about that, but when we arrived thirty minutes later and Rosa greeted us in the drive-way, I understood. She was roughly fifty years old and time had not been kind to her. She was a large woman. She'd prob-ably been quite attractive in her youth, but her face was now lined with deep wrinkles from working in the sun.

She pulled me into her arms while speaking in Italian to Ben. He laughed and conversed with her, though you could tell the language didn't come as naturally to him as French. He struggled for words and nodded along. I worried that I'd be left out tonight if she and her brother spoke only Italian. Extra wine for me then. Rosa held me at arm's length, surveying me from head to toe.

"So nice to see Ben with a real woman," she said at last, her English heavily accented.

I wasn't sure if I should take offense or thank her for the compliment. I chose the second. Ben's arm looping around my waist sealed the deal. He was proud to introduce me to people he considered family friends.

"Emmy's as real as they come." He pressed a soft kiss to my temple.

Angelo came strolling out of the house, a straw hat atop his head, and joined us, hugging and kissing both Ben and me.

His English wasn't quite as clear as Rosa's, but at least I wouldn't struggle tonight.

"Everything set up?" Ben asked, nodding toward a barn in the distance. I wondered what he had planned.

"Yes, please, go, enjoy," Angelo said. "And we'll see you for dinner in an hour or so."

After greeting us, they shuffled back into the winery to attend to their customers. It was a beautiful day and there were several cars in the parking lot. Ben said we'd have dinner with them later, once the winery tours were done for the day. He took my hand and led me toward an old barn on the edge of the property.

The barn appeared to be several hundred years old. It was dimly lit and cool inside. Ben brought me to the back, where we walked down several steps to a rustic wine cellar. Stone floors and shelving units stacked with wine bottles lined the walls. There was a small round table set up in the center of the room with two bar stools, and the soft glow of white Christmas lights strung from the ceiling made the room romantic and alluring. On top of the table were a bottle of chilled white wine resting in a marble ice bucket along with a platter of assorted cheeses and sliced meats. It was a lovely, romantic gesture.

I glanced back at Ben. "Did you arrange this?"

He nodded, silently watching me. "Sort of a private tasting. I thought this might be more relaxing than joining one of their tours."

Very thoughtful of him. He pulled out a stool and motioned for me to sit. Once we were both seated, Ben uncorked the bottle and poured us each a glass of wine.

"Cheers." He clinked his glass to mine, his dark eyes still watching me.

"Cheers," I murmured, bringing the glass to my lips. It reminded me of our first date, sharing a bottle of wine and some polite conversation. Of course, now we were much more well acquainted. And I felt slightly more comfortable around him, though he still sent my pulse spiraling out of control.

We sipped our wine and nibbled on delicious cheeses while Ben told me some of the vineyard's history. It had been in the family for sixty years and run by the various relatives during that time. I liked that family values seemed to be alive and well in Italy. Big family dinners and running businesses together were the norm. It reminded me of the South in some ways. Soon the bottle was empty and Ben rose from his seat to select another from the hundreds surrounding us in the room.

I ventured over to where he was closely inspecting a bottle. "I'm guessing you'd like this *rosato*." The word rolled from his tongue with his Italian pronunciation. "It'll be fruity and light."

"And it's pink," I added, brilliantly.

"Yes it is." He smiled at me sweetly. "My favorite color."

I raised a brow. "Pink is your favorite color?"

His hand pressed between my thighs, stroking delicately. "Pink is definitely my favorite color." He smiled devilishly.

Whoa.

Setting the bottle down on the shelf, Ben leaned in closer, bringing his hand to the nape of my neck to pull my lips to his. He kissed along my mouth, jaw, and cheeks. Feeling light-headed from the wine and the rush of blood pounding in my ears, I clutched his bicep. It was warm and solid under my palm.

He placed sweet, tender kisses all over my lips and neck. He took his time seducing me. It was impossible not to fall under his spell. He lingered at my neck, trailing kisses down the column of my throat, stopping at my chest. I felt his teeth graze my collarbone, and darts of pleasure shot down to my breasts, where I desperately wanted to feel his mouth. I squirmed against him, still clutching his biceps, brushing my breasts against his chest. "Ben . . . we can't here. . . ." I breathed against his mouth.

"Are you only brave enough to tease me through text?" He trailed a finger along my jawline. "Where's your courage, sexy girl?"

I wasn't sexy or courageous. But Ben made me feel like maybe I could be. I glanced around at our surroundings. At least it seemed semiprivate. And if our hosts were busy with customers . . .

He dragged his fingertips down my spine, his knuckles brushing past each vertebra, lighting my skin on fire while he nipped at my lips. He was so unrushed, so sexy and in control, while I felt like I was burning up.

I gripped him through his pants and found him already rock hard. When my hand wrapped around him we each let out a simultaneous groan. Ben roughly pulled my tank top down, revealing my black lacy bra, and pressed a kiss to the center of my chest. My heart thumped steadily as I looked down and watched. His full lips traveled across my breast-bone, pressing delicious kisses. He dragged down the cups of my bra, exposing my breasts to his mouth. His warm tongue circled one nipple while his eyes lifted to watch my response. His tongue flicked back and forth over the sensitive peak and I let out a soft groan. Ben responded by sucking my breast into his mouth, kissing and licking me greedily.

"You taste so fucking good, baby." His hand caressed one breast while his tongue stroked the other. I was lost to the sensations, my panties growing damp and my knees already trembling. My fingers wound their way into his hair, holding him in place as he worshipped my breasts.

His cell phone rang, interrupting our bliss. He groaned a frustrated growl and pulled it from his pocket. "Fuck. One second, baby. It's Fiona. Probably just wanting to check in."

He answered the call, leaving me standing in front of him with my breasts damp and exposed. Ben watched me while he spoke, placing one hand on my waist, his thumb lightly stroking my hip. He asked about her visit to the doctor, and even though I knew he was just being polite, it frustrated me. The conversation dragged on—something about Paris Fashion Week—then Ben's brow crinkled in concentration. He pulled the phone away from his ear and mouthed, *just a few more minutes. . . .*

I tried not to pout. I knew it wasn't attractive, but I hated that Fiona had called him, interrupting our private time together. A sudden idea took hold of me.

Fueled by three glasses of wine and a healthy dose of lust, I dropped to my knees in front of him. His body went as tight as a wire. Ben's eyes widened as I reached for his zipper and tugged it down. I couldn't help the smile curling on my mouth. I liked that he brought out my daring side. Not only were we in a public place where someone could discover us at any time, but he was on the phone with my boss. His hand caressed my hair and he looked down at me with a wicked grin.

I slid his pants and boxers down to his knees. He wasn't fully hard, but as my hand curled around him, stroking him slowly, I felt him thicken and lengthen in my grip. I watched his face as I worked. Pleasure overtook his features, his eyes growing dark with desire.

"Yeah, I'm still here," he said roughly into the phone. "Sorry, what did you say?"

I wanted to claim him, to own him.

Would he tell me to stop . . . or would he get off the phone with Fiona? I wasn't sure which was more likely, but I grinned at myself for thinking up this little experiment. I needed to see who he would choose. If she was more important to him, he'd stop me to continue his conversation. I prayed he made an excuse and let her go.

Now fully hard and long, I stroked him faster and felt his knees tremble. My mouth closed around him and a sigh broke from his lips. I wrapped both my hands around his thick length and suckled the warm flesh of his tip, using my tongue to lavish him in broad strokes before pulling him all the way to the back of my throat. I heard him saying something into the phone, but all my attention was on him. I worshipped his cock, thoroughly enjoying myself. A strangled squeak escaped the back of his throat as he fought for control.

When both of his hands cupped my jawline, I knew he'd ended the call, and I was flooded with emotion as Ben surged forward, filling my mouth. I lifted my eyes to watch him. He pushed his hips forward, invading my open mouth, and retreated, dragging himself in and out of my mouth slowly but deeply. The expression on his face was raw pleasure. His eyelids were heavy, his breathing accelerated. Soft groans escaped his parted lips each time he thrust forward and bumped the back of my throat.

"Fuck baby, that's pretty." Ben's warm hands swept the hair back from my face as his eyes followed my movements. "I love seeing you with my cock buried in your mouth."

I realized I'd never done this start to finish for him, and suddenly I wanted to make him come. I opened my mouth wider to accommodate him, still gripping his length in my hands.

"Emmy, fuck, fuck . . ." His breathing increased and a soft rumble in his chest told me he was getting close.

"Baby . . . I'm gonna . . . baby . . . fuck . . ."

Cupping the back of my head with one hand, he pressed forward as he came, sending hot jets of semen sliding down the back of my throat with minimal effort on my part. He knew what he was doing; that was for sure.

Ben reached down for me, pulling me up to my feet, and kissed my forehead before tucking himself back inside his pants. "That was . . . wow." He smiled sweetly.

I basked at his compliment, happy and proud to have brought him pleasure. "It was okay?"

"I'm about ready to get down on one knee." He chuckled.

There was little time to ponder what his comment meant because almost as quickly as he'd hauled me to my feet, his mouth was traveling down my throat and his hands moved to the edge of my skirt. I hadn't realized just how wet the process of pleasuring him had gotten me, but there was no denying it. I was soaking. His large index finger invaded me, and I let out a whimper. I gripped his shoulders, kissing him greedily as he steadily brought me closer and closer.

Voices just outside the wine cellar broke our kiss as we both looked toward the door. Shit! I struggled to arrange my skirt and cover myself, but Ben's hands stopped mine. Was he crazy? Angelo and Rosa were apparently leading their tour group through the barn.

"Let me finish, sweet girl." His mouth crashed against mine and his fingers continued their sweet assault, sending me spiraling closer to the edge. I didn't know if it was the sense of danger, the possibility of being discovered, or Ben's dominance over my body, but I came apart completely, shamelessly rocking my hips against his hand to ride out the sensation. Ben kissed me to quiet the moans tumbling from my lips.

The voices trailed off, and somehow we weren't discovered.

Afterward, we made our way inside the house and Ben showed me to the guest bath where I washed up and made myself presentable.

As we entered the large dining room with a rustic plank-wood table, the smells of garlic and tomatoes and roasting meat greeted us. Angelo uncorked a bottle of red wine and Rosa arranged several large serving platters in the center of the table.

"*Grazie!*" she greeted us warmly, stuffing each of us into a chair.

I didn't realize it before, but now that I could smell the food, I was ravenous.

Ben's eyes lingered on mine throughout the meal, probably because I couldn't help the moans each time I tasted a new dish.

I can't say the conversation exactly flowed, because well, it didn't. Neither Angelo nor Rosa spoke great English. But the food was delicious. Some of the best things I'd ever tasted— roasted meats, fresh ravioli stuffed with ricotta cheese and sweet basil, all paired with scrumptious local wines. Our hosts were warm and welcoming and it was a lovely meal.

At the end of dinner, Ben called for our car and our hosts walked us to the door. Rosa pulled me in for a hug, thanking me and telling me that Ben was a good man and needed a good girl.

It was clear she was a motherly figure to Ben, and I felt honored that he'd thought to introduce me.

"Thanks for coming," Ben said once we got in the car.

I smiled and rested my head on his shoulder.

The drive back to Milan was dark and I was sleepy. I snuggled against him, full and happy. I hoped nothing would change.

14

Emmy

The following day we had a late flight out, but first Ben had a photo shoot. He urged me to stay at the hotel, sleep in, order breakfast, and take a swim in the deep tub. He'd be back to collect me in a few hours. I didn't argue. After all the wine last night, a little extra sleep was exactly what I wanted.

When I woke an hour later, I called for room service and let the bathtub fill, adding a generous pour of bubble bath. It was nice to have a morning to myself to relax. Usually Fiona had me running around early, so this was a rare treat to be savored.

After a leisurely bath, I dressed in the fluffy hotel robe and ate my poached egg and toast. Then while I waited for Ben, I crawled back into bed and watched the Italian-only TV stations.

I checked the time, and realizing it'd be early morning back home in Tennessee, I decided to try my mom.

My mom's accent burst through the phone. "Emmy Jean, I miss you. How's Paris, honey? Are the French being snooty?"

I laughed. God, I needed this. Needed to hear her voice. It was like a little slice of home and instantly grounded me. "Oh Momma, it's amazing here. I've been to the Yves Saint Laurent offices and Versace castings and got samples from Louis Vuitton. And I'm actually in Milan right now." I didn't mention Ben.

She was quiet on the other end, and I wondered if she knew the names of the famous designers I'd name-dropped.

"Don't get caught up in that world. Those people aren't like us, Emmy Jean."

Her words stopped me. She was right. I'd never felt more out of place, yet with Ben I didn't have to pretend to be someone I wasn't. "Don't worry, Momma. I'm still me." I smiled, knowing it was true.

"Good. I can't wait for you to get home for a visit. With your dad on the road so much, I get lonely."

My dad was an over-the-road truck driver and was gone much of the week. I listened as she droned on about the church potluck and her prized tomatoes, occasionally asking her questions and probing deeper. It was good just to hear her voice. It reminded me that there was a bigger world beyond the glitz and glamour of Fashion Week, that I was destined for more in life.

This was a temporary adventure and the realization unsettled me. I'd been so caught up in this whirlwind; I wondered what would happen once I was back home. Would Ben still be interested in me once we were in New York? I tried to picture him in my little, dingy apartment, hanging out with me and Ellie. It was like trying to envision Fiona dressed in last year's couture. Never going to happen.

"I'll come home soon, Momma. Say hi to Dad for me. I love you."

She seemed so far away—my childhood home in the country was a distant memory in the bustling fashion world of Paris and Milan. And my affair with Ben consumed everything, every waking thought, and even inspired my dreams. I knew it probably wasn't healthy, but it was my reality. I'd been sucked into his bubble, and I didn't want it to end.

After saying our good-byes, I curled up on the bed to await Ben's arrival.

Was I really so shallow that an attractive—albeit stunningly attractive—man could turn me into a pile of goo? But it was more than that, I reminded myself. As much as I enjoyed his outward appearance, I liked him for all the qualities that had nothing to do with his good looks.

He'd been honest and forthright with me about his goals. The way he talked about his future and his financial savvy was sexy. It demonstrated his ability to plan ahead and provide. He put my needs first when we'd been intimate, which was more than I'd expected based on my prior disappointing experiences. Not to mention, the man had the dirty-talking gene. Which meant over the long haul, he'd be the type to keep things interesting. Just enough of that spontaneity to keep the fire burning. I knew I was getting ahead of myself, though. Damn, I was ready to pick out bridesmaid dresses and he hadn't even told me we were exclusive. If this was just sex, why did it feel like so much more?

15

Emmy

Fashion Week was in full swing in Paris. The air buzzed with energy and excitement and there was a flurry of activity. I headed backstage at the Versace show to see if I could find Ben. Guys were everywhere in various stages of undress. Some were seated at the makeup stations, their hair being coaxed into new styles and held with clips to let the creation set; others changed behind partitions, modesty aside.

Ben was easy to spot. He stood several inches above everyone around him. My perfect Greek god. My sexy man. I felt proud watching him. The makeup artist used a foundation brush to dab on concealer, brightening up his skin tone. The dark circles he once had under his eyes had disappeared. Perhaps sleeping next to me at night really had done the trick.

Fiona stood near his side, sipping a glass of champagne and chatting casually with the stylist while the makeup artist worked her magic. Ben was walking in several shows today but was currently wearing a pair of faded jeans that made his butt look adorable and a white T-shirt.

His eyes caught mine and an easy smile bloomed across his pouty mouth. He really was gorgeous. I returned his smile, sending him a silent wish of good luck, and then headed back out to the seating area. I needed to make sure Fiona's reserved seat in the front row was all set. I would be sitting several rows back but felt lucky I'd been able to get a seat at all. Gunnar was watching the show from the hotel via live video feed.

I found my seat and settled in. I wondered if I was allowed to take any photos with my camera phone. But I supposed I could find photos of Ben later online. There were a million photographers here, their flashes already popping like crazy.

I saw Fiona slip into her seat in the front and I knew the show was about to start. Little butterflies danced in my belly in anticipation.

Hot lights and flashing cameras flooded the stage. Loud gyrating music thumped through the sound system. I didn't know the order or when I would see Ben. Some shows lasted only seven or eight minutes; others were closer to twenty. It just depended on how many looks they had to show, and I didn't know how many exits he had.

The first of the models began walking and a slow smile overtook my face. I was here, in Paris, at my first fashion show. The feeling was surreal. I watched in transfixed fascination as the parade of beautiful men marched confidently down the catwalk. This season was all about bold colors, solids, blacks and whites, and lesser-used animal prints . . . apparently snakeskin was going to be big next year.

Suddenly Ben was there, strutting beautifully toward me on the runway. He was utter perfection. Confident, sure, and sexy as hell. His walk was poised, his chin up, and his dark gaze straight ahead. My eyes wandered the length of his body, taking in the charcoal-gray suit and bold red tie. A leather satchel hung from his shoulder. Never had a slim-cut suit and a murse looked more sexy.

I knew he didn't get to keep the clothes, but damn, I wouldn't mind slowly undressing him later, unwrapping him like a present. My pulse kicked up at the thought. With all the afterparties to follow, I only hoped I could get some alone time with him.

Once the shows ended for the day, I scrambled backstage to find him. It was insanity: photographers, designers, and models everywhere. And everyone was in a celebratory mood. Drugs, alcohol, naked people. *Wow*. Giving up any hope of finding him, I sent him a text telling him I'd see him at the afterparty and headed out.

After swinging by the hotel to change into something more evening-appropriate—skinny black ankle pants paired with a silk purple halter top and strappy silver sandals—I navigated to the Metro that I'd grown comfortable taking over the past several weeks.

When I arrived at the hotel where the afterparty was being held, I felt out of place and awkward as I made my way inside the elegant hotel. Stopping at the front desk, the reception staff directed me to take the elevator to the third-floor ballroom.

I was not at all prepared for the scene that greeted me. Low house music thumped from the speakers, and along with the dim lighting, set an evocative mood. Plush white sofas were arranged in a U shape and filled with stick-thin female models chatting amicably. I continued past them, feeling like I was back in my high school cafeteria, passing the cool-kids table to sit alone in the corner.

Needing some liquid courage, I approached the bar before seeking out Ben. Or even Gunnar. Any friendly face would do. But first I wanted a drink in my hands. I preferred an ice-cold beer but opted for a glass of champagne, which seemed to be the drink of choice tonight.

I took a sip of the semisweet, chilled champagne and closed my eyes. I hated how out of place I felt. It was obvious who the models were and who the regular people were. I was too short, too curvy. Never had I been more aware of my body than standing in that room of size-zero women. I headed farther down the bar to an empty stool, where I could sit and take the pressure off my feet. Damn pinching heels. Easing into the modern half-moon–shaped seat, I noticed the man next to me, head down, sipping his beer quietly.

He must have noticed the way I longed for his bottle of beer because, just seconds later, he signaled and nodded to the bartender, and a beer was uncapped and placed in front of me.

I turned to him, all smiles for the first time tonight. "Was I that obvious?"

He smiled easily, his features open and friendly. "Braydon Kincaid." He extended a hand toward me.

"Emmy Clarke." I placed my palm against his. "And thanks for the beer."

"Anytime." It was obvious he was a model. He was tall, at least a couple inches over six feet, and his body, while lean, was toned and firm with muscle. His hair was a shade lighter than Ben's—a mix of warm brown and blond—and his eyes were a striking blue.

Braydon turned fully in my direction, still watching me as I tilted the bottle to my lips and took a long sip. I wasn't much in the mood for conversation, but something about him set me at ease, more than it probably should have.

Swallowing the icy gulp, I turned to face him. "Were you in some of the shows today?"

He took a pull of his own beer, the broad column of his throat working as he swallowed. It was hard not to be affected by this man physically. He truly was gorgeous. "Armani, Prada, Iceberg, Jil Sander, and Calvin Klein. Fun stuff."

"Oh, now I remember. You opened the Jil Sander show. You were the one wearing those hot-pink pants."

He smiled, his eyes sparkling on mine. "You caught me. They were giving out samples after the show, but I don't think

I'll need to wear those ever again. I'd like to keep my man card, thank you very much."

I laughed easily, instantly put at ease around him despite only knowing him a few minutes.

"So what do you do?" he asked. He'd worded it in a polite way, but it was obvious he knew I was not a model.

"I work for Fiona Stone."

"Ah, I see." The knowing smile that tugged at his mouth told me he was familiar with her, but I didn't probe any further. Most people had heard of her or Status Model Management. That was no surprise. But I didn't feel like swapping Fiona horror stories, so I let it drop.

"And I think you should be proud being dressed in pink today. It takes a damn confident man to pull that off," I said, changing the subject away from myself.

He shook his head. "Yeah, I'm sure my parents would be real proud. I had a manicure today and strutted the catwalk in pink. Every father's dream right there."

I laughed, though I wondered if there was any truth in his words and if his dad approved of his chosen profession. "Where are you from?" Mention of his family had me wondering where he grew up. His accent was definitely American.

"Ohio. What about you?"

"Tennessee."

"I should have guessed."

"Why, my accent?" I was used to people commenting on it.

"Yep." He grinned. The small talk relaxed me. We each

took a sip of our beer and let the comfortable silence permeate the air around us.

Braydon's knees brushed mine and I couldn't help but notice the dark wanting in his deep blue gaze. It made my skin tingle.

"I should go look for my friends." My voice had gone all husky and low and I cleared my throat. "Thank you for the beer."

Braydon lifted my hand from my side and pressed it to his lips. "Anytime, jelly bean." His playful words, the glint in his eyes, and the soft press of his lips against my skin sent a zip of heat rushing through my core.

I swallowed roughly, my eyes lingering on his. When I finally moved away, it was on shaky legs.

Crossing the room, I headed straight into the more dimly lit VIP lounge area. Mirrored walls and spinning disco balls threw off little flecks of color that bounced across the room. The effect was disorienting.

I spotted Ben on the far end of the room seated with a group of guys and girls on one of the white leather sofas. He hadn't yet noticed me, and when I got closer I spotted thin lines of white powder drawn on the table in front of them. While Ben and I had never discussed drug use, I had assumed he didn't use. Now I wasn't so sure.

He held a glass of amber-colored liquor and his eyes were a bit glazed. Panic gripped me, my stomach dropping to my feet. Maybe I didn't know him at all. When his eyes met mine, recognition crossed his features. He sat up straighter in his seat, pulling away slightly from the waiflike girl tucked in by his side.

"Emmy." He reached a hand toward me and I took it, easing in between him and the model beside him. I didn't know her name but her face was familiar. I was pretty sure I'd seen her in the Prada show earlier. Rather than squeezing myself between them, I remained standing, wedged between the sofa and low coffee table near Ben's knees. He looked up at me, his smile somewhat somber.

Suddenly I didn't want to be there. I wasn't part of that scene. Drugs weren't okay with me, and sitting back and enjoying a drink felt like I'd be condoning the cocaine use going on around us. And I certainly didn't. Call me stuck up, prudish, whatever you want, but going back to my room and taking a bubble bath sounded a lot more appealing than hanging out with these people.

"I think I'm going to go."

Ben rose, unsteady on his feet. "Then I'll take you back."

I gripped his bicep, keeping him steady. It looked like I'd be the one taking him back. I'd never seen him this drunk. And something in me didn't like it. I was worried for him. How much had he drank, and should he be drinking so heavily on his medications? I helped him maneuver from where we stood in the space between the table and sofa.

As we made our way through the center of the room, I looped an arm around his waist to keep him walking on a straight path. I'd never seen him so smashed, and I couldn't say I was a fan. I knew from experience there was nothing fun about taking care of someone drunk, and likely to be sick later.

Yay, me.

Ben staggered toward the door, clutching a hand around my hip. "Thanks, baby."

I was willing to guess he hadn't eaten a thing all day. I swear, no one fed these models. At least I hoped that was all this was—too much alcohol on an empty stomach. I fought to keep us both heading in the right direction, keeping my hold on Ben, my handbag, and trying to balance on my stiletto heels. I felt a large hand close around my elbow.

"I've got him." The familiar deep voice from earlier— Braydon—said from behind me.

I released my hold on Ben and allowed him to step between us. He tossed one arm under Ben's shoulder, easily guiding him to the elevator.

I trailed behind them, slightly embarrassed.

"Too much to drink, buddy?" Braydon asked him once we were all inside the elevator.

Ben gave a nod, recognition flashing in his eyes as he appraised the man standing before him. "Bray."

Braydon stepped closer, pulling me inside the doors while keeping his hold on Ben.

Braydon's hand remained glued to my hip, holding me near him. The heat from his hand simmered up my side, pushing my nipples against the lace of my bra. My body was curious about him, even if my mind was wrapped up in Ben.

"You gonna share this one with me?" Braydon asked Ben, his eyes still on mine.

Ben shoved an uncoordinated hand into Braydon's shoulder. "No, asshole." His voice was flat, not amused.

Had they shared women before? And why was this information like a shot of adrenaline to my system? These two beautiful men worshipping the same woman? Holy shit. I felt weak.

I bent down to adjust the strap of my sandal digging into my ankle. Keeping one hand on Ben's shoulder to steady him, Braydon reached for me, relieving me of the handbag that dangled awkwardly from my arm. He slipped the strap over his wrist and winked at me. "Let me help."

I met his kind eyes and smiled, seemingly at a loss for words around this tall, fair-haired, gorgeous man. A man who currently had a pink wristlet dangling from his thick forearm.

"Which hotel are you guys at?"

I gave him the name, still wondering how he knew Ben and why he was being so nice to me.

"I'll get a car."

I'd taken the Metro here but figured trying to get a drunk Ben on and off the subway wasn't an adventure I particularly wanted to experience right now. Or ever. Not to mention he didn't need paparazzi. We wouldn't want someone to realize who he was and start snapping pictures—especially given that Paris was crawling with photographers during Fashion Week.

I sat in the back of the car, wedged between the two men.

Ben took my hand and held it in his lap. He leaned his head back against the seat rest and mumbled apologies to me.

"Braydon?"

"Hmm?"

I was too aware of his body heat next to mine, his leg occasionally bumping my thigh. "You don't think he . . . took something, do you?"

"Drugs? Nah. Ben doesn't touch that shit. Never has."

I wasn't sure how Braydon knew that, or the extent of their relationship, but his confidence set my mind at ease.

When we reached the hotel, I woke Ben and he seemed to have sobered up a bit on the twenty-minute ride back. Once inside the room, he fell heavily onto the bed, leaving Braydon and me standing awkwardly at the foot of the mattress, staring at each other.

"Emmy, come here . . ." Ben pulled me down onto the bed with him and nuzzled into my neck, breathing in the scent of my hair. His hand moved from my waist down to my behind, cupping my bottom and giving it a gentle squeeze.

He turned to address Braydon. "Thanks for the lift, but time to go, Bray."

Braydon chuckled softly. "I don't think so, man. It's called whiskey dick. You're not getting any tonight. Besides, you wouldn't be much use to her." Braydon's navy-blue gaze met mine and I shuddered.

Ben's grip on me tightened. "I always make Emmy come."

Gah! "Okay, story time's over." I excused myself from Ben's grasp as my cheeks heated. Apparently Ben needed a muzzle when he was drunk. I crossed the room and grabbed the phone. "I think I'll order some room service. See if giving him something to eat helps." I looked at Braydon. "Would you like something?"

Braydon smiled lightly, removing my purse from his arm and handing it to me. "Sure. I could stay for a bit."

I ordered sandwiches and bottles of water and we sat on the bed and ate. Ben nibbled at his, but I was happy to see him drink an entire bottle of water. He then stripped down to his boxer briefs and lay down on the bed, obviously not shy about getting undressed in front of another man. Braydon and I exchanged a smile. I was relieved to have the company, and to have Ben safely tucked into bed.

The shrill ring of a cell phone startled my eyes away from Braydon's. Ben leaned over the side of the bed and dragged the phone from his discarded pants pocket before groaning and tossing the phone on the bed beside him.

Braydon reached for the still-ringing phone and checked the screen. "It's Fiona."

"It's after midnight. What could she possibly want?" I couldn't help the disdain in my voice.

Ben exchanged a knowing glance with Braydon. There was something big yet completely unspoken being communicated between them. "Don't tell Emmy about Fiona," Ben muttered softly.

"I think you just did." Braydon's eyes met mine, studying, watching for my reaction, but I gave him none. "Call me if you need anything. Ben has my number in his phone," he said, finally.

I nodded, still too stunned to speak.

I wanted to go to my own room, to shower, to change. Maybe have a good cry. But Ben tugged me down to the bed just seconds after the door closed behind Braydon and folded his body around mine.

"You feel so good," he murmured, his lips brushing the skin at the back of my neck.

I let him hold me, unable, or unwilling, to tell him to let go.

16

Ben

I had the next several days off, and now that the craziness of Fashion Week was behind us, Emmy and I enjoyed some sightseeing in Paris. I felt bad about getting so drunk at the afterparty. Emmy had taken good care of me, and I wanted to make it up to her.

We lounged on a blanket on the expansive lawn in front of the Eiffel Tower, she lying in the warm sun and me quietly reading beside her. I felt her watch me as I read. I was used to being looked at, critiqued . . . but the way Emmy looked at me was different. I skimmed the pages, feeling her gaze take in the way my lips moved as I read, watching my fingers turn the pages. She lifted her sunglasses, wanting an unobstructed view.

"What?"

"Have you and Braydon really shared a woman?" she asked, eyes squinting on mine.

I set the book down beside me. "Yes."

"More than one?"

I wanted to be honest with her. "A couple. Does that bother you?"

"No." Her eyes darted away from mine, looking longingly at the sunglasses she'd discarded. There was something she didn't want me to know.

"It is something you'd like to try?" I asked.

She swallowed heavily. "I don't know."

Individually, Braydon and I were no match for a woman. But together, the two of us were devastating. We'd attracted some of the world's hottest supermodels. It was all in good fun, but something about doing that with Emmy felt wrong. She caused the alpha male in me to want to mark my territory. She was off limits, not to be shared. But unless I read her wrong, I could tell the idea of Braydon and me moving against her, two rock-hard cocks to stroke and suck, was getting her hot. I cataloged her reaction. Her pulse quickened, fluttering wildly against her neck, and her nipples pebbled against the front of her tank top.

"Interesting. I wouldn't have taken you for a threesome type of girl."

"I'm not." Her voice was tiny, a little broken murmur of uncertainty. She bit her bottom lip, her eyes blinking up at mine in complete surrender. She may have never considered it before, but it was obvious she was now. I was willing to bet if I reached a hand inside her panties, I'd find her wet.

I wasn't sure how I felt about that. She wasn't mine. I'd

made that clear. And now I was being a selfish prick. If this was something she wanted, I should give it to her. If only to prove to myself that I could.

"Ben?"

"Hmm?"

"Fiona called last night after midnight. And Braydon didn't seem surprised she was calling."

My gaze dropped from hers down to the blanket. *Shit.*

"She's not one of the women you two shared, was she?"

My heart throbbed in my chest. She'd asked me directly about Fiona and I didn't see any way to avoid it. I knew she wasn't going to be happy, though, and I didn't enjoy the thought of hurting her.

"Did you and Braydon sleep with Fiona?" she prompted.

"Would that bother you?"

"To know that you had sex with Fiona? Yes." Her voice was firm and I could only imagine the many thoughts swirling inside her head. "Was it just once?" Her wide gray-blue eyes blinked twice, finding mine.

With Braydon? "Yes." I knew I wasn't being entirely truthful, but my answer to her question was honest. It was the best I could do.

She twisted her hands in her lap.

I couldn't help reaching for her, cupping her jaw to lift her chin. "Hey. Are you okay?" I whispered.

She nodded. "I guess so."

I smiled and leaned in to softly kiss her mouth. "It wasn't a big deal. Okay?"

Emmy stayed quiet. I prayed we could move past this. I didn't want my past with Fiona fucking up my present with Emmy. She straightened her posture, but I couldn't help but notice the movement shifted her farther away from me on the blanket.

Emmy

The fact that Ben had been intimate with Fiona was devastating. I couldn't help picturing Ben kissing her, his mouth moving over her throat, his hands gripping her hips. I squeezed my eyes shut. My breath caught in my throat like someone was sitting on my chest. She was the anti-me, my nemesis. How could he have been with someone like her?

During the last several weeks, I'd convinced myself that Ben and I were growing closer—if not a real couple, at least moving in that direction. But if he was willing to share me with his friend, how serious could he actually be about me?

Maybe that was exactly why I shouldn't question this. If Ben was okay with it, shouldn't I be? This was all just casual exploration. I was in Paris, the most romantic and seductive city in the world with the opportunity to enjoy the company and intimacy of two male models. I knew what Ellie would say. Go for it! So why was my stomach in knots? And why did my mind keep replaying the subtle way his jaw had tightened when I'd acted open to the idea? Part of me wanted this—if only for the chance to read Ben's reaction, to see if this really was okay with him.

I quieted the portion of my brain yelling at me that this was nothing more than a sick little competition. The need to conquer something that Fiona had done wasn't healthy, and I hated myself for thinking that way. I shouldn't need to compete with her. It was childish and petty, but it was how I felt. No denying that fact.

I just needed to shut off my brain and let my body take the lead.

Ben and I hadn't talked about Braydon again, but several days later an envelope was delivered to my room midmorning. I slid out the thick notecard.

Join Braydon and me for dinner and drinks—8 p.m.—
Grand Capri
    I'll send a car for you at 7:45

                                                            Ben

He wasn't asking. He was telling. But before I had time to freak out or ponder his intentions, another knock at the door grabbed my attention. The concierge delivered a large box. I carried it inside and placed it on the bed. Lifting the top, and shoving aside mountains of white tissue paper, I discovered a dress. Not just any dress, but an evening gown. My mouth dropped open. It was a Vera Wang: sleek and expensive-looking black silk, halter-style top with built-in bra cups, and a long slit cut up one side. It was a classic style that I knew would still be stylish years from now. I hugged the soft material to my chest, savoring the feel of it. I'd never owned something so pretty.

Moving aside more tissue paper, I lifted a shoebox from the bottom of the package. A pair of shiny black Christian Louboutin platform heels. There was a note inside of the shoes—on a damn Post-it of all things—that said: *Only what you can handle.*

My blood pumped erratically and a hot shiver ran through my body.

What did that mean? If all I wanted was dinner and then to come back here alone, or just with Ben, that'd be fine? Or if I wanted them both . . . was that on the table, too? God, this was awkward. What had he said to Braydon? No. That was crazy. Just because I was a bit curious did not mean I was going to go through with it. I was willing to go out with them tonight, but that was it.

I had all day to ponder these and loads of other questions before my date. But it also afforded me the luxury of time to get ready. I figured a long bath would help me relax and I could devote some much-needed attention to my neglected e-reader. Pity, my mind was spinning.

A text from Ben that afternoon asked how I was feeling.

Me: Nervous

I chuckled at the brutal honesty in my response. So much for playing it cool.

Ben: Don't be, baby. Remember, only what you can handle

His words did nothing to calm me. He sounded so in control, so certain. I could only hope he was, because I was neither.

Ben: I'm sending someone over to help you get ready. She'll be there at 5:30—if that's okay with you . . .

Me: Sure

I wasn't used to having someone fuss over me, but if Ben thought it would help, this was his world, and I was just playing in it.

I bathed, shaved, and smoothed sweet-smelling cream on my arms and legs. I had just finished blow-drying my hair when Lucia arrived at five thirty. I was slightly worried she'd just be in my way, but I couldn't have been more wrong. She quickly took charge, introduced herself with a friendly handshake, then unpacked her black rolling suitcase full of makeup and various hair-styling instruments. She directed me to sit and then assessed my skin and features. I was relieved to hear she spoke fluent English. Ben had thought of everything.

"What type of look would you like?"

I had no idea. "Oh, just something natural."

"What colors are you wearing tonight?"

"A black dress and shoes."

She nodded. "Special occasion?"

Heat flooded my cheeks as a wave of embarrassment washed over me. How did I explain my situation with a model who wasn't quite my boyfriend, yet I wanted him to be . . . and that I'd be going on a date with him and his equally delicious model friend for an apparent threesome? No . . . that wasn't something you told people. Though I knew Ellie was likely to get it out of me, especially if tequila—or as I liked to call it, truth serum—was ever involved. "Something like that," I offered.

Lucia applied natural makeup: dusted bronzer across my cheeks and forehead, lined my eyes with charcoal, applied several coats of mascara, and dabbed my lips in rosy-pink gloss before handing me a mirror. I loved it. I looked elegant and very pretty. Having this special treatment made me feel confident and put together. A small miracle, considering how nervous I was about tonight.

I felt like a princess getting made up for her wedding day. When in actuality, somehow I found myself headed off for a date with two men. I wondered how Ben really felt about this. I knew he wasn't looking for anything serious with me, but when I'd brought it up, his jaw had gone tense and his whole body posture had changed. Unless I had imagined it.

When I'd learned of his past of sharing women with Braydon, I was surprised more than anything. Heck, I didn't think that kind of thing actually happened outside of porn videos. I'd never been particularly drawn to the idea of ménage. Yet the idea of Ben, and another man—not just any man, but Braydon—both pleasuring me was like system overload. I couldn't deny my curiosity.

After my makeup was done, Lucia curled my hair in big, loose waves and ran her fingers through before setting it with hairspray. I never took the time to style it this way, and I loved what she'd done.

After she packed up and left, I took my evening gown into the bathroom to get dressed. Since the style couldn't accommodate a bra, the only undergarment I put on was a tiny scrap of pink lace, one of the few thongs I'd packed.

The smooth silk glided over my hips and fell into place, brushing the tops of my ankles. I tied the halter straps behind my neck, letting the silky ribbons form a bow. I took in the plunging neckline that hugged my breasts perfectly. I'd been worried about going without a bra, but this seemed to work.

The addition of my little diamond-studded earrings made me feel a little more like me. When I turned to face the mirror, I barely recognized the girl staring back. She looked sophisticated, confident, and sexy. Inside, my emotions were a mess of nerves and insecurity. But at least it didn't show on my face.

I shoved my feet inside the beautiful pumps and wiggled my toes. The peep toe opening showed a glimpse of my red toenail polish. I was ready as I'd ever be.

Ben arrived alone in a black limousine. I was grateful for that. I didn't think I could handle seeing him and Braydon together quite yet. He stepped out of the limo and greeted me on the curb. He looked dashing—smart and sinfully sexy in a black Armani suit and black shirt open at the neck to expose his sexy throat. The dark clothing made his eyes stand out, shining brighter than usual and looking more green than hazel today.

He bent to kiss my cheek, and the intoxicating scent of his cologne washed over me. "You look lovely," he whispered, sending a shiver down my spine. His gaze lingered at my breasts, which were squeezed together by the form-fitting dress, before his eyes finally lifted and settled on mine.

"Are you sure you're okay with this?" I asked.

"This is for you, Emmy. It can be anything you want."

I couldn't help but notice he didn't answer the question. His hand on the small of my back led me to the limo and I climbed inside. It was dimly lit and spacious—the smell of leather and a trace of Ben's cologne were waiting for me inside.

Sitting down across from me, he lifted a bottle of champagne from an ice bucket. "Would you like a glass?"

"Something stronger if you have it," I murmured, arranging the dress around my legs.

He nodded thoughtfully and poured us each a measure of vodka over ice and added a splash of cranberry juice, almost as an afterthought.

"Thank you," I said, accepting the glass and taking a sip. Mother, that was strong.

"It'll be just a few minutes for us to pick up Braydon, and then about a twenty-minute drive to the restaurant."

I nodded. "Fine." I focused on my drink, suddenly unable to meet his eyes at the mention of Braydon's name. Why should I feel guilty for wanting this? It wasn't cheating since Ben approved and he'd be there with us. Nor was I in a real relationship with Ben. Besides, I wasn't entirely certain that anything would even happen.

The alcohol on my empty stomach had an immediate effect, relaxing me despite the quiet intensity radiating off Ben. He didn't once take his eyes off me.

When we arrived at Braydon's hotel, he opened the door and climbed in, choosing to sit beside Ben so they were both facing me.

"Damn, jelly bean." His eyes roamed my exposed skin, taking in my dress and heels.

I smiled shyly while Ben handed him a bottle of beer, seeming to anticipate his drink of choice.

"She looks good enough to eat," he told Ben, accepting the drink and taking a long sip, his eyes never leaving mine. "I bet she tastes even better."

A zip of heat flashed up my spine.

"She's fucking delicious. Sweetest pussy I've ever had," Ben whispered, his husky voice dropping lower as his eyes traveled along my cleavage once again.

Braydon swallowed roughly, his Adam's apple bobbing in his throat. "Is she bare?"

"Completely. She's soft and smooth." Ben's voice was a low growl.

Oh. My. God. My pulse hammered behind my ears. They were talking about my lady parts like I wasn't even here!

Ben moved across the limo, settling on the seat beside me. His fingertips moved to my neck, trailing softly and tilting my jaw so he could press his lips to my fluttering pulse. He laid delicate, damp kisses all along my jaw and throat. His lips moved up my neck, kissing my cheeks softly before pressing a tender kiss to my mouth.

My eyes slipped closed, enjoying the attention. Ben's coarse cheek against my skin sent sparks of heat between my legs. When I opened my eyes, rather than looking at Ben, who continued softly kissing me all over, my gaze wandered to Braydon, on the seat across from us. His beer sat abandoned in the cup holder and the growing erection in his dress pants was obvious. He was enjoying the show.

Ben's hands moved to untie the ribbon behind my neck, and my heart slammed wildly in my chest. Panic gripped me but I was too turned on to stop him. Once I was exposed to Braydon, I knew there'd be no going back. But I didn't want to stop this. Ben's deft fingers did away with the tie and lightly caressed my skin as the halter top was unfastened.

Braydon's deep, penetrating gaze slipped from mine to watch as the dress dropped away from my chest. My breasts, aching and heavy, responded instantly to the cool air conditioning, my nipples hardening.

Ben's eyes met mine as his hands lovingly cupped my breasts, softly stroking his thumbs across my nipples as he watched my reaction. I pulled in a shaky breath, sucking my bottom lip into my mouth.

Hitting the button for the intercom, Braydon spoke in French to the driver, telling him to keep driving, I presumed. Then he came to my other side. I was flanked by two gorgeous men. Never in my wildest dreams had I ever imagined being part of a scene like this, but I was undeniably turned on and excited by the idea of it.

I'd assumed we'd take things slowly, share conversation, dinner, plenty of drinks to up my courage, giving me time to feel out the situation and see if I wanted more. Apparently, they were not okay with waiting. But the damp spot in my panties told me neither was I.

Braydon's hand cupped my breast and he rolled my nipple between his thumb and forefinger, emitting a soft groan when his palm made contact with my plump flesh. "Can I taste you, jelly bean?" The top of my dress rested in my lap, my breasts fully exposed.

I nodded and watched as he lowered his head, his mouth softly closing around the tip of my breast and suckling gently. His warm tongue licked me in easy strokes while Ben moved in to kiss my neck once again. Ben's warm mouth moving against my neck, and Braydon's damp tongue teasing my nipples, was all too much. I squirmed in the seat, whimpering loudly, and gripped a hand on each of their thighs. There was no denying they were both rock hard in their dress slacks.

Ben broke away from the kiss—his breathing accelerated and eyes filled with desire. Braydon slowed his movements, kissing and nibbling each of my breasts while Ben lifted my skirt to find the lacy edge of my thong. He tugged it down to my knees and over my calves, carefully disentangling it from my heels. Then he stuffed it into his suit coat pocket without a word. His eyes held mine and I nearly whimpered at how sexy he was when he was in control like this. I was his to use as he saw fit. And I knew he'd take care of me and make me feel good.

With the dress bunched around my waist, Ben pushed my thighs apart and Braydon trailed ticklish fingertips up my inner thigh. I'd never been intimate with someone I barely knew, but somehow I already felt comfortable around Braydon. He was open and sweet and he'd helped me selflessly the other night with Ben. I already had a certain level of trust with him, and of course he was exquisitely gorgeous. Where Ben was dark and intense, Braydon was open and friendly.

Ben's fingers spread my plump lips, revealing my pink center, and Braydon groaned. "Fuck, that's a beautiful pussy."

I looked down, feeling self-conscious about being so exposed and quite obviously turned on—I was glistening wet.

Braydon's large palm slid up my thigh, stopping just before he reached my sex. He'd paused to gauge my reaction. My eyelids fluttered in weak desperation, and taking that as a sign of reassurance, the pad of his thumb brushed against me. I shivered as the rough digit swept circles around my swollen clit.

"I want to watch you come, see this beautiful pussy get nice and wet." Braydon's voice was deep and washed in desire.

I loved knowing how hot I was getting these two men without even touching them. I nodded and his hand cupped my sex, his palm pressing against my clit. Pleasure shot through me. He slowly slid one finger inside me, groaning as his first then second knuckle disappeared inside as though the act of penetrating me was physically torturing him.

Ben laved attention on my breasts, sucking and licking more greedily than Braydon had. I curled my fingers in his hair and moaned. The action pushed my hips closer into Braydon's hand and his pace increased.

Between Ben's wicked mouth teasing my breasts and Braydon's fingers pumping into me, my orgasm came hard and fast, slamming against me unexpectedly.

Tossing my head back against the cool leather seat, four hands held me steady as little tremors racked my body. Ben's mouth crashed into mine, our tongues tangling as I let out a final cry of pleasure.

Holy shit, that was intense.

More intense than anything I'd ever experienced. And all they'd done was kiss and touch me in a few strategic places. I needed to pull it together. Ben pulled my thong from his pocket and slid it back up my legs, dropping one more soft kiss on my mouth.

The limo stopped and a smooth male voice spoke over the intercom. Braydon pressed a button and answered the driver in fluent French. Ben handed me my purse and took my hand. This was like a well-orchestrated event and I was the main attraction. It was almost too much. It bothered me how proficient they were at this. It was quite obvious other women had been treated to this same ecstasy.

Ben watched me with guarded eyes, checking to make sure I was okay with what had just happened, and I pushed the silent doubts away, determined to make the most of my magical night.

Ben helped me from the car, my legs still shaky, and guided me toward the door while Braydon trailed behind. Ben laced his fingers between mine, the action somehow possessive. Even if he was willing to share me with Braydon, our joined hands said we were a couple.

I felt at ease as we entered the beautifully decorated restaurant. Light tones in creams and whites contrasted with the dark mahogany floor. The lighting was dim; just scattered sconces and soft glowing candles dotted each linen-clothed tabletop.

I felt a little self-conscious being out with two men, like everyone knew what we were up to, what had just happened in the limo. But, of course, they didn't. They were probably just ogling these two male models. And who could blame them? Braydon and Ben glided across the floor like they owned the place. I merely tried not to call attention to my trembling legs and still-flushed cheeks.

Ben pulled out my chair, and he and Braydon waited until I'd slid into the seat before gracefully lowering themselves into their own, like all of our moves were coordinated. Their eyes, still heavy with desire, watched my every move. As the server came by to fill our water goblets, I couldn't help but wonder if they were each still hard and ready under the table.

I could hardly focus on the menu with the memory of our erotic limo ride still clouding my senses. Somehow I heard Ben suggest the filet and an accompanying glass of red wine. I merely nodded. It sounded delicious, even if my appetite was nowhere to be found.

Our drinks were delivered—a bottle of red wine for me and Ben, and a tall glass of beer for Braydon. He made me smile. It seemed that regardless of his opulent surroundings, he was comfortable in his skin. He'd removed his suit jacket and rolled his shirtsleeves to his elbows. Ben remained the epitome of classic handsome sophistication. Forget the filet, he made my mouth water.

Even if they were both sexy models with truckloads of self-confidence, Braydon and Ben were each very different. As we talked, I learned Braydon's upbringing mirrored mine: two loving parents, suburban home, and public school education. Rather than starting in modeling right away, he went to a university for two years before being discovered at the university gym.

"I began small, doing photo shoots for fitness magazines, which eventually led to national campaigns and now international work as well," Braydon explained while peeling at the label of his bottle of beer. He'd refused the pint glass he'd been offered, much to the server's dismay. "Shortly after, I left college, no longer passionate about the business degree I was pursuing, and started living out of a suitcase, traveling the world for various modeling jobs."

"How did the two of you meet?" I looked between them, wondering who would answer.

Ben nodded once to Bray.

"Our paths crossed numerous times over the past several years, usually Fashion Week in Milan or Paris, and of course New York City. We started hanging out and just sort of clicked."

I nodded. I could see that they were comfortable around each other, even if they were quite different. Ben was more reserved, an observer, and when he coolly raked the room with those brilliant hazel eyes fringed in dark lashes, women and men alike took notice. Maybe it was because it seemed like he'd pose a challenge, or because they just wanted to see him direct that haunted gaze their way, but he had women clamoring for him, trying to get him to smile, and men wanting to strike up a casual conversation. He just didn't seem real somehow. He was too stunningly handsome.

Our meal was delivered and my nerves settled just slightly.

"So how long have you two been together?" Braydon asked as we ate.

I expected Ben to correct him. To tell him we weren't together.

"About a month now," Ben said instead, his knee brushing mine under the table.

I forced the piece of meat down my throat. *Interesting . . .*

When dessert was offered, I opted for a berry torte. Ben and Braydon passed, each looking at me hungrily. Oh my, apparently I was on their dessert menu later. The thought was dizzying. The way Ben watched me take slow, tentative bites of the torte made me wonder if he thought I was purposely drawing out our meal. And maybe I was; but the truth was, this dessert shouldn't be rushed. Sweet berries burst on my tongue and the flaky pastry was light enough to melt in my mouth. It was heaven.

"What made you change your mind?" Braydon asked, polishing off the last of his beer. "I thought you said you didn't share Emmy."

Ben exhaled slowly, his gaze settling on mine. "Tonight is for her. Whatever she wants."

Braydon nodded slightly.

All too soon, we'd finished our drinks and Ben paid the check. Then he rose to help me from my chair. Which was good because I didn't think my legs could be counted on to work properly just then. I pulled a deep breath into my lungs, wondering how the rest of tonight would play out.

Ben

Emmy was silent on the limo ride back to our hotel. And I was grateful for Braydon's nonstop chatter on the latest basketball stats for his favorite team. It wasn't something I followed, but I appreciated his effort to fill the silence. I had no fucking clue what I was doing. The idea of anyone else touching Emmy was fucking giving me a migraine. She'd come so easily for Braydon, and I knew that shouldn't bother me, but it did. I could tell how proud of himself he'd been, that smug smile on his face. My hands had clenched into fists with the desire to wipe it from his face.

Shit. I'd agreed to this—for her—but damn if I wasn't having doubts. I needed to man-the-fuck-up. She wasn't mine. I'd told her that time and again. This shouldn't matter to me. Yet it did. It'd be a serious lesson in restraint to keep from punching Braydon in the jaw when he touched her later. Even the way his hand reached for her, resting against her lower back as we led her to and from the car, annoyed me. How was I going to handle him putting his dick anywhere near her?

I poured myself another healthy measure of vodka and downed it, hoping to turn off my brain for the night. It clearly wasn't working correctly. It wasn't the head I was supposed to be thinking with, anyhow.

I met Emmy's wide eyes from across the limo. Her breathing was shallow and fast, and her eyes moved between each of our forms. She didn't seem bothered by what had happened earlier—more like turned on, curious, and eager. I both liked that and didn't. She was this sweet girl from Tennessee, loving and tender, but with a naughty side, too. It was confusing as hell.

Fuck it. I slammed another drink just as our limousine pulled to a stop. I needed to be more drunk to deal with this shit.

17

Emmy

Once inside his hotel room, Ben seemed to need to mark his territory, to claim me as his before anything else took place. While Braydon poured us another drink, Ben lifted me into his arms, held me snugly against his chest, and kissed me deeply. His actions confused me. He was so tender, so loving, it seemed contradictory to what tonight was all about. But I wasn't about to complain. This was Ben. This was what I'd wanted all along.

He pressed one more soft kiss to my mouth then lowered my feet to the floor. Though with these sky-high heels I was still several inches shorter than him, we were a bit more on a level playing field. The top of my head at least grazed his chin. He kissed my forehead and his eyes locked on mine. I tried to read whatever he was trying to tell me but couldn't determine whether his haunted gaze was indecision or just concern for me. I swallowed and stepped away.

Braydon turned to face us, directing his attention to Ben. "You sure you're okay with this?"

"Why wouldn't I be?" Ben asked, his voice flat.

I pulled in a shaky breath as Braydon crossed the room to stand directly in front of me. He brushed his fingertips past my jaw and dropped a light kiss on my lips. It was so light, I wondered if I'd imagined the contact. He dropped to his knees and removed my heels one by one. As I stepped out of them, my height was reduced by a good six inches.

"Fun sized," he said with a chuckle and rose to his feet again.

I smiled at him. He made this feel so easy and relaxed me instantly. It was like we weren't getting ready to have a three-some, but just three friends hanging out, flirting, and seeing where the night took us. Realistically, I think we all had a good idea where it was headed.

They each softly petted me, smoothing hands up my bare arms, brushing the hair off my neck to tenderly kiss me there, caressing my hips. Ben cupped my bottom and squeezed. Their dual attention was dizzying and turning me on.

Braydon tilted my chin up to meet his eyes. "Are you ready for me?" I let my gaze wander down to the large erection tenting his slacks. "You've already got me hard," he growled.

I bit my lip, sizing up the rather impressive bulge. Braydon gave it a squeeze and adjusted himself.

"I want to see." I surprised myself by finding my voice.

Braydon smiled lazily and began unbuttoning his pants. "Anything for you, jelly bean." He pressed my hand against the bulge in his pants. "See what you do to me?" I squeezed him and he released a soft groan. He began slowly pulling his belt free from the loops. "You want to see what a real man looks like?"

Ben gave his shoulder a playful shove, and my tummy turned with nerves. My nervousness evaporated as Ben tilted my chin up and kissed me. Sure, it felt a little strange to be kissing one man while I stroked another, but not as strange as I would have thought. It was Ben after all, someone I had totally fallen for, and he and Braydon had done this several times before. It was obviously something they were comfortable with. I loosened up and went with it.

Now free of his belt, Braydon slipped the pants down over his hips. I noticed several things at once: He went commando. His size was comparable to Ben's. Long and firm, but with a thick vein coursing up his length. Shaved completely. And a silver barbell piercing the head. *Whoa.*

"What the fuck is that?" Ben asked with a frown, looking at Braydon.

I followed his gaze down to the silver ring piercing the head of Braydon's cock. "It's an APA." Braydon shrugged, like having a piercing down there was no big deal. "I'm not allowed to get piercings or tattoos," he explained, meeting my eyes.

Except, apparently, on this forbidden part of him. I remained speechless.

"He didn't have that last time," Ben explained, turning to me before directing his attention back to Braydon's offending member. "What the fuck, man? That's not going to hurt her, is it?"

Braydon laughed and tossed his head back so a rich,

throaty chuckle tumbled from his lips. "Fuck no. She'll be begging you to get one next." He smiled confidently, his hand reaching down to find his cock, stroking it slowly up and over the head and the piercing.

I had to admit, I was curious. I had no clue how that thing would feel inside me. But I was hesitant to touch him for fear of doing something wrong. He could read the indecision on my face, his eyes zeroing in on my mouth, where my teeth grazed my bottom lip.

"Come here, Emmy," Braydon whispered, his eyes heavy with desire. "Touch me."

His hand closed around mine, showing me what he liked. Light grip, long measured strokes moving up and down to caress his whole length, include the piercing. His head dropped back and his eyes slipped closed.

I looked to Ben for his reaction. His face remained calm, his expression unreadable as he watched my eyes. I continued slowly stroking Braydon as his breathing stuttered in his chest. He felt foreign in my hand. His skin was warm, as was the barbell, but he was different. I'd grown used to Ben in these last several weeks.

I felt Ben move behind me. His hands captured my hips and he tugged my ass back to greet his hardened length. He untied the knot in my halter dress just like he had in the limo. But this time he let the dress fall away completely so it pooled at my feet. His cock nestled into the crevice of my bottom, his hands coming up to cradle and massage my breasts.

Braydon's lips moved over my throat and collarbone

while Ben's lips moved against the back of my neck and be-tween my shoulder blades. I'd been so worried over how I could possibly please two men, but the reality of the situation was that they were pleasuring me, treating me like a god-dess. Four large hands moving over my skin, two soft mouths pressing damp kisses all over me. The sensations were over-whelming. I released my hold on Braydon to bring my hands up into Ben's hair as he kissed the back of my neck.

I sensed there was something happening between me and Ben, but I had no idea what. *Stop being delusional, Emmy; he's repeatedly told you he doesn't want a relationship!* I fought to turn off my brain and take Ellie's advice. Have fun. Don't get emotionally invested.

Ben slid my thong down my thighs and lowered himself to his knees in front of me, edging Braydon aside. "I get the first taste," he said to him.

Braydon motioned for him to go ahead, as though I was some rare and fine delicacy to be sampled and savored.

Ben kneeling before me was a beautiful sight. He raised one dark eyebrow, then without warning pressed his mouth to the juncture between my thighs. He dragged his tongue slowly across my center, sending warm darts of pleasure up through my belly. My knees buckled, but Braydon's strong grasp on my hips kept me from going down.

Ben licked and suckled in that slow, maddening rhythm I'd come to appreciate from him, while Braydon held me from behind, offering soothing caresses along my spine. Holy God, this felt amazing.

Ben was almost too good at this. My body couldn't handle the direct contact, but he knew what he was doing and he alternated lapping against my clit and pressing soft kisses against my plump lips and pubic bone. All too soon, I dug my hands into his hair and came loudly, thankful for Braydon's firm grip on my hips.

Ben rose and lazily smiled, kissing my lips. His mouth was damp from my juices and something inside me found that incredibly sexy. They each shed their remaining clothing and I stepped away from the black silk pooled at my feet.

The three of us moved to the bed. I needed to taste Ben, to show him he was mine and I was his. No matter what he said, I felt that truth deep in my heart and I was going to show him. I pushed him back against the bed and moved over him, taking his rock-hard length in my hand and letting my mouth sink down all the way until my lips met his taut stomach. He sucked in a breath, his abs tightening.

"Shit, baby," he cursed. His hands cradled my hair and I stroked him enthusiastically from base to tip while I suckled his firm length. "Fuck, Emmy . . . yeah . . . just like that."

I felt the mattress dip as Braydon moved behind me and buried his face in my upturned bottom. *Holy crap!* His tongue circled my entrance, teasing me, and I let out a small groan around Ben's thick length.

All too soon, Ben pulled himself free from my mouth. "You're going to make me come, Tennessee." My heart leapt at hearing his old nickname for me. It made things feel more intimate between us, hearing him refer to me like he did when we'd first met.

Braydon moved from the bed and sheathed himself in a condom, and I was hit with a wave of nerves, wondering what they had in store for me. Wondering if I could really go through with this.

Ben tugged me closer so that we lay facing each other in the center of the bed. "Are you sure?" he whispered, his hazel gaze searing into mine.

"Are you?" I watched him closely, determined to understand what was going on inside his head.

Rather than answer me, he looked over my shoulder and gave Braydon a nod.

I was lying on my side, half-draped over Ben, when I felt Braydon lay down behind me. Braydon kissed the back of my neck, smoothing his hands over my generous backside. "Fuck, I love this ass, jelly bean."

A nervous squeak escaped my throat as he parted my legs, positioning me so that my top leg rested over Ben's hip and Braydon's cock brushed against my center.

I whimpered as Braydon pushed forward, slowly, carefully filling me. My breath caught in my throat. It was a snug fit already, but the piercing provided added friction. There was just something so naughty about the thought of his piercing inside me. I liked it. I squeezed my eyes closed and groaned as he sunk all the way in.

"Shit," Braydon cursed. "She's so tight."

"I know," Ben bit out.

Ben hugged me to his chest, cradling me against his warm body. He kissed my forehead and allowed me to adjust to the fullness of Braydon penetrating me. When I opened my eyes and met Ben's, the tension in his jaw and blazing possessive look in his eyes caught me off guard. I kissed him, unsure what he wanted in that moment.

After several moments, he grabbed my hand, bringing it down to his cock. "Stroke me, baby," he whispered, his voice ragged.

I reached between us and gripped him, letting my hand slide all along him, gliding from base to tip.

Braydon surged forward, rocking my body against Ben's. The moment was incredibly erotic, being sandwiched between two men. Two sets of legs tangled with mine, their large hands caressing and petting me. Ben kissing my mouth, Braydon's tongue lavishing my shoulder . . . I lost myself to the rhythm, stroking Ben in the same measured tempo of Braydon's movements against me.

Ben's hand moved between my legs, pressing small circles against my clit, and already it was almost too much. I moaned out his name and he smiled, watching me closely.

"Not yet. Come with me, baby," Ben whispered against my mouth.

My body broke out in chills as I fought to slow the impending orgasm threatening to overtake me. My hips moved of their own accord, pressing against Ben's hand and pushing Braydon's cock deeper inside me. Pulses of pleasure shot through me.

"Slow up . . ." Ben's hand reached across me to press against Braydon's hip, forcing his thrusts to slow.

The tension in his expression told me Ben wasn't particularly thrilled with touching another man when they were both naked, but he did it for me. Since Braydon didn't possess the ability to read my body's reactions quite like Ben did, he directed him, ensuring my pleasure was put first. Even if another man was fucking me, he would make sure it was being done properly.

Having both of their complete attention undid me. I came harder than ever before, burying my face in Ben's chest and crying out. Ben's hand took over my disjointed movements and he firmly stroked himself until I felt warm semen flowing over our laced fingers. My pussy clenched and Braydon pressed in deep once more, groaning out his own release.

I remained cradled in Ben's arms, resting my cheek on his firm chest, enjoying the sensation of just being held. I knew it was stupid, but in that moment I felt so loved, so protected. I never wanted to leave this warm spot. And I didn't have to, because Braydon returned with warm washcloths and cleaned me off while I remained nestled against Ben. And after ditching the condom, Braydon crawled back into bed with us.

Ben lifted his head from the pillow and frowned. "What are you doing?"

"Going to sleep. Your girl drained me." Braydon tossed me a sexy smile.

"Get the fuck out. I get to hold her."

"Ben." I shoved his shoulder. It was the middle of the

night and we were all a little tipsy. Was he really going to send Braydon away? "The bed is plenty big enough."

He narrowed his eyes at Braydon. "Fine, but stay on your own fucking side. No one cuddles with Emmy but me."

"Damn cuddle hog," Braydon muttered.

"At least he's not a cock block," I joked, smiling at Braydon.

Braydon and I shared an easy laugh. I couldn't help but notice Ben's stark expression. I found it rather curious that he just let his friend fuck me but cuddling was apparently crossing the line. However, Ben had said I was his insomnia cure, so maybe he just wanted a good night's sleep. I didn't get to ponder it for long because after two men and three orgasms tonight, my body was done with all nonvital functions. Breathing and cuddling were the extent of my talents at the moment.

Sleeping in a big bed between two men was another new experience for me. I curled into Ben, relaxed and exhausted, and let him hold me.

18

Emmy

The next morning I was relieved to see Braydon had slipped out and left at some point. Even if I felt bad for Ben trying to throw him out last night, I didn't think I could handle facing him this morning. I had the man I wanted, warm and solid beside me.

Ben lazily blinked open his eyes and his mouth twitched with a smile.

"Morning." I tried not to be self-conscious about my just-woke-up appearance.

"Morning, beautiful. How are you feeling?"

I stretched and surveyed my body, taking stock of how I felt. I felt good. Better than good, actually. "Fine."

"Not sore or anything, are you?" he asked, his expression concerned.

I shook my head.

"I honestly didn't know he had that piercing." He frowned.

I smiled. "It was fine, Ben." And *fine* was code for "mind-blowing," but Ben didn't need to know all that. "Would you ever consider . . ." I looked down at the sheets, nudged up by his semierect length.

"Fuck no. I'm not crazy, sweetheart." His hand went protectively over his manhood and I giggled, snuggling into his arms. Ben wrapped me tightly in his embrace and kissed the top of my head.

The truth was, I didn't need him pierced, inked, or with any other embellishments. I loved him just the way he was. Whoa. *Liked*. I liked him. Not that other L-word. That would be very dangerous. And stupid.

Our late-morning cuddling session was interrupted by a knock at his door. Our eyes locked together in confusion. Was he expecting someone?

Ben climbed from bed and looked through the peephole. "Fuck. It's Fiona."

A cold chill zipped up my spine. What was she doing here?

"Get in the bathroom," he commanded, pulling the blankets back, urging me from the bed. The warm, safe nest we had just shared.

Without complaint, I allowed him to guide me into the bathroom. He shoved my clothes and shoes at me and hung my purse strap over my shoulder before shutting the door. I was too stunned to move. Too stunned to think. Instead, I gripped the bundle in my arms and stared at the back of the door as it promptly closed in my face.

A moment later, I heard voices fill his room. I stood naked on the cold marble floor holding the bundle of my dress and shoes.

"Messy bed . . . someone's been a busy boy," she teased.

"I was sleeping, Fiona. Did you need something?"

"I tried calling you last night. You never come see me anymore. . . ." The pout in her tone was clear. She missed him.

"I told you. It's time we both moved on."

I held my breath, waiting for her response, but she was quiet. The soft murmur of voices continued, but I struggled to make out their words. I pressed my ear to the door, trying to hear. I imagined him holding her, whispering soft words to her, knowing I was probably listening. My knees felt shaky and my stomach flipped at the thought of him touching her. He didn't want to share me with Braydon last night, but now I was getting shoved in a bathroom when Fiona came knocking? *Oh hell no . . .*

A moment later, I heard the hotel room door close, and Ben opened the bathroom door, his expression concerned.

I exited the bathroom and shoved my feet into the shoes still in my hands. I made quite a sight—dressed in an oversized T-shirt and Louboutin heels, silk Vera Wang dress wadded up in my fists.

"I'm sorry you had to hear that."

I swallowed a massive lump in my throat. "Ben, have you been fucking her?" My voice came out surprisingly calm, considering every nerve ending in my body was firing at once. I felt sick, dizzy, heartbroken, and slightly homicidal. I knew there was that one time with him and Braydon, but I couldn't handle the thought of anything more.

"She and I have a history," he said carefully. "I'll tell you anything you want to know, but now isn't the right time. I have to get ready. And if I know Fiona, she's probably ringing your room looking for you." He squeezed my shoulders softly. "Go."

I nodded.

I couldn't concentrate on anything but the impending conversation Ben and I needed to have. I showered, dressed, and went through the motions at work, but my mind was elsewhere. The beautiful evening we'd shared. The way Ben made me feel. The devastation of knowing he'd quite possibly been with Fiona this entire time.

Thankfully, Fiona didn't seem to suspect that I'd been hiding in Ben's bathroom that morning while she droned on about not seeing him anymore. I could barely look at her, but she didn't seem to notice or care how coolly I was behaving toward her.

Finally, I made my way back to the hotel and collapsed onto my bed. My phone pinged with a new text.

Ben: Are you back?

Me: Yes

Ben: Can I take you to dinner?

I considered his request. I knew I should be hungry. I'd barely eaten all day. But food was the last thing on my mind. Not to mention, if we were going to have an emotionally charged discussion, I'd rather not do it in public.

Me: I'd rather just talk.

Ben: Okay, I'll come down to your room in a few.

Me: See you then.

Nerves took flight in my belly and I paced the room waiting for him. I had no idea what he would tell me. Would this be the end of us? Even though I had been expecting it, the knock at my door startled me.

Ben looked exhausted. The dark circles under his eyes and his defeated posture indicated he'd spent the day worrying, much like I had. I wanted to hug him, collapse against his chest, bury my face in his scent, and forget about everything else. Forget that Fiona had invaded our peaceful bubble this morning, forget that he'd rudely shoved me into the bathroom. And most important, forget how he'd continually held me at a distance, insisting this was merely physical when I felt so much more.

"Can I come in?"

I realized I was just standing there, blocking the doorway. I stepped aside and motioned him forward. Ben sat down next to me on the bed and sucked in a deep breath.

"I have some questions." My voice was tiny and unsure.

He nodded, solemnly looking down at his hands. "I'll tell you whatever you want to know."

My stomach knotted into a painful mess of nerves. I wished I could live in blissful ignorance but I had to know. Straightening my shoulders, I met his eyes. "Are you and Fiona lovers?" No sense beating around the bush.

Ben didn't flinch, didn't give away any physical clue that

this line of questioning made him uncomfortable. "We were, yes." He watched my eyes, checking for my reaction.

I suddenly felt sick, my worst fears confirmed. I fought the urge to curl into the fetal position and stared back at him, too captivated to look away. I gulped in a lungful of air. I had to know. "When . . . how often . . ."

Ben shifted on the bed, the first sign that he was uncomfortable. "We've spent a lot of time together . . . occasionally it got physical."

"And you and Braydon . . . together . . . you shared her?"

He nodded. "Yes, that was just once, as I told you."

I unconsciously scooted away from him. "How long has this been going on?" My voice was tiny, just a rasp as my throat threatened to close.

"Fiona was my first. So . . . since I was eighteen."

Holy fuck! He was twenty-three now. Five fucking years? He'd been sleeping with her for five years? Not to mention you never forgot your first. Never. *She* was the friend of his mom's that had taken his virginity. I felt physically ill. They were forever linked through their ongoing and obviously intimate affair.

I'd always had this underlying suspicion that she was in love with him, and now I understood why. Their relationship was so much deeper and more complicated than I'd ever imagined. It wasn't some drunken hookup after a Fashion Week party with Braydon like I'd originally assumed. It was so much more.

Ben shifted closer and reached for my hand. I quickly snatched it away, fisting my hands in my lap.

"It was just sex, Emmy. It didn't mean anything."

I wanted to hit something. If he honestly believed sex didn't mean anything—especially an ongoing relationship with the same person for five years—he was an idiot. "I hate that she knows every intimate detail about you . . . things I thought were ours . . . she's felt you inside of her . . . many more times than I have."

He hung his head. "I'm sorry. I should have told you sooner. I haven't been with her in months. Since before you and I got together."

I felt so naïve. It was too much to take in. He'd never said we were exclusive . . . yet still, I'd never imagined something like this. I felt hurt, betrayed, shattered into a million pieces. My poor heart thumped unevenly in my chest.

"How dare you wrap me up in this . . . seduce me . . . say it was just sex . . . all the while knowing Fiona is my boss, who I already have a tough relationship with. Did you ever even think about my career? What she'd do to me when she found out you weren't sleeping with her because you had a new plaything?"

He didn't respond but his eyes widened, telling me he hadn't considered it.

As I sat on the edge of my bed, my knee bouncing wildly, several things clicked into place at once. Suddenly everything made sense. The fact that he'd only slept with three girls before me was a result of his ongoing affair with Fiona. He didn't need to date, or go looking for a hookup. She traveled with him wherever he went, cock-blocked him from dating other girls, and gave him regular sex. God, I hated her.

"Ben, I can't do this."

He bit down, his eyes blazing with fire. "I've spent the whole day trying to figure out how to tell you this. . . . I don't want anyone else, Emmy. And after last night with Braydon, I don't ever want to see anyone touch you again. I want you to be mine. I want a real relationship—just you and me. And now I've apparently fucked it up before we even got started."

I didn't argue; I just twisted my hands in my lap, unsure how I felt about his little declaration. Was he just saying all that because I was mad about Fiona?

"Do you want me to go?" His voice was soft and low.

I nodded, unable to meet his eyes. "Yes. I need to think. Alone," I added.

He released a slow breath. "I'm sorry, Emmy. I told you my past was fucked up. I knew I'd ruin things somehow. But I swear, I never slept with her once you and I started seeing each other."

I had no doubt she'd propositioned him several times, so his abstaining should have made me feel better. But it was a shitty consolation prize. "I need time." And I needed an ugly cry. No one needed to see that.

"Okay," he said softly, rising from the bed. He bent down and pressed a tender kiss to my forehead. "I'm sorry."

The door closing behind him was an ominous sound. I curled into a ball on the center of the bed, wrapping my arms around myself. I felt sick, humiliated, completely disoriented.

I let myself fall apart, sobbing quietly into a pillow until it was thoroughly soaked and I'd given myself a headache.

Sometime later, I rose from the bed, heading off in search of a pain reliever.

When I caught my reflection in the bathroom mirror, I winced at the girl staring back at me. My eyes were puffy and swollen; my hair was tangled and damp around my face from the onslaught of tears. I needed to pull it together.

I swallowed two pain relievers with a glass of lukewarm tap water and splashed cool water on my cheeks. I grabbed my phone and crawled back into bed. It was stupid, considering I'd kicked him out, but still, the ache in my chest intensified at seeing I had no new messages.

I dialed Ellie, too dazed to even calculate what time it was in New York.

She answered on the third ring. "Emmy!"

"Hi," I croaked. Damn voice sounded like a man. *Awesome.*

"Em? What's wrong?"

In some ways I was relieved she instantly knew something wasn't right. I didn't think I was capable of pretending, or making polite small talk right now. I took a deep breath and pulled the covers up to my chest. "You know my bitch of a boss who I hate?"

"Fiona, right?"

"Yeah. Well, I just found out Ben's been sleeping with her on and off for five years."

"Christ."

"Yeah." I let that sink in and fought off a fresh wave of tears. Speaking the words out loud was about to turn me into a faucet again.

"So he's been seeing you both? Fucking asshole."

"No. He said he hasn't been with her since he and I began . . . whatever it was we had."

"Do you believe him?" she asked, her voice rising in uncertainty.

I swallowed the lump in my throat. "Yeah. I think so. I don't think he'd lie about it. He's told me whatever I asked. And he's been with me pretty much every night, so . . ."

"Ohh-kay . . ." Ellie drew out the word, like she was mulling something over. "You guys were just casual . . . physical . . . no strings attached . . . not exclusive . . . right?"

"I guess," I confirmed.

"Hmm. And he said the relationship with her is over . . . now that he's seeing you?"

"Yeah."

"I'm sorry, Emmy. You're my girl and I've got your back no matter what, so if you tell me we need to castrate him, we will. We'll put it on the fucking calendar and it's done. But babe, honestly . . . you knew how he approached relationships. And this was something he was doing long before he met you. And then stopped once he started seeing you."

I blew out a frustrated breath. "You think I'm overreacting?" I quickly remembered the date and noted it was possible that PMS was rearing its ugly head a few days early.

"Well . . . it's possible that this feels like a bigger deal because it was with Fiona—who you despise. But it's totally up to you. Do you even want to continue this fuck-buddies relationship if your heart's in the game and his isn't? That can be dangerous, too."

I remembered Ben's solemn look when he told me he wanted to do this for real—no one but us. "Actually, he told me today that he wanted a real relationship with me. Just the two of us . . . no one else."

Ellie remained silent for several long seconds. "Wow."

I didn't know how to interpret her awestruck silence. "What?"

"It sounds like this is what you wanted all along. You said he's a great guy and you're falling for him. And now he wants a relationship, but because of who he slept with before he ever started seeing you, you're going to hold that against him?"

It did sound stupid when she put it that way. But I wouldn't cave. Even if I was tempted to. Not that easily. Him sleeping with Fiona for five freaking years was a huge deal. She was my boss. His boss, too, in a sense. That was messed up.

It wasn't something I could just overlook and laugh off. I had to see Fiona every day, knowing they'd been together. I shuddered at the thought. Realizing Ellie was still on the line, I thanked her for the advice and said good-bye, needing time to process.

I shuffled into the bathroom and turned on the faucet to fill the tub. Escaping into a steaming hot bubble bath and shutting off my brain was the only thing I wanted tonight.

19

Ben

I didn't want Emmy to think I'd brought up the idea of a monogamous relationship between us to smooth over my past with Fiona. That wasn't the case. Not at all. I should have told her about Fiona sooner, or not answered the door that morning. It was a shitty thing I'd done—shoving Emmy into the bathroom and closing the door. Like that would erase the problem.

I knew Fiona and I had a fucked up past. But honestly, it never bothered me. She was an attractive woman, and neither of us was looking for a relationship. We stayed in the same cities where we didn't know anyone else, and we were both typically single. Sex was nothing but convenient—a purely physical release. But I understood why Emmy hated that Fiona had experienced the pleasures of my body. I considered Braydon a good friend, and I fucking hated that he'd seen Emmy's gorgeous, plump breasts, that he'd tasted how sweet she was and heard the soft whimpering sounds she made when she came. That experience had opened my eyes. I didn't ever want to share her again. She was mine, and selfishly I wanted her all to myself.

I'd never wanted a relationship before, but this hit me like a smack to the head. I wanted all that and more with Emmy. My sweet southern belle. The idea of calling myself her boyfriend put a stupid little grin on my face. And now, before we'd even started, I'd fucked it up already. It almost made me rethink what I was doing. Almost. But I knew I would fight for her. I just had no idea how. My texts over the last few days had gone unanswered and I wasn't bold enough to show up at her door and risk getting sent away. I missed her. And once again, I wasn't sleeping for shit.

I decided to call Braydon. He knew me and he'd gotten to know Emmy a little, too—too much, in my opinion. But maybe he'd have some advice. He was in London doing a small fashion show, and I had no clue what his schedule might be. I'd opted not to do the show. I had the luxury of being a bit more selective with the jobs I took. I sent him a text, unsure if he had time to talk.

Me: Hey . . . I need help with Emmy. Call me.

Braydon: I'm in. ;)

Me: No. Not for that, fucktard. Call me.

A few minutes later my phone rang. "Hey, man," I greeted him.

"I was just thinking about you guys. Well, not you. But Emmy. Mmm . . ." He made a low humming sound in his throat.

"Well, stop thinking about her, asshole. That's never happening again."

"Whoa, getting a little possessive, aren't we? That's new for you."

"Yeah, no shit. All this is new for me. I think I'm falling for her, man."

"Wow. Big Ben's growing up. That's huge, man."

Dick. "Well, she's not talking to me right now."

Braydon chuckled. "What'd you do? Lemme guess . . . she wants you to get an APA now and you won't?"

"This isn't about your dick or its stupid-ass jewelry, dude. And no, I'm never getting my junk pierced." I stood from the bed and began pacing the room, suddenly restless. I explained Emmy's already strained relationship with Fiona and the hurt in her eyes when I told her about our past. Braydon stayed quiet, listening to the whole thing. I blew out a heavy sigh. "I need to get her back. What do I do?"

"You need to show her what she means to you. Make her understand how special she is to you. Make her forget all about Fiona."

That did make sense. "So how do I do that?"

"You have to think about the things she likes . . . if she's into poetry, you write her a poem . . . or if her favorite food is sushi, you find the best Japanese restaurant to take her to. Shit like that."

Okay . . . that was pretty good.

"Thanks, man." Now I just needed to think about what to do to show her how I felt.

Christ. I wasn't good with feelings. This should be interesting. . . .

20

Emmy

That week after Ben's confession about his relationship with Fiona was hell, but I threw myself into my work. Being Fiona's bitch was the perfect distraction. I thought about Ben often, a dull ache always present inside my chest, but I did my best. I woke groggy and unrested, went about my day, and collapsed into bed each night clutching my phone. I had to talk myself out of calling him at least six hundred times. I called Ellie instead.

I'd successfully ignored his few texts, one adorably addressed to "Tennessee." It was difficult not to cave, but I deserved better. I knew I did. And the daily pep talks from Ellie helped remind me. Ben would need to try harder if he actually wanted a go at a real relationship. I needed to make sure he was committed to this idea. I wanted to see him work for it. I needed to make sure he was serious about me before jumping back in, because I was his, body and soul.

Slipping out of my heels, I was ready to collapse on the bed when a knock at the door stopped me. My heart thumped unevenly, and I wondered who it could be. It was a delivery from the concierge.

Opening the door wider to accommodate him, the concierge wheeled in a cart and unloaded several items onto the table: a glass vase of flowers, a six-pack of Hap & Harry's Tennessee Lager—one of my favorites from home—and a white bakery box full of blueberry muffins. What in the world?

Once the concierge had left, I tried to make sense of this delivery. The deep purple irises on tall, vibrant, green stems had a light, floral scent that reminded me of home. The notecard attached to the vase of flowers said, "State flower of Tennessee." Oh . . . that was interesting. All my favorites from home. Did irises even grow in France? And I doubted they sold this brand of beer. Had Ben done this? Flown these in just for me?

I lifted an ice-cold bottle of beer from the carton, twisted off the cap, and took a long sip. Mmmm . . . My taste buds did a little happy dance. Looked like I'd be having muffins and beer for dinner. Which suited me just fine.

It was strange how these little comforts of home improved my mood. I smiled for the first time in a week. Everything looked brighter.

My phone rang and I crossed the room, beer in hand, to fish it from my purse. "Hello?"

"Hi." It was Ben.

The coarse sound of his voice surprised me. I had been so

wrapped up in my own little world, I hadn't even thought to check the caller ID. I didn't say anything else and neither did he right away, but I could hear him breathing.

"Did you get a delivery?" he asked, tentatively.

"Yes, thank you. It just came. That was very thoughtful of you."

"It's nothing. I just wanted to show you that I was thinking of you, that I care about you, Emmy. You're all I can think about. We should talk. I miss you."

I missed him, too. Every hour of every day. "Okay."

"Okay?" His hopeful, happy tone made me smile.

"Yeah, come have a beer with me. I'm guessing you've never had Hap & Harry's."

He laughed. "Be down in a minute."

When Ben arrived, the urge to crush myself against his body was nearly overpowering. Instead, I opened the door wide and invited him in. Handing him a beer, I couldn't help but notice the deep, dark circles under his eyes. He hadn't been sleeping well, and I felt a pang of guilt at that realization.

He took a slow sip from the bottle, tilting his head back, but his eyes remained on mine. His scrutiny was too much. I busied myself at the little table, removing two muffins from the pastry box, and placed them on napkins for us. Ben's large form loomed just behind me, and I felt the heat radiate from his skin, felt him breathe my scent against the back of my neck. He reached around me to set his beer on the table then took mine from my hands and placed it beside his.

"Emmy . . ." His gruff whisper sent a rush of goose bumps

breaking out over my skin. His hands captured my jean-clad hips and he tugged me back a step until my back met his firm chest and his arms closed around me, hugging me from behind. He buried his face against the side of my neck. "I can't do this anymore. I miss you so fuckin' much, baby. And I'm so sorry about everything with Fiona. I should've told you sooner." His soft, whispered apology murmured against my skin made tears spring to my eyes. I missed him, too. Terribly.

I turned in his arms, feeling the first of the tears roll down my cheeks. Ben looked at me, a pained expression on his face, and brushed away the drops with his thumbs, capturing my cheeks in his palms. I didn't say anything, didn't need to. The look we shared communicated so much; there was no need for words. Ben watched me in wonder, smoothed the hair back from my face, and ran his fingers through the long strands before he eventually bent down and brought his mouth to mine. "I'm falling for you, Emmy," he whispered just as his lips pressed against mine.

Endorphins, lust, love, and desire flooded my system all at once. I kissed him back—hard—crushing my mouth to his. His words were everything I'd wanted to hear, but actually hearing them, in his deep, sexy voice, was too much.

I clawed at his clothes, pushing my hands under his shirt, tugging at his belt. Ben groaned against my mouth and his hands helped me. He tugged off his shirt, only breaking our kiss for a second, then removed my top. He cupped my breasts over my white lacy bra, groaning as his palms made contact with my skin. I'd missed that; I'd missed him too much to go slow. And Ben obviously felt the same way. I felt his rock-hard erection press into my stomach. Desire coursed through my veins and I groaned into his mouth. Ben lifted me off my feet, carrying me in a cradle hold over to the bed.

He laid me down against the center of the mattress and looked down at me. My breathing came much too fast, my chest rising and falling rapidly. His eyes lingered on my chest, moving over each curve. He delicately traced a fingertip along the lacy edge of my bra before reaching behind me to unclasp it.

He petted and kissed me gently all over. Sliding down the bed so he was even with my chest, he placed tender kisses along my collarbone, ribs, and the center of my stomach. He lifted my hands to his mouth, kissing the inside of each wrist, right where my pulse slammed violently in my veins. I twisted restlessly underneath him, trying to press my core against his heavy erection. He chuckled against my skin, lighting me up like a damn Christmas tree. I was so turned on, so unabashedly horny. I wanted him. I needed him to claim me. Even if he wasn't good at using pretty words or big emotional displays, I needed him to show me.

He came to rest beside me, laying so we faced each other. Stroking my cheek softly, his eyes watched mine with wonder. "God, I've missed you."

I placed my own palm against his rough cheek and my thumb skittered past the bruise-colored skin underneath his eye, acknowledging that this past week had been rough on us both. "You said that night with Braydon made you realize some things?" I whispered.

He swallowed and nodded. "Yes. I'm not good at expressing my feelings, but fuck, I wanted to punch him square in the face when I saw him touch you."

I smiled. "We didn't have to do that, you know . . . I'd never even thought about having a threesome before you suggested it."

"That was stupid of me. He and I had done it before, so I figured it was no big deal. If it was something you wanted, and I could give it to you, I didn't want to deny you anything. But then when it was actually happening, I don't know. All this emotion and regret just hit me like a brick. I didn't want him touching you. I wanted you all to myself: your sweet laugh, your beautiful, lush body. I don't want to share you, Emmy."

"You don't have to."

He leaned forward and rested his forehead against mine, lightly kissing my lips. "Never again."

I nodded, agreeing completely. It was sort of a bucket list thing, and once had definitely been enough for me.

"I need to be inside you," he whispered, hoarsely.

I let out a ragged breath. "Bennn . . ."

His fingers fumbled with the button on my jeans, and I found myself helping him to push them down my thighs.

Once I was stripped of every last stitch of clothing, Ben curled his hand around my pubic bone, his fingers lightly brushing my sex. "This pussy's mine. No one gets to fuck this but me."

"Yes, Ben. Just you."

He shed his boxer briefs and jeans in one quick movement, sending them over the edge of the bed.

I gripped his smooth, firm length in my hand, slowly stroking him, and was rewarded by a husky moan tumbling from his parted lips. My body responded with a surge of moisture between my legs.

"I need to fuck you, Emmy."

Reading the tension in the firm set of his jaw, I knew this would be hard and fast, and that was exactly what I needed. We both needed to chase away any lingering thoughts of Braydon, or Fiona. This was just us, wild and passionate.

His body slanted over mine. Ben kissed my mouth hard and inched himself forward, the head of his cock parting my folds as he pushed inside me slowly, allowing my body time to adjust.

He sank all the way in, inch by delicious inch, until he was fully buried within me. I sucked in a sharp breath at the same time he released a low groan, cursing under his breath.

"Fuck, baby, that's so good."

I was doing little more than lying underneath him but I took the compliment, pressing a kiss to his neck. I loved his scent, the weight of him on top of me. Finally, Ben started to move—little shallow thrusts until he was sure I was stretched around him and ready for more. I wrapped my legs around his back and Ben gripped my ass in one hand, angling my hips up to meet his thrusts. The sensation was almost too much. He was so deep inside me.

He drove into me, pounding hard against my core. I clung to his broad back while he moved against me, pushing me into the mattress with each deep thrust, claiming me, owning me, making me his.

Ben

Afterward, I held her, feeling her body tremble and pulse after her final orgasm. Being intimate with her helped to chase away some of the memories of Bray. That wasn't something I wanted creeping around the edges of my memory, because I'd meant every word I'd said. She was mine. I'd never needed anyone quite like the way I needed her.

After her heartbeat had recovered, she rolled to face me in bed so we were laying side by side.

"We should talk, Ben."

I nodded. I didn't know what more there was to talk about. In my mind things were pretty fucking clear. I had Emmy back. That was all that mattered. "What's on your mind, baby?"

She brought a hand to my cheek and rested it there. She sighed deeply. "Are you sure you want this . . ." She motioned between us.

"I just came twice, I'm with the most beautiful girl in the world, and I'm about to get the best sleep of my life. I'd be a fuckin' fool not to want this."

She swatted my arm, a smile blossoming on her mouth. "I know what I want . . . but you're not the relationship type," she reminded me sternly.

"I told you, it's not a choice. I need you." I didn't know the right words to make her understand. But she watched my eyes and seemed to take it all in.

"Relationships that start with sex don't work, Ben."

I tilted her chin up to meet my eyes. "Nothing about my life has been conventional. Let me do this my way."

Unwilling to even allow her the time to answer, my mouth captured hers in a hungry kiss. I couldn't wait a second longer to feel her lips on mine. She was so soft, so sweet. I didn't know what it was about this girl, but I wanted her. Needed her.

After our third round of sex in as many hours, we were both worn out. Emmy showered and changed into little sleep shorts and a tank top while I got two fresh beers for us and the muffins we'd forgotten about earlier. Neither of us had eaten dinner, but they would do the trick. When Emmy emerged, with damp hair combed straight down her back and freshly scrubbed pink cheeks, she smiled at the little picnic I had set out on the bed.

I fed her bites of muffin—she liked only the tops—and we sipped our beers, made small talk, and snuggled together in the bed. I navigated the conversation around any mention of Fiona, happy that my peace offering seemed to work. My little beer-drinking, blueberry-muffin girl.

I continued to give Fiona her injections but worked hard to keep things purely professional between us. I was expecting her in the next few minutes and made sure I turned my phone to vibrate. Emmy would probably call now that she was done with work for the day. I wanted to talk to her, but I needed to help out Fiona first. And since Fiona and Emmy mixed about as well as oil and water, I didn't want to upset either of them right now.

Emmy wouldn't understand me helping Fiona like this, and Fiona was in a delicate enough state of mind with all these damn fertility drugs. Her first two attempts at getting pregnant hadn't worked, and I began to wonder if putting her body through all this was really worth it. But I wouldn't question her. I could see the determination blazing in her eyes when she handed me the syringe. Fiona lifted her shirt and I swabbed the area clean, watching her inhale sharply at the cold alcohol.

"Sorry," I murmured. The goose bumps faded and I flicked the vial, pushing up the plunger until a bead of liquid formed at the head of the needle.

"It's okay," she whispered, her eyes solemnly regarding mine. "Thank you for doing this. There's no way I could inject myself."

"It's no trouble, Fiona. I just hope for your sake this is the last time we have to do this."

She nodded, her eyes going misty.

Using the distraction, I pinched her skin and stuck the needle in, trying to be as gentle as I possibly could, burying the tip in her flesh. Fiona always jumped a little, but other than that we had this little routine down to a practiced science. Securing the small bandage in place, I discarded the needle in the Sharps Container.

"Doing okay?"

She nodded. "What would I do without you?"

A thousand times, I'd wanted to tell her about Emmy, but something inside me kept putting it off.

Emmy

During the day, I dreaded my time with Fiona. I still couldn't look her directly in the eye. Every time I saw her, I thought about her and Ben. It was torture. He wanted to tell her that we were together, but I kept dragging it out. I knew she'd flip out, and since she already treated me like crap, I didn't want to see what would happen once he told her. She'd probably end up firing me.

In the following weeks, Ben and I became nearly inseparable. During the week, each of us worked, but we spent every night together in Ben's bed. We ordered room service, fed each other, talked about books, music, movies, our childhoods, and future dreams. And we had a lot of sex. The closer we got, the more we seemed to crave each other. Once or even twice a night wasn't enough.

Oftentimes after sex, I felt like I'd run a marathon. My muscles trembled and became woozy, and I was drenched in sweat and come. I hadn't known I was capable of multiple orgasms, and I never thought men were, either. Well, perhaps *men* weren't, but Ben Shaw, a god in bed, was, and even he came two or three times during our crazy hours-long sex bouts. We leapt past any and all physical boundaries, making love constantly. We showered together, soaked together in the bathtub, and slept nude in his big bed. He refused to let me feel self-conscious, constantly petting me, kissing me, and telling me I was beautiful. It was perfection. A dream come true, really.

I realized with absolute clarity that I was falling in love with him. It was impossible. But I was. He was sweet and caring and made me laugh. I wanted to share his bed every night, sleep wrapped up in his arms, chase away his demons, and make sure he was well fed. I wanted to be the one to take care of him. The last person he saw before bed and the first person he saw when he woke. He was mine. Totally and completely. Even if he didn't know it yet.

When I looked at him, I didn't see the model in the magazines. I saw a man with basic needs and desires I wanted to fulfill. I wanted to be the one he called out for in the night, the one who caressed and soothed him back to sleep. The one who fed him, who cared enough to get him off those shit pills. It pissed me off that no one had cared enough to do these things before me.

At the same time, I was entirely grateful that I got to be the one.

He was mine. And I knew then that I loved him. Not the idea of him, not the model, or the prestige or luxurious lifestyle. I loved this man, this broken, sensitive, dirty-talking man.

I wanted to give him everything: all of me, my family, and everything he never had. But it still wasn't enough because he deserved all that and more.

Loving Ben Shaw was the most terrifying feeling. It was like being on a roller coaster with no lap bar, freefalling without a parachute, and dying of heart-squeezing breathlessness all at once. I had no idea if he was even capable of a committed, traditional relationship. But it didn't dampen my feelings. I loved him with my whole being, whether or not it was returned. It wasn't a choice. And that scared the ever-loving shit out of me.

With the TV humming low in the background and providing the only light, Ben spooned his big, firm body around me. We'd dined on some of the best fresh ravioli I'd ever had and were full, sleepy from sex, and drifting off to sleep. Ben pressed a sweet kiss against my neck and murmured about how good I felt in his arms when three dumb little words tumbled from my lips: "I love you."

I held my breath after I said it. It was entirely true, but crap, I hadn't meant to just drop it on him like that. Now, or maybe ever.

Ben remained silent but I knew he'd heard me. I'd felt him stiffen just slightly when I'd uttered those three little words. After a few heartbeats' time, he pressed another kiss to my head and said good night again, his tone final.

My heart thumped wildly in my chest. I didn't plan to just blurt it out like that, but when I did say it, I certainly didn't expect to be met with utter silence. My stomach cramped with nerves, and I was wired and nowhere near sleep. But I had to lie there, acting like nothing was wrong. . . . Shit! I wanted to cry. Instead, I bit my lip and stayed quiet, focusing on keeping my breathing deep and even.

All too soon, Ben's body shifted closer and his arm around me became dead weight. He groaned softly in his sleep. I envied that he could fall into a peaceful sleep right now. My mind churned with unanswered questions as I tried to relax. It was going to be a long damn night.

21

Emmy

Ben had promised that this evening's afterparty would be much tamer than the crazy Fashion Week parties. Tonight was a private affair celebrating designers on the rooftop of the La Manufacture hotel, located in the textile district of Paris. Many of the major clothing brands would be there. Ben mentioned that Braydon was back in town for a shoot, but apparently I wasn't supposed to get excited about the possibility of seeing him tonight. I assured Ben it had nothing to do with our night together; I was just relieved that I'd know someone there besides him and Fiona.

Ben, Fiona, Gunnar, and I rode together in a limo to the event. A smug little grin curled on Gunnar's lips as he watched the way Ben pressed a hand into my lower back; anyone could see that his eyes and hands seemed to know me intimately.

Fiona silently pouted the entire ride there.

It was awkward, to say the least.

The chilly night air enveloped the rooftop. Strands of little twinkling white lights adorned the terrace, and the view to the city beyond was breathtaking. Tuxedo-clad waiters circled the crowd, holding silver trays of peach-colored cocktails. I didn't know what they were, but Ben and I each took one.

He took a sip and shook his head. "You can have mine."

I tried the drink. It was fruity and sweet. Delicious. "Happily."

Gunnar and Fiona each headed off across the party and mingled. Fiona annoyingly air-kissed the cheeks of the industry people she greeted.

I spotted Braydon across the rooftop, leaning against the railing as he took in the views. I tugged on Ben's sleeve and nodded toward him.

Ben chuckled. "Go on and say hi. I'm going to grab a real drink and then I'll come join you."

Braydon happened to turn just as I approached, like he could somehow sense me coming.

"Jelly bean!" He carefully lifted me off my feet. And although I was double-fisting the two peach cocktails, I didn't spill a drop.

I chuckled at the silly nickname. "Hi, Braydon."

"Where's your man?"

I nodded to the bar. Ben was on his way toward us, holding a glass of amber-colored liquor for himself and a bottle of beer I presumed was for Bray.

"Hey, buddy." Braydon clapped him loudly on the back and took the beer from him. "Got her back, huh?"

"Yep. Thanks for your advice, man." Ben smiled and pulled me to his side to kiss my temple.

I was a little self-conscious of him touching me in public. Fiona still didn't know about us, and I was worried what she'd do when she found out. Ben and I had discussed it and decided to keep things quiet for a little while longer.

I noticed a glass of champagne marked with lipstick sitting beside Braydon's empty bottle. "Is someone here with you?" I asked, nodding toward the glass.

His eyes went to Ben's, and his expression looked pinched. "Yeah. London's here. She just went to the restroom."

Ben tensed beside me. Before I could ask who London was, Gunnar came to retrieve Ben. "There's a designer from Gucci here, and he wants to meet you."

"Sure." Ben looked directly at me. "Is that okay if I leave you with Bray?"

I nodded. "Of course. Go."

I eyed the champagne flute again. The lipstick was a pretty shade—blood red. I could never pull off that bold of a color. I'd look like Bozo the Clown. I tended to stick to sheer glosses mostly. "So, who's London?"

"London Burke. Victoria's Secret supermodel."

"Are you two dating?"

"Not really."

"Oh. Did she and Ben . . . date?"

"Something like that." Ben's ex was a Victoria's Secret

supermodel. Translation: Fuck my life. He didn't offer any further explanation, and I didn't press. There was something about the situation he didn't want me to know.

London never returned for her glass of champagne, and Braydon did his best to distract me. He asked about where I lived in New York and talked about his drunken adventures over the past couple of weeks, but my eyes continually watched for Ben's return. An hour later, with still no sign of him, I excused myself from Braydon. After consuming three of the little peach cocktails, I was in desperate need of a restroom. And I wanted to find Ben.

I ventured inside, used the restroom, and reapplied my lip gloss, studying myself in the mirror. I was wearing a little cream-colored dress with a scoop neck and the black pumps Ben had gotten me. I felt cute but a little unsure. I hated how working around models caused me to constantly need reassurance from Ben that I was enough. I turned away from the mirror, frustrated. I just wanted to find him.

Reemerging into the night air, I scanned the rooftop for Ben. It should have been easy to spot him in the large, open, rectangular area. I saw Fiona talking to Braydon where I'd left him but no sign of Ben anywhere. Where had he gone? I noticed two girls exit the rooftop through a door I assumed was a stairwell into the hotel, so I decided to follow them.

The girls headed down the flight of stairs, gripping the banister as they navigated the steps, wobbling on their stiletto heels. I followed them inside one of the hotel's top-floor suites. It seemed the party had slipped into this space, too.

Club music thumped in the background, and the kitchen counter was littered with liquor bottles, lime wedges, and mixers.

People stood talking in the living room, mostly girls in too-short cocktail dresses who were no doubt freezing outside. I crossed through the room, still not finding Ben. Blood pumped erratically in my veins as I realized a hotel suite also meant bedrooms . . . and if Ben wasn't on the roof, and he wasn't in the living room . . . Oh God . . . I felt weak, but I pushed my legs into action, heading down the hallway.

There were three doors—two were open, revealing an empty bathroom and a bedroom, and the third door was closed.

Not hearing any sounds from inside, I reached for the knob. It felt cool in my palm. I turned it slowly and pushed the door open. The lights were on but the room was empty. At the far end of the room a sliding-glass door was open; the sound of voices from the balcony outside drew me forward.

My stomach danced with nerves and my heartbeat thrummed dangerously fast in my chest. I was terrified of what I might find, but I had to know.

"Are you honestly saying you don't miss me at all?" a female voice asked.

"London . . ." Ben's voice answered, his tone a playful warning. "I didn't say that."

She laughed a soft, calculated laugh—the laugh of a woman used to getting exactly what she wanted. "Because no one fucks like you, Ben."

"That's a good point." He chuckled.

"We had fun together, right?" Her voice had dropped lower, gone all sultry.

"London . . ." His was a soft plea.

I couldn't listen anymore but rather than exit gracefully, I turned and slammed right into the glass balcony door, rattling it loudly. Ben turned suddenly and caught my eyes. "Emmy."

I fled, feeling the first of the tears already threatening to spill over. I retreated the way I'd come, back toward the living room. I would hail a cab back to the hotel. Alone. Ben and London trailed behind me, and once we reached the living room I ran smack into Braydon.

He reached out to steady me, gripping my upper arms. "Jelly bean? You okay?"

He must have come in search of us, and unfortunately he'd brought Fiona with him, too. More people had crowded the living room, like the party was slowly but surely moving inside. Braydon's gaze wandered behind me to Ben and London and he winced. He must have known all about their history.

"Emmy . . ." Ben reached for me. "That was nothing, just London and I catching up. I promise you."

London stepped closer on precariously high heels. Her dress, if you could call it that, was a swatch of red satin that barely covered the important bits. Plenty of cleavage, incredibly long legs, long blond hair, and that red lipstick I'd noticed on the glass earlier. Tears blurred my eyes, but what I did see of her was stunning.

"I'm sorry, I didn't mean to cause any drama," London

spoke up, sounding sincere. "I'm London." She offered me her hand.

Oh God, she was nice, too. I just stood there, uselessly staring at her hand. Ben stepped closer.

"This is Emmy, my girlfriend."

Fiona made a strangled cry at hearing the word *girlfriend*. I had to admit, it surprised me, too.

"Nice to meet you. I've never known Ben to have a girlfriend." London smiled widely at me.

"Ben?" Fiona's raspy, accented voice pierced the awkward silence. No one said anything for several long moments, but I could see tears filling Fiona's eyes. She and Ben watched each other intently, her features awash in hurt. A second later, Fiona turned and fled, elbowing partygoers out of her way as she made a mad dash for the front door.

Ben gave me a sympathetic look then darted out after her.

Watching him go after Fiona felt like a knife was being shoved into my chest. After hiding me from Fiona all this time, he chose this horribly tense moment to announce that we were together, and then ran out after her?

My heart stopped.

I felt sick. Sicker than I had when I heard his flirty banter with London.

Black spots clouded my vision. Oh fuck, I was going to pass out.

Braydon's hand lightly stroked my lower back and kept me from collapsing. London still watched me curiously, and the hush that fell over the room told me several others were too.

"Get me out of here, Bray," I whispered.

His warm arm encircled my waist and he guided me away from the carnage.

The party on the rooftop had died down significantly, with just a few people lingering. Braydon led me to an out-of-the-way seating area in the corner. I stopped by the bar and grabbed a bottle of Jack and two glasses. His brows shot up but he said nothing and motioned to a couple of plush chairs situated around a stone fire pit.

I sank into the chair and poured us each a healthy measure of whiskey. I wasn't near drunk enough to deal with all the confusing feelings Ben stirred up within me. I'd told him I loved him, and he'd said nothing . . . and now tonight I catch him flirting with his ex—who, oh, happens to be a supermodel. Then there was Fiona. I gulped the liquor, just wanting to feel numb.

"Whoa, easy there, jelly bean." Braydon's hand on mine stopped me from pouring too much into my already-empty glass.

I leaned back into the plush cushions, kicked off my heels, and rested my feet in Braydon's lap.

"Are you cold?" He started to remove his suit jacket.

I waved him off. "I'm fine. The fire helps." Little blue flames danced from the rocks inside the elegant gas fireplace, gently warming the air around us.

"Tell me how I can help. You want me to kick his ass?" Braydon asked finally.

I'd really just wanted some company while I got intoxicated, but his willingness to help made me smile. "You'd do that? I thought you two were friends."

He shrugged. "We are, but I like you better. You have better tits."

I still couldn't believe I'd had sex with Braydon. That was random. "Nah... you better not. His face is his money maker. I wouldn't want to be responsible for taking down his career. Of course, if you wanted to chop off his ..." I glanced at Braydon.

"Baby maker?"

"Yeah." I laughed for the first time that night. "That'd be fine with me."

"I don't know what that was with London earlier. I know he thinks with his dick most of the time, but he's different with you, Emmy. You have to see that."

I thought it over silently. I wondered if he was over London. She seemed like she was looking to get lucky tonight. "How many women did you and Ben share?"

Bray looked down. I could tell he didn't want to betray guy code by telling me their secrets, but I also trusted he'd be honest with me. "Just Fiona and one other. A girl named Mia."

So they hadn't shared London. Interesting. "Was Mia a model, too?"

Braydon shook his head. "No, she was a girl in New York that Ben dated briefly."

I winced. I didn't know if that made it better or worse that she wasn't a model. It might have been worse, because I liked the idea of being the first.

"For the record, I think he only shared to avoid getting too close to girls . . . he's never been the type to want a relationship."

The whiskey was working too well already, and suddenly I wished I was sober for this conversation. Did Ben, at one point, want a relationship with Fiona? I needed to pay attention and figure out all these little clues Braydon was dropping.

Braydon leaned forward and gave my knee a squeeze. "Hey, it's going to be okay. He's crazy about you. I know it."

I sniffed. I wouldn't cry. "Thanks, Bray. We'll see."

A short while—and three glasses of whiskey—later, Ben appeared in front of us. "There you are, Emmy. I've been looking everywhere for you."

I lifted my chin, glancing out at the city lights of Paris below. It might have been childish to ignore him, but I had nothing to say at the moment. "How's Fiona?" My tone was bitter. I didn't care.

"I wouldn't know. I asked the concierge to see that she got a cab, and I've been looking for you." He knelt in front of me. "I need to talk to you, please, baby."

Dammit. The desperation in his eyes and the rough tone of his voice had all my resolve melting away.

I nodded. "Okay."

"Braydon . . ." Ben tipped his head toward the exit.

"No, I want Braydon to stay."

Ben's gaze narrowed. "Fine," he bit out.

I grabbed Braydon's hand and gave it a squeeze. His gaze locked on Ben and he shrugged, as if apologizing. I didn't want to kick Braydon to the curb. He'd been there for me to-night. And in our brief encounters, I'd grown to trust him. He was a good guy. The jury was currently out on Ben.

Ben sat in the chair next to me with his body fully turned toward mine. "I'm so sorry about earlier, but baby, nothing happened with London."

"I heard you, Ben. You weren't trying real hard to dissuade her."

"That wasn't it. Will you listen to me? There was nothing to dissuade, because she had no chance with me. I'm yours, Emmy."

His words tugged at something in my chest, but I couldn't be distracted by my pesky heart right now. "You were flirting."

"No, I was trying to be polite."

I rolled my eyes and emptied the contents of my glass down my throat.

Ben took the glass from my hands. "A second before that, I was telling London about you. Did you hear that part?"

"No," I admitted. "What did you say?"

"I told her I'd fallen for a sweet southern belle." Ben's hands captured mine. "You've stolen my heart, baby. No one and nothing's going to change that. I belong to you." He brushed the stray tendrils of hair back from my face, looking at me adoringly. "I don't want to spend a single day without you. I've never needed anyone, Emmy. But I need you. I love the way you take care of me. And I want to take care of all your needs. If letting this dickhead into our bed showed you anything, it's that I'll give you anything, baby."

Braydon snorted, complaining under his breath that he wasn't a dickhead.

"When I saw Bray's hands on you, I wanted to punch him. I've never felt that way before. Sex was never an emotional event until you. I need you by my side. In my bed each night. The thought of my day without you to brighten it is the most depressing thing I could imagine. I'm falling in love with you, Emerson."

My lips curled into a smile. My eyes met his deep, hooded gaze, and for just a heartbeat's time it was just us. No one else existed; no one else mattered. His palms cupped my cheeks, drawing me closer. His mouth stopped just millimeters from mine, his warm breath dancing over my lips. "What's your middle name?"

"Jean."

"Really?"

"Shut up."

"I'm in love with you, Emerson Jean," he murmured, his lips brushing mine.

My heart thumped wildly in my chest. I'd waited so long to hear those words, and now actually hearing them in Ben's deep, sexy voice, with his warm lips brushing mine, it was even better than I could've ever imagined.

"I love you," I whispered back just before his mouth crashed against mine.

Ben lifted me from my chair, planting me in his lap, and kissed me roughly. It was as though he was starved for me. His mouth moved over the skin of my neck, my jawline, and then settled over my mouth. His tongue battled mine, sucking and tangling until I was writhing in his lap. My dress was hitched up my thighs and I ground closer, pressing my core against the straining bulge in his pants.

His hands moved to grip my ass and tug me against him. I released a breathless moan, my body shuddering at the contact.

From somewhere beside us, Braydon cleared his throat. Ben's mouth left mine just long enough to bark an order to Braydon. "Get them out of here." He nodded to the last of the people who lingered on the rooftop. Apparently Ben didn't want an audience for whatever was about to happen. I was too drunk and too turned on to stop him.

While Braydon escorted the group to the exit, Ben's mouth captured mine again in a devastating kiss. "I love you, Emmy. I love you. I need you," he murmured in between kisses. The possessive way he said those words sent sparks of desire shooting through my system. I wanted to be his. My hips rocked shamelessly against his lap, my center wet and ready. The way his hands roamed my writhing body made me feel sexy and seductive. I was alive with heat and sexual desire.

When I found his belt buckle and began restlessly tugging at it, Ben groaned. Finally freeing the belt buckle from hell, I slipped my hand inside his pants and boxer briefs, closing my fist around his hard length.

"Oh, fuck," he groaned into my mouth as I began stroking him.

I stopped my motions long enough to allow Ben to lift

the clingy shift-dress off over my head and deposit it on the empty chair next to us.

Grinding against him in my bra and tiny lace panties, I didn't care that we were in the open night air or on a rooftop. Ben had just told me he loved me, and I needed him. Now.

The sound of a buckle unlatching next to us caught my attention. I looked up to see Braydon standing beside us, undoing his belt.

"Not happening," Ben growled out. "Go guard the door."

Braydon pouted but redid his belt and dutifully walked back toward the exit.

Not bothering to undress either of us any further, Ben fucked me hard and fast. He pushed the material of my panties aside and buried himself inside me in an excruciatingly slow thrust that stretched me so fully I cried out, the sounds echoing in the night air. He gripped my waist and lifted me up and down on him.

Whispering sweet and naughty things to me the entire time, Ben pumped into me. "You're so fucking sexy. . . . I love the sounds you make. . . . That's right, beautiful, I want to watch you come."

Within minutes, his words pushed me over the edge. I came, loudly calling out his name.

Ben buried his face against my neck and groaned. "I love you, Emmy."

I felt his warmth flooding my hot entrance as little aftershocks pulsed through my body.

Pulling some tissues from his pocket, Ben cleaned me

and arranged my panties so I was covered once again. Just as I was pulling my dress back on, Braydon appeared.

With a large erection tenting his slacks. *Whoa.*

I couldn't help but giggle. I guess I was still pretty tipsy, but I found that funny. Our lovemaking had gotten him hot and bothered.

"Are you guys fucking kidding me?" He adjusted his pants and winced. "Don't do that shit in front of me if I'm not invited to play."

I hadn't realized that Braydon had been watching, or at least listening from his guard post at the door. *Oops.*

"That's never happening again, man. Emmy's not your plaything. She's mine." Ben possessively pulled me to his lap again, nuzzling into my neck.

"You two are fucking mean." Braydon sighed loudly. "I could go find Fiona, cheer her up. She hasn't seen my piercing yet."

My gaze snapped to Braydon's. "No, Bray. Anyone but her."

It was bad enough both Ben and Braydon had already been with her. Some tiny part of me liked that she hadn't experienced his piercing like I had. If we were keeping score, that little thing afforded me extra points. Stupid, I know.

"You got it, jelly bean."

I fell asleep in Ben's arms that night while he continued to pet and caress me softly, whispering over and over again that he loved me.

22

Emmy

Ben and I lay around relaxing much of the day until there was a knock at the door in the late afternoon. It was a bottle of champagne delivered from the concierge. The notecard read:

> *For Ben and Emmy. Enjoy!*
> > *Love,*
> > *Fiona*

"See, I knew she'd come around," Ben said, uncorking the champagne with a loud pop.

She was being too nice. Something was up. Ben didn't see it—but I did. I also found it interesting she had addressed the notecard to both of us. Like she knew I stayed in his room and only went to mine to change clothes. But I smiled and accepted a glass of the bubbly.

"I love you, Emerson."

He couldn't seem to stop saying it. Which was just fine with me. "I love you, too." I smiled at him and then sipped my drink. Mmm. Fizzy and sweet. "Ben?"

"Hmm?"

"I want you to come home with me, see where I'm from, meet my parents."

His gaze softened. "I'd like that."

We hadn't yet spoken about what would happen once we left Paris, but I held out hope that we'd make a go at a real relationship back in New York. I knew he traveled a lot for work, but with Fiona's approval maybe I could travel with him.

My phone chimed from my purse, and I glanced at it. It was Fiona. That was strange. She rarely called me. She usually sent a text.

"Hello?"

"Hi, darling. Did you guys get the delivery?"

Darling? That was new.

"Yes, thank you. Ben's already poured us each a glass and it's delicious. That was very thoughtful of you." My voice sounded light and cheery. *Good job, Emmy.* I silently patted myself on the back. Way to be civil with your boyfriend's ex. I felt proud. Very grown up.

"Wonderful. Well, you guys enjoy it, and then later I'd love for you to swing by my room. I'd like to talk about adding more responsibilities to your role. You've proven to be quite capable."

What? Seriously? "Oh, okay. That sounds great. I just need to shower, and . . ."

Fiona cut me off. "Nonsense, we're all practically family now. Just come by whenever . . ."

"Okay, I will. See you soon."

I hung up the phone, deep lines of confusion etched across my face.

"Who was that?" Ben asked, taking a sip of his champagne.

"It was Fiona. I think she wants to promote me."

His smile lit up his face. "See. Told you everything would work out, baby. I love you."

"Love you, too," I said, distractedly. I didn't trust Fiona for a second. I just needed to figure out her angle with this move.

I was too distracted to enjoy the champagne with Ben, and after several minutes he chuckled, urging me to pay her a visit. "Just go." He laughed. "Call me after."

"I will. Thanks." I pressed a quick kiss to his lips and headed out.

When I reached the penthouse suite, I paused before the ornate cream and gold enameled door. I smoothed my hands over the black dress pants I'd changed into and straightened the hem of my burgundy blouse. This would turn out okay—it had to. I knocked at the door and lifted my chin. I wouldn't let her intimidate me. Couldn't.

When Fiona opened the door, she looked like shit. I'd never seen her dressed so casually—in black yoga pants and an oversized sweatshirt that hung to her knees. Her hair was in a sloppy ponytail and she wasn't wearing any makeup.

"Fiona?" My voice croaked. "Are you okay?"

She swallowed and nodded. "Fine, love. Come in." She retreated into the large living room and I followed, closing the door behind me. She slumped down onto the sofa and curled her legs up underneath her.

I sat opposite her on the lounge chair. "Are you sure you're feeling okay?"

She laughed uneasily. "I look like shit, don't I?"

I bit my cheek. *Shut it, Emmy!*

"I'm fine, honestly. I've just had a slew of doctor appointments lately, and it's worn me out."

"Oh, well, I'm sorry, and I didn't mean you looked bad. I've just never seen you, you know," I stammered, "not put together."

"It's quite all right." She waved her hand dismissively. "I wanted to talk to you about your position at Status."

My stomach did a little flip. "Okay."

"It's quite obvious you've been more than capable with your assigned duties. Ben trusts you—and you know I trust his judgment. So . . . I'd like to expand your role, give you a bit more responsibility. Of course, it would come with a pay raise as well. How does all that sound?"

What were you supposed to say when your boss found out you were dating her ex-fling and offered you more money? There was no guidebook for that, but I was pretty sure I was supposed to feel grateful. "It sounds fabulous. Thank you for the opportunity."

"Wonderful. I was hoping you'd say that. I'm going to

need help with New York Fashion Week, especially because of all these doctor appointments I mentioned."

I wanted to ask again if she was okay, or if there was anything I could do to help, but something in her posture made me pause. It wasn't any of my business so I just nodded. "Absolutely."

"Attending castings, talking to the designers, helping to prepare the boys."

"I can do that. Anything you need." Wow, maybe my assistant job was finally going to pay off. I was moving up in the world.

"Brilliant. I'll email you later tonight with more details. But for now, if you'll excuse me, I'd like to take a nap."

"Of course." I let myself out, leaving Fiona curled up on the couch.

When Fiona finally emailed me that night, I was lying in bed with Ben, using his iPad to video chat with Ellie. But when the email from Fiona came through, I sat straight up and told Ellie I'd talk to her later.

It began with my new pay—a healthy increase from my previous salary. And then went into detail about my duties in preparation for New York Fashion Week.

On the last line of the email I finally uncovered her ploy. I'd be leaving Paris in two days.

Our relationship was so new, so fragile, I feared what the distance might mean. If this were a Lifetime movie, I'd run away with this man and never look back. But sadly, life didn't work that way.

The entire ride to the airport, Ben kept telling me he was proud of me, and that I should be excited about this opportunity. I couldn't help but think it was just a ploy for Fiona to get rid of me since she had learned of my relationship with Ben.

I trusted him, but that didn't mean I was happy about him spending three weeks alone in Paris with the woman he'd had an ongoing affair with. I didn't trust her. Not at all.

Ben paid to upgrade my seat to first class, even though I told him it wasn't necessary, and then walked me as far as security would allow.

"Hey, it's just three weeks." He cupped my cheeks in his big palms, meeting my eyes with a worried stare.

"Three weeks and two days," I pointed out.

Ben smiled and pressed his lips to mine. "We'll talk every night. I'll send you dirty texts."

I giggled despite my sour mood. "Did you just tell me you'd sext me? Spoken like a true fucking romantic right there."

"Anything for you, baby. I love you, Emmy."

"I love you, too," I told him, drinking in that brilliant hazel gaze I'd miss so much. "Behave."

"I will, I promise. You too." Ben pulled me snuggly into his arms, lifting my feet from the floor so he could cradle me in a full-body hug. I melted into his embrace.

We could do this, right? It was just a few weeks.

23

Emmy

Ben was increasingly hard to get ahold of in the weeks that followed. Maybe it was the six-hour time difference or our work schedules, but we were rarely afforded the time to talk. The only thing that helped me pass the time was that I'd taken one of Ben's T-shirts with me from Paris. His masculine scent still clung to the fabric, and each night I'd buried my face in the cotton and inhaled deeply. When the scent finally wore off, I worried that it was somehow a sign of things falling apart between us.

Ben had trouble sleeping through the night again and told me he had started taking his pills. It disappointed me, but I understood. The man needed to sleep. He ate dinner most nights with Fiona, which I tried to be mature about—they were the only two left in Paris since Gunnar had returned to New York a few days after me to prepare for another big campaign. But my old doubts and insecurities about their relationship started to creep in again.

I'd been working so much since I'd returned that Ellie and I hadn't had a proper girls-night-out yet. So tonight she'd insisted we were going to do something. Admittedly, it was exactly what I needed to get my mind off things.

We ventured uptown, even splurging for a cab so we didn't have to deal with walking to and from the subway in footwear that was more cute than comfortable. Ellie was dressed in skinny black jeans and a beautiful pair of Jimmy Choos. I was in jeans and a pair of tall, black, high boots.

I loved fall in New York. There was a whole new wardrobe needed. I'd thrown myself into shopping, owning it like it was my job. It was the perfect distraction. Ellie was all too happy to help. She showed me the best shops in the city where we could get a deal on the latest fashions.

We entered the overly loud club and elbowed our way to the bar. It'd been a long week and nothing sounded better than an ice-cold beer. Unfortunately, the bar was surrounded three-deep with waiting customers waving bills in the air, trying to capture the overworked bartenders' attention. It would be awhile until we got our drinks.

"Ugh. Apparently we didn't get the memo it was douche-bag night tonight," Ellie said over the music.

"What?"

"I hate guys like that." She shot an annoyed glare at the group of guys tucked into a corner booth in the sectioned-off VIP area.

The guys seemed to be celebrating something. Bottles and shot glasses littered their table, and they laughed loudly and shared fist bumps.

"Oh my God. That's Braydon!" I tugged Ellie's hand. "Come on."

"You know him?"

I chuckled at Braydon. For some reason he was stripped down to a tank top and jeans and wore a pair of sunglasses. Inside. And not just any glasses. Women's heart-shaped, pink, glittery sunglasses.

I stopped in front of their table. "Braydon?"

His crazy-glasses-covered gaze snapped up to mine. "Jelly bean?" He leapt from his seat and tackled me in a hug. "What are you doing here?"

I felt like blurting out that Fiona had banished me from France once she learned Ben and I had gotten too close, but instead I politely explained that I was back to work on New York Fashion Week.

He slipped off the silly shades and his gaze wandered behind me and latched onto Ellie. "Introduce me to your friend." His tone was decisive and he was practically eye-fucking her. Clearly Braydon liked what he saw. All that dark mahogany hair and pretty olive-toned skin made lesser men weak. And drunk Braydon was no match.

"Oh, right. Braydon, this is Ellie."

Ellie surveyed him coolly, her expression bored and unimpressed.

"Hiya, kitten." Braydon smiled.

Ellie rolled her eyes at the cheesy pickup line. "Do you have ears? She just told you my name. Use it."

Braydon turned to me and his uneven grin told me he was several drinks ahead of us. "Ohh . . . she's a firecracker. I like that."

"Embracing your inner douche tonight?" Ellie retorted, her eyes widening as if to make a point.

One side of Bray's mouth curled up. "Is Ellie short for something?"

Her chin lifted. "Elizabeth. But if you'd like your testicles to remain attached to your body, you'll stick to Ellie."

Braydon reached down, unconsciously cupping his manhood. "I've become quite fond of these boys, so Ellie it is."

I didn't know what had made her claws come out, but watching their fiery exchange was entertaining.

"Well . . . we were trying to grab a drink at the bar . . ." Ellie looked longingly in the other direction.

Braydon shook his head. "We have a waitress, she'll be by in a minute. It'll be faster."

I sat down in the booth next to Braydon, and Ellie reluctantly slid in next to me.

Braydon introduced us to his friends, who, based on their height and features, I guessed were also models. I was now used to being around models, and Ellie, blessed with a healthy self-esteem, didn't bat an eyelash.

Braydon signaled the waitress and we placed our order. He asked for our drinks to be added to his tab.

"What's with the glasses, Bray?" I nodded to the pink glasses that lay discarded beside him.

He shrugged. "Found them on the table. Aren't they cute?" He slipped them back on and grinned at me. Oh yeah, he was trashed. He was funny and playful when he was drunk. Ellie rolled her eyes, clearly not amused.

Braydon leaned closer, throwing his arm around my shoulders. "Big Ben's not here to bust us . . . you can play with my APA again later." He flashed his white teeth at me, smiling brightly.

I shook my head and laughed. While some would have thought it was crass the way he'd practically propositioned me for sex, I knew Braydon was only kidding. Ellie shot me a questioning look, but I just laughed it off.

I checked my phone again, wondering why I hadn't heard from Ben at all that day. I tried not to think about the fact that he was alone with Fiona in the most romantic city in the world.

24

Ben

I opened the door to my hotel room to find a tear-streaked and sobbing Fiona.

"What happened? What's wrong?" I guided her inside and closed the door. She crashed against my chest, burying her face in my shirt as she cried. I brought an arm around her, doing my best to comfort her.

"I had my last insemination today." She sucked in a breath to steady herself, her eyes gazing down at the floor. "They won't do any more on me because it's not safe to be on those drugs for longer than twelve cycles. That was my thirteenth. I had to beg them," she said, her voice just a small rasp.

I'd never seen her so down. "So there's still a chance, right?"

"No. I just know this isn't going to work. Why would it? The other twelve didn't. Maybe God or whoever's up there"— she looked up at the ceiling—"doesn't want me to be a mother."

I remained silent, unsure of how to comfort her. I was completely out of my element.

"And even if I could find a new doctor to convince to work with me and take another round of treatment, we'll be leaving in a few weeks and you'll be back in New York, busy with your new girlfriend, too busy to help me with my injections."

"Hey." I reached out for her hand. "I'll never be too busy for you."

She laced our fingers together. "I know. You're too good to me."

Unsure of what else to do, I pulled her to my chest for a hug, and Fiona nestled against my neck. After a few moments, the sobs racking her chest had quieted and her hands slid down my sides to cup my ass.

I stepped back. "Fiona," I pleaded, my tone a weak excuse for a warning. It would be so easy to slip back into our old roles, to fall into bed together, to comfort her that way. But I realized that it never made me happy. I never could sleep for shit the times we did share a bed. That was reserved just for Emmy.

She wiped the tears from her cheeks and blinked up at me. Fiona was a beautiful woman—even with her tears. But I couldn't do this.

"Ben . . ." She didn't say anything else, just continued pleading with me with those intense brown eyes.

"If I could fix this, Fiona, I would. You know that."

Recognition seemed to click for us both at the same time as our gazes snapped together and she took a step closer.

"Ben, you could fix this. You could give me a baby. The most beautiful little baby."

"Fiona . . ." I shook my head.

"Ben . . . no one has to know . . . Emmy doesn't have to find out. . . ."

I released a frustrated sigh. Fiona had worked hard to build my career, to make me wealthy and successful over the past five years. She'd worked nonstop for me, forgone dating and relationships . . . and I couldn't help but wonder if she hadn't been working so hard for me, perhaps she would have settled down into marriage and kids by now.

I led her over to the bed and we each sat on the edge. I hated the hopeful look in her eyes. Growing up without my own father made me damn sure that when I did have kids someday, I wanted to raise them.

"No one will ever know," she whispered softly.

I gave her hand a squeeze. "I'll run you a bath. Do you want to stay here with me tonight? Watch movies? Order room service?"

She smiled weakly. "Thanks, dear. That's brilliant. Exactly what I need."

"No problem." I rose from the bed, leaving her to run a bubble bath in the big Jacuzzi tub. I needed to call Emmy but settled for sending her a quick text while the tub filled.

Me: Something came up tonight. Too busy to talk. Miss you.

25

Emmy

I didn't like going even one day without talking to Ben. So even though his text said he'd be busy, I couldn't resist calling him a few hours later. Of course, as soon as I dialed, I wished I hadn't.

Fiona answered his phone.

But worse than that, she said he was sleeping and she didn't want to wake him. Then she promptly hung up on me.

I felt like murdering someone after that. I settled instead for a five-mile jog, a steaming hot shower, and then went about my day. He'd certainly have a lot to explain when he called.

The shrill tone of my cell phone woke me in the night. I fumbled to find the phone and quickly answered it to stop the ringing.

"Hello?" I croaked, my voice rough from sleep.

"Emmy, baby . . ."

"Ben?"

"I'm sorry baby. I'm sorry for everything."

"Ben, what's wrong?"

His long pause reminded me just how far apart we were. "I needed to hear your voice."

His tone was somber, sad. Something was wrong. "You don't sound well. What time is it there?"

"Six in the morning."

He was either up early or really late from the night before. "Did you sleep okay? Why did Fiona answer your phone last night?" The memory came rushing back with resounding clarity.

"She did?"

"Yeah. She said you were asleep."

"I must have had too much to drink and passed out. I'm sorry."

"Ben, did something happen with Fiona?" I couldn't shake the unmistakable feeling of panic creeping into the edges of my brain.

"You know I would never do anything to hurt you, right?"

I swallowed the thick lump in my throat. "Yeah, I think so."

"I wouldn't, baby. I promise. Just trust me, okay?"

I didn't answer, my mind abuzz with questions. There was something he wasn't telling me but I wasn't brave enough to ask just then.

"Okay?" he asked again.

"Yeah, Ben. I trust you. I just don't trust Fiona."

"I can handle Fiona. Just don't worry, okay?"

"I miss you," I admitted, my voice a tiny whisper.

"I miss you more. Not long now and then I'll be home."

I could not freakin' wait. I hated the feeling that Fiona thought Ben and I were getting too close and had purposely created this distance between us.

26

Emmy

The day Ben was due home, work dragged by at a horrible pace. I tried to focus, I did my best, but my gaze constantly wandered to the clock. Ben's flight was due in later that morning and he'd promised to come straight into the office to see me. We were going to lunch. Unless I could talk him into taking me straight home for a midday romp between the sheets. Eating was overrated. And I'd missed him terribly.

At ten o'clock, Gunnar stopped by my desk. "Come on. Fiona wants everyone gathered in the conference room to make some big announcement."

I looked at him curiously. Maybe she was announcing my promotion. I rose from my desk and stood a little taller in my heels. I'd done well in Paris, and I put up with all her diva demands with a smile on my face. It was paying off. "What do you think it could be? Heard any rumors?" I asked as we ventured down the hall.

Gunnar nodded, a sly smile overtaking his mouth. "Yeah. Rumor has it she's finally pregnant."

What? "Fiona? Pregnant?" I couldn't picture her as a mother. Not at all.

Gunnar's brows pinched together. "I thought you knew Ben was helping her—giving her those fertility injections, taking her to her doctor appointments."

Holy Mother. All the air was sucked from my lungs but I managed to draw a small, shaky breath. "He never told me." My voice was a harsh rasp.

"Her meds were flown in from the U.S., delivered on ice, and had to be refrigerated. I thought for sure you were coordinating all that."

I shook my head. "No." They'd kept it all some big, elaborate secret. I was beyond hurt. He may have said he didn't have feelings for her, but by spending his time caring for her, his actions painted a different story.

Something about the entire situation made my scalp tingle.

Gunnar and I stood at the far end of the narrow conference room while everyone filed in. The large table in the center sat empty as everyone gathered around. It would be standing room only—and a tight squeeze. This must be some big announcement.

Fiona appeared a moment later with Ben beside her. I wanted to run to him, throw myself in his arms, but the crowded room prohibited that. He met my eyes and I sucked in a breath. He looked terrible. Tired and upset about something. Like he'd just gotten some horrible news. I'd wanted nothing more than to see him for the past three weeks, but suddenly I felt unsure. Unsure about where we stood, unsure about his distant calls these past couple of weeks. Had he changed his mind about me? About wanting a relationship?

In contrast, Fiona stood next to him looking bright eyed and bushy tailed. Whatever had been ailing her in Paris had obviously cleared up. She looked well. Happy. Happier than I'd seen her in a long time. I wondered if what Gunnar had said could be true. . . .

Before I could process all of the tangled emotions overtaking my system, Fiona cleared her throat to speak.

A hushed silence fell over the room.

"Thank you all for your work while we were away. Our lovely boy Ben killed it as usual." She smiled fondly at him. "But the reason I wanted to assemble the group today is to share some very exciting news." When she smiled at Ben again I was struck with an overwhelming urge to hit her in the face. With a chair. "I'm expecting a baby."

My stomach twisted violently, turning sour as my breakfast threatened to make an appearance. If Gunnar had been right about this . . . was he also correct about Ben taking an active role? I was already uncomfortable with their relationship, but being lied to for months on end . . . I felt sick.

"Who's the father?" someone asked from behind me.

A slow smile curled on Fiona's mouth and her eyes met Ben's. "Someone ever so dear to me."

Holy shit.

She and Ben shared a look that communicated so much.

They were carrying on a private conversation without exchanging a single word. It was unnerving, and even more so because I had no idea what was being said.

I elbowed my way through the crowded room and headed straight for the women's restroom.

Tears blurred my eyes as I locked the door on the handicapped stall and slid to the floor. It was disgusting to sit on a public bathroom floor, but I had little choice. My legs weren't working at the moment.

The entrance door flew open. "Emmy, we need to talk." It was Ben.

Ten minutes ago I'd been so desperate to see him, to feel his arms around me. And now I felt completely devastated and unsure about everything.

I didn't want to face him, didn't want him to see me cry. But I needed some answers. There were signs all along. Signs I ignored. The phone calls he wouldn't take in my presence. I wondered if they were from Fiona. That time she was in his room and he wouldn't let me in . . . all those nights he'd been short with me on the phone when he was alone with her in Paris . . .

Still hiding in the end stall, I cleared my throat, fighting to keep the tears at bay. "Gunnar told me you'd been helping her. You lied to me."

"I'm sorry about that, baby. So sorry. When Fiona came to me and told me about her fertility struggles she asked me not to say anything to anyone. I gave her the injections, but I swear it was harmless."

"Ben . . . are you the father?"

He didn't answer for several of the longest moments of my life. Eventually he slid down the wall, sinking to the floor until he was sitting across from me. I could see his feet from my view underneath the door. "Will you come out so I can talk to you?"

That was not the answer I needed. My heart thumped erratically in my chest. "Do you really think that'll make this easier?"

He sighed deeply. "I suppose not."

Several long seconds ticked past before I spoke again. "Tell me, Ben. The truth." I deserved that much at least, but I held my breath, unsure if I would be able to handle his answer. I wiped the tears from my cheeks, wondering where this story was going and if it could possibly have a happy ending for me and Ben. Maybe I was being foolish hiding from him in a bathroom stall.

"Shortly after you left Paris, Fiona was devastated about the artificial inseminations not working. She'd had many rounds, and none of them took. She asked me to sleep with her."

A tortured cry escaped my throat and I clasped a hand over my mouth to silence it.

"She was a wreck emotionally, so I told her she could spend the night in my room. I didn't think she should be alone just then. But that's all I was planning on—sleeping. I ordered us dinner and we watched TV and shared a few bottles of wine. I drank too much and passed out. Sometime later, I woke in the middle of the night with Fiona on top of me. She had . . . she was . . ." He hesitated. "She was riding me."

I didn't try to stop the cry that escaped my throat. I hung my head and wept, gulping for air. "That's rape, Ben. You can press charges."

"I'm not pressing charges. I invited her into my bed. We were both drunk. She was severely depressed. . . ."

I didn't know what there was to think about. Whether they were drunk or not, that was *not* okay. I hated Fiona. She could burn in hell for all I cared. "She took advantage of you . . ." She should be punished for that.

"Emmy . . . she and I used to be lovers. That type of thing was normal—her waking me up that way. . . ."

Gross.

Oh my God . . . that could be Ben's baby inside of her. Silent tears streamed down my cheeks. Panic gripped my heart. I wished I could plug my ears, pretend none of this was happening. Instead, I gripped my chest, pressing my palm against my heart, begging it not to falter. It thumped unevenly as pain surged inside my chest. I swear I felt the exact moment my heart broke, shattering inside me with a sharp, distinct pain.

Ben continued, "I threw her off me and cursed her out. But I'm not pressing criminal charges. She apologized and said she wasn't thinking clearly . . . she was crazy from the wine and fertility drugs . . . and she's been my friend for a long time, Emmy. I can't do that to her."

The weight of the knowledge that he didn't want to see her punished was crushing.

"So, you're going to be a dad."

"Maybe. Or a sperm donor. She says I can be as involved as I want to be," Ben added.

Holy shit. I couldn't bear the thought that he'd be forever tied to Fiona. Hell, maybe they'd even give a real relationship a go. For the baby's sake. I fought off a wave of nausea and suppressed a groan with my fingers pressed over my lips.

"Emmy? I'm sorry, I never should have let her stay the night, share my bed. But I didn't plan on this. . . ."

I needed to be away from him. I didn't even want to share the same air. Rising on shaky legs, I wiped my eyes and exited the stall. Ben leapt to his feet, his gaze holding mine in worried suspense. The adrenaline coursed through my system and pushed my body into action. I needed out of this room.

His hands darted out to stop me, resting on my shoulders.

"Don't. Touch. Me," I bit out.

He dropped his hands, looking hurt. Good. Served him right. He'd lied to me for weeks. He'd been inside Fiona and had helped her for months before that.

"I wanted to tell you. But I knew you'd get mad. And I don't think it's possible she got pregnant from that night, Emmy. I told her I couldn't be the father. I didn't even . . . uh, come . . . but she just keeps insisting she has a *feeling*."

My hands flew to my hips. "Ben, you don't have to come to get a girl pregnant. Didn't you pay attention in ninth-grade biology?"

He bit down, his jaw tensing. "I don't think the baby's mine."

"Oh you don't *think* it is—how comforting." *What a fucking moron.*

"Emmy . . ." He fisted his hands and shoved them in his pockets.

"You know what, I hope it is. You two will be very happy together."

Ben frowned. "This is exactly why I didn't want to tell you. I've asked for a paternity test. We'll get this worked out. I promise you. Just trust me."

"I'm sorry. I can't do that. There's been too many secrets. Too much deceit where that woman's concerned. I can't. I can't do this anymore." I lifted my chin and shoved past him, exiting as quickly as my shaky legs would carry me.

Ben

I took one last glance in the mirror after the makeup artist had finished with me and saw Fiona approach from behind. Just fucking great.

I spun to face her, my expression impassive. I was here to do my fucking job. Nothing more.

"Have you had sugar?" Fiona asked, her fingers reaching out to touch the dark circles I knew lined my eyes.

"Of course not." I stepped back out of her reach. I was barely eating, I wasn't sleeping for shit, and my work was reflecting it.

Fiona noticed my movement and frowned. We hadn't talked much after I requested the paternity test and mailed her a check to cover the costs. It was cold, but so was what she'd done to trick me into bed with her.

I didn't need some big declarations of feelings—I knew how Fiona felt about me. And how I would never feel about her. Especially now.

We worked together. That was a necessity for the time being. She'd already booked me for several upcoming campaigns and I would see them through. That didn't mean I was okay with her touching me, trying to act like we were still friends, or inviting me out to dinner after a shoot. I showed up to the shoots, did my job, then took off for the hotel. I didn't socialize with her, or anyone, for that matter.

I had become something of a loner in the last few weeks. Drinking enough to pass out at night just so I could shut off my brain and escape the constant memories of her. *Her*. My beautiful, sweet girl.

I missed her. I missed the soft beat of her heart lulling me to sleep at night. I'd booked every job I could, trying and failing miserably to keep Emmy from my head. I didn't want to be home alone in the quiet solitude of my apartment, a place I'd once loved for being so serene. Now it was too quiet, lifeless, and I wasn't man enough to be alone with my thoughts, so I threw myself into my work. I'd considered traveling to Tennessee, knocking on the door of every Clarke in the state if that meant finding her. Until Braydon reminded me they were fond of guns down south, and not-so-delicately pointed out that Emmy didn't want to see me. She'd been the only girl to bring out these emotions in me, the only girl to crush my heart when she'd left.

27

Emmy

Unwilling to get out of bed just yet, I curled myself against the sheets, remembering the way Ben's hands would tunnel under the blankets until he found my sleeping form. He'd tug me closer, scooting my body across the bed until he could spoon his body around mine. I smiled sleepily at the memory. His warm palms would caress my skin. With one hand resting flat against my belly, he'd burrow his face into my neck and inhale against my skin.

In bed at night in the silent darkness, the memories refused to fade, somehow growing in their intensity each day I wasn't with him. When my brain would stop replaying our intimate moments, I didn't know. But I hoped whenever that happened, it'd also take away the deep ache in my chest.

"Emerson Jean, get outta that bed," my mom drawled, pulling the blankets off my legs.

"Ugh," I groaned, rolling over and curling into a ball. Getting out of bed had become surprisingly difficult in the weeks since my breakup with Ben. I'd fled for Tennessee, quit my job at Status without any notice, and packed only one small bag.

I felt bad because Ellie was holding my room open, paying my half of the rent in the hopes I would soon return to New York. I had no plans to do that. There was nothing for me there now.

"Come on. Enough of this. I made your favorite pecan buns with caramel sauce and coffee. No more moping."

It was easy for her to say. Her heart hadn't been put through a blender. To make matters worse, my brother, Porter, was living at home again after ending his lease with a roommate. As if I needed any more spectators to my demise. My mom hadn't had us both under the same roof in years. Porter was now twenty and though he'd yet to determine his direction in life, my mother cherished having him around. And I was half-worried Porter was going to drive up to Manhattan in his beat-up old pickup truck and hunt Ben down to kick his ass. I may not have objected much.

Ben had called and texted me nonstop until I changed my number. I couldn't get sucked back into his world. I didn't belong in it from the beginning. I was a simple southern girl. I wasn't cut out for the level of drama that followed him around. And if he was the father of Fiona's baby, they'd be linked for life. Even if he wasn't, I doubted he'd ever cut ties with her. He didn't see things clearly when it came to my old boss. I couldn't be with someone who didn't put me and our relationship first.

I was left to mourn the loss of him in my life, knowing the ache I felt would never fully heal. But I couldn't hide in Tennessee forever. I needed to go back to New York, if not to stay, to at least see Ellie and collect the rest of my things.

Ben

One Week Later

Seeing Emmy standing on the curb at the airport was surreal. I'd been seeing her everywhere—imagining every long-haired brunette was her—so it took me a second to realize that this time it was real. She really was here.

It took every ounce of restraint I had to avoid pulling her into my arms, holding her against me, pressing kisses all over her pouty mouth. Her expression was weary—guarded. And I hated how she seemed to be on high alert around me. I wanted to hold her, to comfort her, but I knew I'd lost that right.

"Emmy..."

She stared straight ahead, looking determined to ignore me. I watched the way the wind lifted the strands of hair that had escaped her ponytail. I wanted to bury my face in her neck and kiss that spot just below her ear.

My feelings for her hadn't changed. Not one bit. I loved

her. To the very depth of my being. I needed her in my life. I knew I'd fucked up time and again with Fiona, but I needed Emmy to hear me out.

Ignoring me, she raised her hand in the air, waving at a cab. It zoomed on past.

"Emmy, wait." I reached for her but stopped myself. She wasn't mine to touch anymore. The thought was sobering. To be near her again and not have the right to reach out and take her in my arms was a strange realization. I didn't like it.

"How's the baby?" she asked, her voice cold and unemotional.

That was what I wanted to explain to her. "We should talk, Emmy."

"I have nothing to say to you."

"Well, I do. There are a few things you should know."

When she spun around to face me, all the venom in her expression dissolved. She'd been suffering just as much as me. She closed her eyes briefly and drew a shaky breath. I wondered if she was being hit with a barrage of memories like I was. Her soft laughter, sharing a glass of wine at a sidewalk café, teaching her curse words in French, feeding each other in bed at night. And, of course, making love. Her willingness to experiment sexually and the chemistry we shared were off the charts. There were so many things I missed about her, and I wondered if she missed me, too. Or did she only remember the bitter way things ended between us?

"Please. My driver's here." I indicated the black sedan

parked at the curb. "Let me take you home and explain." I had no fucking clue where to start, but I couldn't let her walk away, for fear I'd never see her again. I picked up her bag without waiting for her response.

She straightened her mouth into a polite line and allowed me to help her into the car.

28

Emmy

I'd never been to Ben's apartment, and even though I knew visiting was a terrible idea, I was completely helpless to say no. Part of me was curious about where he lived, and all of me was curious about what he wanted to tell me.

The car stopped in front of a beautiful brick building on a tree-lined street. The doorman greeted him and smiled warmly at me. I couldn't help but wonder if Ben brought women here often. Surely Fiona had been here. I shuddered, shaking off the thought.

Riding the elevator to Ben's floor, I found myself wanting to wedge myself against the far wall. I hadn't been alone with him since I found out about the baby, and I had no desire to share the same small space, the same air with the man who had broken my heart so completely.

Ben quietly appraised me with his intense hazel eyes that always saw too much.

When we reached the ninth floor, he stepped off the elevator, still carrying my bag, and I dutifully followed.

Unlocking the door, Ben held it open for me to enter ahead of him. His apartment was spacious and open. The kitchen was to my right, and straight ahead were the combined living and dining rooms. It was neat and orderly, though a little stuffy with stale air.

I wasn't sure where he was coming from, but it appeared he hadn't been home in a while. He flipped through a large stack of mail that had been handed to him by the doorman and motioned for me to go ahead and take a look around.

The dining room held a round mahogany table and four cream-colored leather-upholstered chairs. I continued to the living room and the large bay window with a view of the city. The room held a chocolate-brown sofa, modern and sleek in its design, and two armchairs. There wasn't much in the way of decorations, just a few black and white architectural photographs hung on the wall and a brick fireplace filled with tall white candles. It was simple but nice. Classic and elegant without being pretentious. It suited him.

Ben stowed our bags near the entryway and asked if I wanted something to drink. He pulled a couple of bottles of mineral water from the fridge, and I gave him a nod.

Something to distract me would be good. I fiddled with the cool bottle once he handed it to me, taking small sips.

Ben sat in one of the armchairs across from the sofa. "Sit down, Emmy."

My body, accustomed to pleasing him, immediately lowered to the couch. I couldn't meet his eyes so I stared down at my hands instead. It was too painful to look at him. Too many memories. As quickly as we'd started our relationship, it had been snatched away. Just sitting across from him was throwing me for a loop.

"I've asked Fiona to have the paternity test done," he said, cutting straight to the chase.

The air in my lungs contracted painfully, pinching in my chest.

"She said the in-utero testing has some risks associated with it. She also gave me a speech about how she's wanted this baby . . . dreamed about this for two years and wouldn't do anything to jeopardize it. She's agreed to do the test just as soon as the doctors say it's safe, which will be after the birth."

"Oh." I should have felt something here—worried? Relieved? But, strangely, I was devoid of all emotion. Nearly eight months more of not knowing. "Are you still working with her?"

"I am," he replied, casually.

"I see." I didn't know why he wouldn't just quit. She was clearly toxic to him . . . to us. . . .

"I have a contract with her. It doesn't expire until next spring," he added.

And just as he wouldn't press charges against her for taking advantage of him, I was willing to bet money he wouldn't take her to court to end their contract early, either.

Ben leaned forward, resting his elbows on his knees and pinning me with a heated stare. "Emmy . . . I miss you." His voice broke into that deep, husky tone.

I felt his anguish. It was the same anguish that had haunted me for the last month. I missed him, too. There was no denying that. But I worried we were all wrong for each other. Too much drama. Not enough normalcy.

"Ben, you really think a relationship between us would have ever worked out? We're from two different worlds."

"Of course I do. I know it would have."

"And you still think that after living through the cata-strophic levels of drama Fiona stirred up for us?" I hung my head; I couldn't stomach seeing the hope in his brilliant eyes. "I can't do this again." I couldn't put my heart through the wrenching feelings that had owned me for the past few weeks. If and when I was ready to date, I promised myself I'd choose someone safe. A nice, normal guy with a normal job. Not an in-sanely sexy and intense man who turned my insides into a pile of goo. I'd been defenseless against Ben. That couldn't happen again. With time to reflect, I knew that the way I'd become totally fixated on everything he said and did wasn't healthy. Every tiny emotion he made me feel—and let's not forget my body's response to him. I'd never had such an intense relation-ship. When I was ready, I knew I needed something like my parents had. Slow and steady. Something stable and reliable.

"You don't have to see her. You don't have to talk to her. I'll be represented by her agency for the next several months, but that's it. I've cut out the personal shit. No more doctor appointments, no more hanging out. . . . You were right. She wanted more with me. Probably always has. It was time to end it."

"Ben, she jumped you in your sleep. You could just quit working for her."

He released a deep sigh and scrubbed one hand over the back of his neck. "It's not that simple. Just trust me, okay?"

I smiled smugly. "I tried that. It didn't work out so well for me."

He frowned. "Fuck, Emmy. I'm sorry. I was trying to do the right thing, do the committed relationship thing with you . . . be a friend to Fiona. *Fuck*." He twisted his hands in his hair.

Realization struck me like a smack to the head. Ben hadn't truly done anything wrong. Fiona had asked him to keep her fertility issues a secret. And he'd honored that. He hadn't cheated on me—well not purposely, anyway. She'd taken advantage of him. Maybe I was being too hard on him. God, this was confusing. My head was a mess.

When I looked up and met his eyes I saw that he was telling the truth. He wanted to make this work. He wanted me.

Each time I saw him, it was like the first time. His strong jawline, defined chest, broad shoulders, and full mouth were such a sensual combination; it destroyed my presence of mind to stay away. Even if it ended up destroying me, I couldn't stay away from him. Wouldn't. "What will you do if it's yours?"

"I honestly don't know."

"Would you . . . want to be with her? Raise the baby?" I held my breath.

"No. I'm with you. I want you. Even though she and I were romantically involved in the past, I never considered actually being with her. It wasn't like that between us."

"Okay. I guess we'll . . . figure it out together. . . ."

"Yes. Together." His hand reached out to take mine. It seemed harmless enough. But when the warm weight of his palm slid against my skin, one touch was all it took. I realized in an instant that even without knowing if the baby was his, I was willing to accept him and all his baggage.

Memories that refused to fade rushed in, overwhelming my sense of clarity. His touch pushed away the hurt and betrayal and flooded me with warmth and awareness. We'd always had this raw, chemical reaction. Time hadn't changed that. I didn't know why I thought it'd be safe to come here with him. No way was I immune to this man. And his home was very much *him*. His light male scent clung to the space, and the interior exuded his sexy, confident charm.

Ben laced his fingers between mine, the move possessive and sure. My whole body clenched, tightened—my breathing coming in shallow pants. Ben read my reaction all in a single heartbeat, and I could see how affected he was by me, too. My lips trembled. I knew I should say something to his revelation. That was why we were here—to talk—but somehow all I could think about was that his bedroom door was less than twenty feet away, and how the incredible pressure of his thick cock pushing into me always stole my breath.

"What do you want?" he asked, his voice a low whisper.

"I . . . I don't know," I murmured. I wanted to go back in time to tell Fiona to shove the promotion up her ass, and I'd stay with Ben in Paris. Unfortunately, life didn't work that way.

Ben moved to sit beside me on the couch. One hand gripped my waist while his other combed through my hair. It had been so long since he'd touched me and my body was on fire with want. Want for this beautiful, sexy man who destroyed me from the inside out.

"Emmy . . ." My name was a broken murmur; his voice, raw and husky. "You can't look at me like that with those pretty gray eyes." His thumb caressed my cheek. "It brings back too many memories." He leaned in closer, his lips brushing the outer shell of my ear. "It makes me want to take you to bed and fuck you until you scream my name."

I didn't answer. Couldn't. My voice had failed me. Cognitive thought had failed, too. Acting on instinct, I placed my palm against his cheek, skimming my fingers lightly across his stubble-roughened skin.

His breathing hitched.

I wasn't saying no. I wasn't saying yes.

Ben's eyes roamed to my mouth.

He wanted to kiss me.

I wanted to forget all the fucked up things that had happened and capture what we'd lost. I bit my bottom lip, letting my teeth pull against the tender flesh. Ben growled and his mouth came down on mine. His kiss was frenzied, his tongue stroking mine in a desperate way.

His mouth left mine only to travel down my throat, his tongue leaving damp kisses along my sensitive skin. His hand traveled north from my waist, moving under my shirt to press against my side. His thumb skittered along the underside of my bra but he didn't go any farther. My heart thundered in my chest, waiting for him to make contact with my achy breasts.

"Emmy . . . tell me this is okay . . . I need to be inside you baby, so bad. . . ."

My sex clenched with his admission. I didn't know where we stood, didn't care. I wanted him just as badly. Wanted him to chase away all the hurt and confused feelings, and nothing would do that better than feeling his body overtake mine with raw lust and sensation.

His hazel eyes burned with passion. "If you want me to stop, tell me now."

I stayed quiet, afraid of what I might say.

Ben lifted me like I weighed nothing at all, securing one arm under my legs and the other around my back, and carried me to his bedroom.

His room was spacious with a king-sized bed in the center, dressed in slate-gray sheets with plenty of fluffy pillows. The last of the sunlight was fading, giving the room a pretty, pink glow.

A cozy-looking, leather armchair was pushed into the corner and had several copies of *Vogue* scattered around it on the floor. But best of all, it smelled like the crisp, masculine scent of his cologne.

He lowered me to the bed carefully and sat on the edge.

His fingers tugged at the hem of my shirt and I dutifully lifted my arms so he could remove it. After a flick of the clasp at my back, he slid my bra straps down my arms, disposing of my bra on the floor at the foot of the bed.

Ben's eyes left mine to roam down my naked chest. He sunk to his knees in front of me and pressed a soft kiss to my belly. Then his eyes lifted to mine and he began peeling my yoga pants down my hips, taking my panties with them. I lifted up a bit off the bed, and he slowly slid the clothing down my legs, removing it completely. I was exposed and vulnerable, but I didn't feel that way. His darkened gaze looked over me hungrily, making me feel beautiful and desired. I wanted him to touch me, to put his mouth and hands on me, but he just knelt in front of me, watching my eyes with his hungry gaze.

"Ben," I whispered, unsure of how to ask for what I wanted. His hands captured my hips and he forced me to lay back against the bed, but I supported myself on my elbows, unsure what he was about to do. Ben crawled up my body, tugging his shirt off quickly. His warm skin pressed against mine and I gripped his strong shoulders. His lips pressed against my collarbone, the top of my chest, my upper arm. He trailed gentle kisses all over my skin, my breasts tingling in wait for him.

Finally his mouth kissed along the swell of my breast, his fingertips making feather-light touches around my nipples. He pressed my breasts together, admiring the generous cleavage it created, and brought his head down to lick and nip at my sensitive nipples. I let out a throaty cry. I didn't know how this could feel so good.

I squirmed beneath him, desperate to grind my center against him. But Ben was relentless. He licked and sucked at my breasts until I was writhing and moaning his name. Then he lifted his head and a tiny smile danced in his eyes, like somehow the sound of me moaning his name was his goal all along. Like it somehow made this moment more real.

I sat up and tugged ruthlessly at his belt, fighting to get his pants off. Ben, seemingly in no hurry, lifted onto his knees so I was face level with his groin. My trembling fingers finally succeeded in undoing his pants and I tugged them and his boxer briefs down his hips. He was rock hard and swollen. And even bigger than I remembered. His heavy length stood ready and waiting for me. Leaning forward, I took him in my mouth, sucking at him greedily, gripping him with both hands. As soon as my mouth closed around him, we each groaned. Ben's palms brushed my cheeks as he watched me work, his eyes at half mast and filled with desire.

"Fuck, baby. You give such good head." I licked all along his shaft, letting him watch the sexy way I was kissing his most sensitive part. I felt like I must be doing something right because he groaned low in his throat, his body making little thrusts into my mouth. "Emmy, ah . . . fuck . . . fuck . . ." He pressed deep to the back of my throat and I felt a warm rush signaling his release.

Still kneeling, he came down on top of me, pressing my back into the mattress once again.

Even after he'd come, he was still rock hard and I felt him nudging against my lower stomach.

His fingertips lightly circled my sensitive clit as he whispered sweet and dirty things in my ear. "You're so wet for me, baby. . . . Good girl . . . I want to fuck you so bad. . . ."

I whimpered as the pleasure built inside me. Taking him in my hand, I guided him to my entrance. Ben let out a throaty groan as the head of his cock met my warmth. I froze then scrambled toward the headboard and away from him.

His eyes widened. "Emmy?"

I shook my head slowly. "Condom . . . you have to wear a condom."

His brow knit in confusion. We hadn't used condoms in months, ever since we'd had *the talk*.

"I haven't been with anyone else, baby. Have you?"

I shook my head. Of course I hadn't. But he had. "Ben . . . you were with Fiona. I don't trust it. I need you to wear one."

His eyes dropped from mine to the rumpled sheets. "Fuck," he cursed under his breath. After a long silent moment, Ben went into the bathroom, leaving me alone on the bed, giving me time to cool off and think. Neither of which were good. I just wanted to lose myself in the moment and not be reminded of all the crappiness of the past couple of months.

I lay still, trying to quiet my thoughts, to silence the doubts rushing in. I was already falling back into him, pulled into his bubble, consumed and unable to walk away. And I couldn't regret that. This is exactly where I wanted to be.

He emerged a minute later carrying a box of condoms. He met my eyes and I knew he could read my reluctance.

I was sure it was written all over my face. Perhaps jumping into bed with him was the exact wrong thing to do. I'd once told him that starting off a relationship with sex would never work. It needed to be built on something stronger in order to last. But the scent of his skin and the way that he touched me was almost enough to make me forget any and all rules. He was too tempting.

He approached the side of the bed then paused, waiting for my lead.

My brain, now working a bit more clearly, knew that this wasn't the solution. I couldn't fall into bed with him so easily again and expect our steamy hot sex to blossom into a real, trusting relationship. I lifted my chin and met his eyes. "*If* we're going to do this . . . there can't be anymore hiding things from me. I need brutal honesty between us."

"There's no *if*. We're doing this, baby. You're mine." He stepped closer, tipping my chin up to meet his eyes.

The haunted man I'd grown to care so much about stared back at me. I didn't argue.

"I think we should take things slow," I murmured, a statement made all the more awkward by the fact that we were both naked.

"Fuck going slow. I love you. I'm in love with you, and I need you. I'm going to spend every day showing you just how much you mean to me. I'm not letting you go without a fight this time. We belong together."

Rather than answering him, I tugged the sheet up around my naked chest, hugging it to my body as I maneuvered from the bed to stand before him. "I need to call Ellie. She was expecting me at our apartment."

Ben stepped closer, but I continued past him, silently grabbing my pants from the floor and tugging them on.

After dressing, I dug my phone out of my purse and discovered I'd missed six phone calls from Ellie and three texts. The last was:

WHERE THE HELL ARE YOU!?

I stepped out into the living room and stood near the floor-length windows to return her call.

"Emmy, where the hell are you? I checked your flight—it landed on time. Are you okay?"

"I'm fine." I was reluctant to admit I'd gone home with Ben. He was firmly at the top of Ellie's *Dead to Me* list. I spun around and met Ben's eyes. He'd dressed in jeans and a worn sweatshirt that looked soft. "I'll be home in a bit."

Ben's mouth tightened into a line and he shook his head.

"Where the hell are you?" Ellie's worried tone pulled my eyes away from Ben's.

"I'm, uh, at Ben's."

"What the fuck are you doing there? Better yet, let me grab my pitchfork and I'll join you."

"Ellie. I can't just walk away from him." Even as I said it, I knew it didn't explain anything.

"Okay . . ." She paused. "I'm listening."

I pulled in a deep breath and held it for a moment before releasing it slowly. "We're talking. I'll call you in a bit. Don't worry about me, okay?"

"I just miss you."

"I know. I miss you, too. See you soon, all right?"

Ellie mumbled her good-bye, and I could tell she was clearly not happy with me. I'd have some friendship mending to do later. Not only had I moved out suddenly last month, but I'd sort of been bad about picking up the phone when she'd called, too. I'd just retreated into myself while in Tennessee. Sleeping a lot, gardening with my mom, and eating plenty of home cooking, enough to offset the obligatory five-pound weight loss I'd experienced when I first got there. Stuffing the phone back into my purse, I could still feel Ben watching me.

"Come sit." He motioned me toward the sofa and I joined him, being sure to keep plenty of space between us. "Are you hungry? I could order out."

I shook my head. "I'm fine." It was late evening, and though I hadn't eaten dinner, food was the last thing on my mind. I was still spinning over what had just happened in his bedroom. I'd basically freaked out when I remembered he'd been inside Fiona. Maybe I shouldn't blame him so much— he'd been passed out drunk according to him, but he'd still comforted her, let her spend the night. I shook my head to clear the thought.

"Where were you flying in from today?" I asked, suddenly remembering he was at the airport.

"I had a shoot in Miami."

Oh. He didn't say if Fiona was there with him, and I wasn't about to ask. We were talking, making progress. I didn't want to shut that down just yet.

"I'm sorry if I pushed you too fast . . ." His eyes wandered to his bedroom door and a shiver raced down my spine.

"It wasn't your fault. I wasn't thinking clearly, either. It's just . . . been so long . . ."

He laced his fingers with mine and gave my palm a squeeze. "Talk to me, baby."

My shoulders relaxed a little, the stiff posture I'd been holding easing. "It's just going to take me some time." I didn't add that I wasn't sure we could ever get back what we had, though the thought filtered through my mind.

"I've got time. We'll take as long as you want." He lifted my hand to his mouth and pressed a tender kiss to my palm. "I'll wait as long as you need."

I realized that Ben and I had rushed right into the physical. Again. I had so much to figure out—where we stood, where I was going to work. . . . I needed to sort things out before I could rush back into this.

"I need to go slow." My voice was firm, and I silently patted myself on the back.

"Slow?" he asked.

"Like, we'll date . . . and wait to have sex. . . ."

"Waiting . . ." His eyebrows lifted. "Hmm . . . that's *different. . . .*"

He'd never waited for sex in his life, that I was sure of. He could have any girl he wanted dropping her panties in a matter of minutes.

"What, you don't like the idea?" I asked.

"If it's what you want, I will do it. Gladly."

I nodded. Good. "It's what I need."

"Will you sleep over?"

I chewed on my bottom lip. "I don't know, Ben . . ." It probably wasn't the best idea.

"Just sleep. I won't touch you unless you ask me. Please."

He looked tired—exhausted, really—and it felt selfish to say no when I knew sleeping beside me worked wonders for his insomnia. Besides, it wasn't as though I actually wanted to leave. Curling up in his bed, breathing in his scent, feeling warm and secure in his arms sounded fabulous.

"Okay," I acquiesced.

"Okay?" A lazy smile overtook his face.

I returned his smile and placed my hand in his. Ben pulled me from the couch and guided me back to his bedroom, the room where things had grown too heated just a few moments before.

Ben carried my suitcase into his room, and I sent a text to Ellie telling her I'd see her in the morning. I fished out my toiletry bag then joined him in the bathroom where we brushed our teeth side by side at the dual vanity. Ben cast glances at me in the mirror. I liked being in his space. It felt domestic and very normal after everything we'd been through.

Back in his room, I knelt on the floor in front of my suitcase to locate some pajamas. My mom had insisted on washing everything before I packed so I didn't arrive back in New York with my luggage full of dirty laundry. I pulled out a pair of navy silk sleep shorts and a pink tank and saw Ben frowning as he emerged from the master bath.

Surely he wouldn't forbid pajamas. He'd said this was just sleeping.

He crossed the room to the tall chest of drawers and pulled out a T-shirt. "I want you in my clothes or nothing at all." His voice left no room for argument. He handed me the shirt. It was ultrasoft cotton and smelled like his laundry soap. I resisted the urge to bring it to my face and inhale. "Thanks."

Ben cut the lights while I quickly undressed in the darkness.

When I stood, he was still standing beside the bed waiting for me. His eyes lowered to the hem of the T-shirt that hit me midthigh. "Beautiful," he whispered.

He peeled back the sheets and covered us with the fluffy white down comforter that was folded over the end of the bed, wrapping us both in warmth.

In the moonlight, I saw Ben smile. "Everything okay?"

"Fine." My voice was a tiny whisper.

"Thanks for staying."

"Have you been taking your pills again?"

He nodded. "They haven't worked for shit, but yeah."

My heart tugged for him. For us both.

"Come here," he whispered, opening his arm so I could move close to him. "I want you close. I need to hold you."

I rolled onto my side and edged closer. Resting my head against his chest, I felt it rise and fall steadily with each deep breath he drew. His hand trailed along my side until it rested on the dip in my waist. Something about him touching me grounded me, made me feel whole. Ben's hand glided down to my hip then slowly smoothed back up to my ribs.

"God, baby. You have no fucking idea how much I missed you."

There was still a lot for us to talk about, but I missed him, too. "I'm here, Ben. Just sleep," I whispered.

"I feel bad that I got off and you didn't. Let me take care of you, honey." His hand trailed along my side again, moving down to caress the skin at my hip under the T-shirt. His rough hand on my bare skin sent a warm tingle through my belly, and my breath caught in my chest. "Then starting tomorrow, we'll begin the waiting . . ." he added.

"It doesn't work that way." I needed to remain strong. If only to prove to myself that I could, and that there was more to our relationship. My libido had taken a backseat when I realized we needed to use a condom. I didn't know where Fiona had been, and I wasn't taking any chances. Besides, that realization had killed the mood completely. Now with Ben touching me, promising to make me come as I knew he could . . . my judgment was slightly more clouded.

His thumb traced a light pattern along my hip, caressing me in slow circles. "You sure you don't want this?" he asked, his voice deep and husky.

"I'm not ready yet," I admitted.

He removed his hand from under the T-shirt, hugged me close, and kissed my forehead. "Okay. Sleeping only. And cuddling. I just didn't want to be a dick and leave you hanging."

I chuckled silently. "It's fine. I just don't want to rush things this time."

"I told you, we'll take all the time you need. I'm not worried. The most important thing is that you're still here with me."

I tangled my legs in between his and snuggled into his broad chest.

He curled himself around my body, nestling in snuggly. The warm weight of his calf draped over my thigh pinned me to the mattress. His chest rose and fell in long steady breaths, signaling that sleep was already pulling him under.

"Don't leave me, Tennessee," his sleepy voice rasped.

I squeezed him tighter. I didn't know how a relationship could survive the threat of Fiona's psychotic presence looming in the background, but I'd try. I had little choice. I needed this man. And it seemed he needed me.

I exhaled heavily and burrowed my face against his neck, breathing him in. His delicious, masculine scent filled my lungs and relaxed me.

"Emmy . . . mine . . ." he murmured in his sleep.

For now, I thought. My wrecked heart wasn't ready to sign up for this, but my body wouldn't heed the sensible advice. I was his. He was mine. This beautiful, damaged, intense man was mine. For better or worse. I needed to see what happened next.

Acknowledgments

I would not survive this process without my readers. I wish I could give you all a unicorn and a big ol' tacklehug. Thank you for continuing to support me and my writing. I am in awe. I owe you guys everything and I LOVE YOU! So much. Thank you for making all this possible. The best is yet to come!

I have to give a BIG thank-you to the amazing models who supported this book. Thanks to the awesome Don Hood, the superfriendly Levi Allen, and the dedicated Scott Mosley for sharing their insights into the modeling world. They each took the time to answer my questions and provided an honest look at their adventures so far. In addition, thank you to Sophie Campbell, who chatted with me about her experience of dating a model. So helpful, little miss! You are all rock stars in my book.

My beta readers are my own little superheroes, helping me to turn my manuscript into a novel. Dropping to my knees to thank the beautiful Sali Powers, and the incredibly talented Kylie Scott. I don't think it's any coincidence that you're both Aussies. Clearly they're putting something in the water down there. Thank you also to Miss Ellie for your constant encouragement and love. Heather Maven, you're an incredibly helpful critique partner and a wonder at creating striking book trailers! Yay! Carmen Erickson, thank you for the editorial guidance.

To my dear husband, who inspires so much of what I write. True love is removing spiders for me, bringing me chicken noodle soup when I'm sick, and letting me wake you in the middle of the night because I had a bad dream, knowing you won't get back to sleep. Love you to pieces, cutie. Best. Husband. Ever. I'm so blessed to be on this journey with you! *Mwah!*

Ben and Emmy's story continues in the next
Love by Design novel by Kendall Ryan

Craving Him

Available in Atria eBook in March 2014
and Atria Paperback in June 2014

Ben

Having Emmy back in my bed was a fucking thing of wonder. I trailed my hand lightly over her hip and backside as she lay asleep on her stomach. I loved her body . . . it was so soft, so smooth . . . it just invited my touch. Last night she said we'd need to go slow. But I was thankful she had spent the night with me. I loved cuddling with this girl. God, I sounded like a pussy.

I gave her butt a gentle pat. "Wake up, baby." I should let her sleep in, relax, but I was too selfish. I was up, and knowing she was here, back in New York and back in my life, made me want to seize the day. *Carpe diem*, or some shit.

Emmy let out a small groan and stretched before rolling over toward the sound of my voice. She blinked up at me sleepily. "Morning."

"Hi." I continued letting my hand skim over her body, lightly dancing along her exposed skin where my T-shirt that she'd worn to bed had ridden up. I knew I was just torturing myself. I needed to keep my hands to myself or I was going to have a massive case of blue balls later. "What do you want to do today?" I had visions of bathing her in my deep tub, taking her out for brunch at my favorite place in the city and then maybe cuddling up in front of the fireplace later.

"I need to get home," she said, flinging the blankets off her legs to climb out of bed. "I left Ellie hanging last night, and besides, I haven't been home in months."

Disappointment coursed through me. She was fleeing already. "Can I at least feed you first?" I asked, rising to stand behind her and pull her back against my chest. I couldn't resist letting my hands slide down to the curve of her hips.

"Just coffee," she murmured.

"You got it." I kissed the back of her neck and slowly released her.

While Emmy dug through her suitcase, I headed into the galley kitchen. It wasn't a room I used often. I liked to cook, but cooking for one was a waste, so I tended to order takeout rather than prepare a depressing meal alone. And besides, I hated doing dishes. That was why I'd hired Magda, my housekeeper. She was fabulous.

I added coffee to the machine and set it to brew. Emmy emerged a few minutes later, her hair combed and secured in a low ponytail, dressed in jeans, sneakers, and a long-sleeved T-shirt. She looked adorable. I was going to have a hard time letting her go. Especially because she'd just returned from an extended stay in Tennessee.

When I'd told her about Fiona's pregnancy, Emmy had quit Status Model Management without a word and fled for the comforts of home. I couldn't say I blamed her, but after running into her at the airport last night and convincing her to come home with me, it seemed she was willing to give me another chance. Now that she was back, my body wanted to make up for lost time. I'd never felt this way about anyone before. I was desperately in love with this girl. I needed to show her that she could trust me. I wouldn't fuck this up again.

I added milk to her coffee, remembering how she liked it and handed her the mug. "I don't even know where you live," I admitted.

She took a sip of the brew and smiled at me. "This is good coffee."

"I have it flown in from Italy."

"Wow." She took another sip. "Why don't you come over, then? You can see my place and meet Ellie."

I leaned in and kissed her forehead. "Perfect. I'm going to jump in the shower, and I'll give my driver a call. About fifteen minutes, okay?"

"Sounds good."

Emmy

Approaching the door to my apartment, I was a bit self-conscious for Ben to see my place. The apartment itself was located in an older, run-down building in a not-so-charming neighborhood in Queens. Compared to Ben's luxury apartment in Gramercy Park in the heart of downtown, this place was a piece of crap. But it was all Ellie and I could afford. And it was home. For now.

Yellowed walls scuffed with marks and worn gray carpeting lined the narrow hallways. Green paint was peeling from our front door, and the smell of three-day old Indian food permeated the corridor as soon as you entered the building. Charming, I know.

Ben attempted a reassuring smile as I fumbled with getting the key in the lock, but I could tell his eyes were assessing every detail. He'd nearly choked when I'd told the driver to head towards the Queens Midtown Tunnel. Not all of us could afford to live in the insanely expensive heart of Manhattan like he did. I didn't know what he'd expected.

Finally freeing the second dead bolt securing the door, I pushed it open.

I'd hoped perhaps Ellie would be in her bedroom and I could have a word privately with her about Ben before he was accosted by her questions. Sadly that was not the case. Ellie was standing in the living room wearing only a towel, hair thrown in a messy bun, mustache remover cream spread above her top lip.

She spun around, hearing our entrance. "Geez! Thanks for the warning, Em." Clutching the towel tighter to her chest, she scurried down the hall for her room.

Oops. I guess I should have texted and told her that Ben and I were on our way over. I was out of practice on the etiquette of being a good roommate after living at home with my parents for the past month, and alone in Paris for a few months before that.

"Sorry, Ellie!" I called out to her retreating backside. I knew she was going to be mortified that a guy as hot as Ben had seen her with depilatory cream on her face.

Ben smiled weakly. "I take it that's your roommate?"

"Yeah, that's Ellie. And I think I'm in trouble with her."

Giving Ben the grand tour took all of about three seconds. Dumpy living room with beige couch, *check*. Small, but neatly organized kitchen, *check*. Hallway leading to our bedrooms and a shared bathroom, *check*.

He smiled politely but I knew this wasn't the type of living quarters he was accustomed to. I wondered if he'd ever stay over, or if he'd insist we stay at his place. Before I had time to ponder it further, Ellie came charging out of her bedroom.

Her eyes were bright and determined, her dark hair flowing in loose waves over her shoulders. "You." She poked Ben in the chest. "Are on my shit list."

He cocked up his eyebrow. "Uh . . . excuse me?"

"You heard me," Ellie said, her tone firm and unwavering. "I'm onto you. And Emmy will not be your plaything until you get bored. She's the fucking shit. You got that, mister?" She poked his chest one more time for emphasis before I caught her wrist and pulled it away.

"I completely agree. Emmy's the best," he said.

Ellie lifted her chin, throwing her shoulders back. "Good. We're on the same page then. But just know, I'm watching you."

"You're Ellie, right?" he asked.

She nodded, seeming to realize that she hadn't yet introduced herself.

Ben stepped in closer, meeting her intense gaze. "I'm going to take care of this girl. She's mine. And I'm not going anywhere."

"Okay then." Ellie's tone had softened.

My heart soared at hearing his sweet declaration.

Ellie met my eyes, looking for any signs of trouble. I kept my face neutral and gave her a small smile. She returned my grin and headed off into the living room, leaving Ben and me standing alone in the hall.

He pulled me into his chest and pressed a light kiss to my forehead.

"I'm sorry about that. She means well," I offered.

"I know, babe. No worries."

Ellie was a tough-ass New Yorker. That was for sure. She spoke her mind, and didn't take crap from anyone. Apparently, she was also fiercely protective of me. It was flattering and a little bit scary.

Ben leaned down to angle his mouth against mine, kissing me tenderly. "I love you. I'm going to go, so you guys catch up and talk, okay?"

"Okay. Thanks for the ride home. You didn't know you were coming all the way to Queens today, did you?"

He smiled and pressed his lips to mine once more. "Nope. But you're worth it."

He'd have a forty-five minute subway ride back, unless he called his driver again. Was that guy just at the ready, waiting for Ben's call? No time to ponder it. I walked Ben to the door. He gave a brief wave to Ellie and kissed me one last time.

"Call me later, baby."

"I will," I confirmed.

Closing the door behind him, I found Ellie in the kitchen, fishing a can of Diet Coke from the fridge.

"So . . ." I leaned against the counter. "How much trouble am I in?"

Ellie straightened and popped open the top of the can, taking a long sip. She looked me over thoughtfully. "For your supermodel boyfriend seeing me with mustache remover or for getting back together with said boyfriend in the first place?"

I smiled unevenly. "I didn't plan for this to happen. It was by complete coincidence that I ran into him at the airport yesterday. He convinced me to hear him out, and I'm glad I did. I missed him, Ellie. Like missed him, missed him. And as for the pregnancy, that really wasn't his fault. He plans to have a paternity test done as soon as it's safe."

"And that's . . . okay with you?"

I'd researched paternity testing extensively online, and found most people waited until after the baby was born to do the test, as it was less invasive and much easier. No wonder Fiona was digging her heels in on this. I couldn't help but imagine her using some excuse to wait until after the baby was born simply so that in her head Ben can be the father for a little longer. It made me sick to even think about it. Yet I clenched my jaw and nodded to answer Ellie's question.

"He's also cut off his friendship with her," I quickly added like that made it all better somehow.

"But he's still going to keep working for her agency?" Ellie shot me a curious glare.

"Yes, for now. He's under contract." I didn't mention that this little fact also drove me mad. I didn't want him working for her, but I didn't want to give Ellie another reason to hate him, so I held my face impassively, trying to pretend it didn't bother me. That it was all just some harmless business arrangement. The truth was, I didn't trust Fiona and never would. Ben had a weakness where she was concerned, giving her too much leeway, being too accommodating.

Ellie released a deep sigh. "It killed me when you took off

for home. I felt helpless, and I just don't want to see you go through something like that again with him."

"It won't happen again. I'm here to stay. In fact, I need to start looking for a job so I can pay you back for rent."

Ellie waved me off. "Psshh . . . I'm not worried about the rent. I'm just glad you're back and doing well." She opened her arms. "Come here."

I stepped into her embrace and gave her a hug. She wasn't a hugger usually. "It's good to be home."

Not much had changed around the apartment, and I was glad to see it felt nice and cozy to be back.

After unpacking, I logged onto my laptop, ready to look for jobs. I was set on paying Ellie back for the rent. I knew she didn't have much extra money just lying around, and I wanted to pull my fair share. Not to mention, I'd go positively crazy without a job. A pang of regret coursed through me at how my job at Status had ended. I certainly wouldn't be getting a recommendation from my former boss. And God, what would I say if someone asked why I'd left my last job? *Crap!* My male model boyfriend got my boss pregnant and I quit. *Ha! Yeah right.* That'd go over about as well as a fart in church.

I supposed I'd have to spin it . . . say I went home for a family emergency. They didn't need to know the emergency was me having a complete emotional breakdown.

About the Author

Kendall Ryan is the *New York Times* and *USA Today* bestselling author of the contemporary romance novels *Unravel Me, Make Me Yours, Hard to Love, Resisting Her,* and *The Impact of You.* She's a sassy yet polite midwestern gal with a deep love of books and a slight addiction to lip gloss.